"Children! Children! What are you doing?"

Then, of course, the natural superiority of die male asserted itself. For I simply left off and scowled, while Laura burst out crying.

"The little b-beast," she blubbered, "he's puttin' flies in the s-spider's web."

"T'ck! t'ck! You naughty boy, Tom," said stepmother mildly. "Well, you mustn't fight and make all this to-do, anyway. Come inside and wash yourselves; you'll be late for school"

When I look back upon the memory of my stepmother; I am bound to acknowledge that, as stepmothers go, she was undeniably a success. Laura and I both rather liked her, but we did not, of course, appreciate at that time with what delicacy of feeling and adroit management she filled her vicarious position. She must have appeared to our father somewhat in the light of a placid harbour after a gorgeous storm. Laura and I had only dim recollections of our mother. I remember her scolding me, and then in the night she would come and wet my face with her tears and kisses. Laura remembered more. She remembered going to the exhibition with mother, and the way that people stared at them both. "I'm not surprised. They looked so drab beside her," Laura explained. Also she remembered some of the songs mother used to sing, and on Sunday evenings curious people came in and ate and drank, and mother sang and played the mandolin. Some of the men who came were Spanish too, as mother was. Father tolerated them for mother's sake, but Laura could see he didn't like them. Father was frightfully English. He used at one time to travel about the world buying and selling horses. He met mother at a place called Bio. Father must have done a lot of things in his time before he settled down to the splendid position he occupied when I was ten.

II

My father had a genius for enjoying life. It is a quality only possessed by simple people. And he was remarkably simple. Every little commonplace action throughout the day appeared to give him a quiet satisfaction . . . doing things properly. He enjoyed washing, brushing his hair, cleaning his teeth, polishing his brown boots—an operation which occupied him twenty minutes every morning and was conducted through the media of most elaborate accessories, like a high-church service; he enjoyed folding an umbrella, blowing his nose, opening a newspaper. Lighting a pipe was a complete ecstasy. And yet he was frugal and restrained, scrupulous in his dealings and direct in his actions. The simplicity of his outlook was emphasised by almost childish beliefs. He appeared to float in a mental archipelago studded with the little islands of prejudice and superstition. He would do nothing of importance on a Friday, or on the thirteenth of the month. He would never pass anyone on the stairs. If he spilt salt, he immediately threw some over his left shoulder. I am glad that I never remember him breaking a mirror. He would have been distracted. His justification for this attitude was that "you never knew." He enjoyed a kind of wistful reverence for the established thing. He believed in God in the definitely anthropomorphic sense, as a Being who, though He would not probably have selected the licensing trade, would have conducted it decently. And in his humble way he tried to conduct it decently himself.

He was very regular in his habits and methodical. He rose at seven in the morning; went into the garden and took deep breaths, and indulged in a few cumbrous exercises. Then he lighted his pipe and polished his brown boots. He breakfasted at eight, read the newspaper, and went for twenty minutes' walk. On his return he devoted the rest of the morning to attending to the business of the House. Book-keeping in the office, of the yard, interviewing spirit salesmen, checking the great barrels of ale delivered by enormous draymen. He had dinner at one o'clock punctually. After dinner he indulged in an hour's nap on the horsehair chair in the parlour upstairs. He usually spread a lace antimacassar over his head to keep the flies from biting him. At half-past three he went out for a walk. Sometimes he called at places on business, but he was always at home at five o'clock for tea. This was our great time—Laura's and mine; we always had tea together, father and stepmother and Laura and I. Tea, of course, is the nicest meal in the day. There is something exciting about the very sound of a tea-cup touching a saucer. It excites me still. And then there are the round plates with piles of bread-and-butter, and brown cakes with black sultanas peeping out, and always one pot of jam, and sometimes crumpets.

And father was always at his best at tea-time. It was as though he had reserved this hour for us. He would call up to the play-room on the third floor, where Laura and I were, and in his enormous voice boom forth:

"Children, what was it the King of North Carolina said to the King of South Carolina?"

And Laura and I, who had been coached for the part, would chant in unison:

"We—want—our—TEA!"

And stepmother would smile and say: "Oh, you silly things!"

And then we raced downstairs to the parlour, and father would express unlimited surprise that there was the tea all ready for us. The drawing-room and the parlour were large rooms and were connected by folding-doors painted in two shades of green. The wood-work in the parlour was painted brown, and the drawing rom white and yellow. Both rooms were richly furnished with every kind of furniture in gold, walnut, and mahogany. It was indeed very difficult to move about for the furniture. Over the fireplace in the parlour was an enormous steel engraving representing "The Death of Wolfe" On either side were cylindrical glass bowls covering a cluster of wax fruit most tantalisingly real. Apart from all this, of course, we had a dining-room. But that was downstairs, leading off the kitchen. We used to have dinner and breakfast there, but the parlour was our favourite room, consecrated to tea only.

When we sat down, father would look very solemn, except for his eyes, which couldn't be, and he would talk and ask us impossible riddles. He had rather a bald head, with large, prominent grey eyes, and a deep chest. When he threw back his head and laughed, everything had to laugh with him, including people and furniture and even the wax fruit itself. He had a habit of buying us little presents, and hiding them, and making us look for them. He would suddenly exclaim:

"Goodness gracious me! What's that awful thing growing out of the wall behind the piano?"

And Laura and I would rush for it. And there indeed would be a huge brown-paper parcel. Feverishly we would break the string. Inside would be a box. Inside more brown paper. Then another box and more paper, and so on till we got down to—possibly an old mouse-trap. Then father would slap his leg and laugh, and Laura and I would pretend to be angry. But we should not be really angry, because we knew by experience that father never let us down like that. Somewhere in a more inaccessible place would be another parcel containing—a railway-station, or a splendid puzzle.

At six o'clock father's busy time would commence, for the bars would begin to fill, and he would be down there till very late at night, when they closed. I believe he used to do a certain amount of serving, but most of the time he talked to customers and attended to things generally. He employed all sorts of people. There was Mrs. Beddoes, the bar manageress, a very stout lady with a white-

One After Another by Stacy Aumonier

Stacy Aumonier was born at Hampstead Road near Regent's Park, London on 31st March 1877.

He came from a family with a strong and sustained tradition in the visual arts; sculptors and painters.

On leaving school it seemed the family tradition would also be his career path. In particular his early talents were that of a landscape painter. He exhibited paintings at the Royal Academy in the early years of the twentieth century.

In 1907 he married the international concert pianist, Gertrude Peppercorn, at West Horsley in Surrey. A year later Aumonier began a career in a second branch of the arts at which he enjoyed a short but outstanding success—as a stage performer writing and performing his own sketches.

The Observer newspaper commented that "...the stage lost in him a real and rare genius, he could walk out alone before any audience, from the simplest to the most sophisticated, and make it laugh or cry at will."

In 1915, Aumonier published a short story 'The Friends' which was well received (and was subsequently voted one of the 15 best stories of 1915 by the Boston Magazine, Transcript).

Despite his age in 1917 at age 40 he was called up for service in World War I. He began as a private in the Army Pay Corps, and then transferred as a draughtsman in the Ministry of National Service.

By now he had four books published—two novels and two books of short stories—and his occupation is recorded with the Army Medical Board as 'author.'

In the mid-1920s, Aumonier received the shattering diagnosis that he had contracted tuberculosis. In the last few years of his life, he would spend long spells in various sanatoria, some better than others.

Shortly before his death, Stacy Aumonier sought treatment in Switzerland, but died of the disease in Clinique La Prairie at Clarens beside Lake Geneva on 21st December 1928. He was 55.

Index of Contents

ONE AFTER ANOTHER

CHAPTER I

"THE DUCHESS OF PLESS"

What I used to like about my father's garden in Camden Town was the spiders. Especially in the autumn when they got big and greedy. I used to like to creep out there in the morning before school, when no one was about. Their webs, sparkling with tiny drops of dew, stretched cunningly between the yellowing leaves, always gave me a thrill. The tool-house door was a good spot to catch flies, and I became quite clever at it I used to throw them into the spider's web. The spectacle which followed always sickened me—I felt my heart beating—but it was tremendously moving and exciting. The spider is surely the most efficient thing alive ... so masterful, 80 well equipped. He is always worth watching, if only for his craftsmanship. The sensitive control over the skein of web effected, then the pounce, and those appalling long circular legs that must seem to attack the victim all round. He appears to do what fighting there is to be done right away from any vital portions of his own anatomy. But it's all over in a second. The victim is rolled round and round and round, bound up and trussed, given one good bite, and left. It used to annoy me sometimes that he left it so soon, and went back to stage centre. You could see the thing struggling in its mesh. Sometimes they caught bees and wasps. This would appear to be a fairer fight, but the spider always won. The most satisfactory thing to throw into a spider's web is a daddy-long-legs. They always stick. They have such clumsy legs and long wings, and you feel that they must make such a fine meal for the spider. If you throw a fly too hard it goes right through....

One day Laura found me doing this. She had been watching me from the bathroom window. She called me "a disgusting little beast." She rushed at me and scratched my face, and pushed me over some flowerpots. She was thirteen then, three years older than I, but I was a man. I suppose women will never understand men. I was in a blind fury as I squared up to her. Ingrained in me was an instinct that it is man's business to understand about killing things. Women are fools. Laura and I were always fighting, but we never fought with such venom as we did that morning. Neither spoke. Occasionally we groaned or screamed with pain as some chance blow or scratch or kick got home. Quarter was neither given nor asked. Laura was fighting for some vague and silly sentiment, and I was fighting for the prerogative of sportsmanship, for manhood, and, incidentally, for the spider himself.

Laura was taller than I, and quite unscrupulous in her methods of fighting. I made her nose bleed, but otherwise I was undoubtedly getting the worst of it. She had scratched my face, bitten my thumb, torn my hair, and kicked me on the shins and knees. It was with something of relief then that I heard stepmother's voice call out:

powdered face, and a kind of pyramid of fair gold hair kept together (or perhaps kept on) with bands of black velvet. There were two barmaids, Olive and May, both tall, both fair; Olive of the willowy, clinging kind, and May more rigid and assertive. I fell in love with May when I was eleven, and I used to go and peep at her through the skylight above the private bar. I had to get a pair of steps to do this and lean it against a clothes-stand in a dark passage. It was an adventure fraught with peril, for neither Laura nor I, not even stepmother, were allowed to go into the bars under any circumstances, and father was very strict about it Then there was a potman named Jingle. He was the object of my idolatry for many years. He had been a prize-fighter. He had a flat, shapeless face and little twinkly eyes. He would often play with Laura and me in the garden and tell us thrilling stories of his victories in the ring. He must have been the greatest fighter who ever lived. In any case, he never told us of any occasion when he had been defeated. And he was so good-tempered and gentle. Of course we were under no delusion as to the principal reason of his employment; neither was he. There was very, very seldom any trouble in "The Duchess of Pless"; father was far too strict. He established a kind of code which had to be observed. No one was served who gave the slightest sign of having had too much, and, indeed, those who gave no sign were limited in the amount they were allowed to consume in one evening. He boasted that he only supplied the best, and that in limited quantities. He would not allow bad language, and though he was fond of horseracing and often went to the races, he would not allow betting or book-making on the premises. I believe "The Duchess of Pless" used to be known in the neighbourhood at one time as "Old Purbeck's Paradise." I know a lot of the men used to laugh at him and call him a crank; nevertheless, he sustained a reputation for honesty and incorruptibility, and was held in great respect in the neighbourhood. I have heard him say on more than one occasion: "I am a fully-licensed man, sir. It is something to be proud of. It entails responsibilities as well as privileges. I have been a fully-licensed man for seventeen years. It's a trade, like any other trade, serving a public purpose, and liable to abuse. I hope I have always conducted it decently."

If any untoward incident did occur to jar this creditable programme, any unseemly attempt to abuse the privileges of his house, my father would bring his fist down on the mahogany bar and in his enormous voice cry out:

"Silence, gentlemen!"

If this were not sufficient, he would bring his fist down again, and call:

"Jingle!"

When our potman appeared, grinning and amiable as ever, father, his eyes blazing with anger, would point to some individual and say:

"That man!"

And Jingle, leering pleasantly, with his long arms swinging below his knees, would sidle up and say:

"Come on, my lad!"

They very seldom showed fight They hardly seemed to have time to. Jingle was like the spider, so wonderfully equipped. He did not appear to hurt them. He seemed to twist them round and tie them up, and then gently shoot them into the street. On two occasions I had the great privilege of observing this operation from my vantage-point in the dark passage. For it occurred at the time when I was spending restless nights on account of May.

In addition to Jingle, our establishment consisted of a cellar-man named Waynes, a quite insignificant individual; a large and flabby-faced cook called Grace, who whenever I entered the kitchen was always either eating or shedding tears on a letter she had either just received or just written. She was a good cook, with a limited repertoire. I remember that for years she used to make us what she called a "Zulu pudding." It is curious that, as we had it nearly every day, I cannot remember what the pudding was like. The title must have been more impressive than the pudding itself. I remember her discussing the meals for the day with stepmother, and with a rolling-pin pressed into her left cheek, saying in her tearful voice: "Well, what do you say to a nice Zulu pudding?"

It was, of course, inevitable that in the end Laura and I always referred to her as "the Zulu pudding." Various housemaids came and went, stole things, quarrelled with Mrs. Beddoes, irritated father to distraction—he hated fresh people and innovations—tried to make love to my adored Jingle, with varying degrees of success, and eventually vanished into the Ewigkeit I hope in any case that I have impressed you with the fact that we were people of considerable importance and prominence in Camden Town at that time; that our establishment was no ordinary establishment; that Laura and I were reared in an exceptional atmosphere of luxury and refinement and wealth. We realised our position more fully when we first began to attend the Grammar School. Some of the other children were dressed almost as well as we, if not so expensively; but we soon learned from little things that were said that their home-life conditions were quite different. Very few of them had cake and jam for tea, very few of them had a parlour as well as a drawing-room, and a dining-room and a play-room. The majority of them only had one "general," and even the Beldams, whose father was a solicitor, had to acknowledge that they only had a cook and a housemaid. They didn't keep any barmaids or prize-fighters at all. None of the others were taken to a box at the pantomime at Christmas; none of the others were given such costly presents. Laura was the only girl who had private lessons on the piano from a gentleman who wore a tail-coat and spats, and who came to our house at half-past six on two evenings in the week.

Laura in those days was something of "a cure"—as stepmother described her. There was certainly nothing about her to denote the kind of woman she was to develop into later on. She was very dark, queer, elfinesque, with a broad, rather plain face and eyes remarkably wide apart. She was tall for her age, with skinny legs and very quick movements. In fact, quickness was her principal characteristic. She was almost incoherently quick in speech, quick to grasp situations, and very quick-tempered. She would be sweet, companionable, and delightful one minute, and then something would happen, and her eyes would blaze and her nostrils quiver. She would cry, or fume, or sulk, till suddenly another wind would blow it all away.

There was no love lost between Laura and the rather rigid, well-groomed young man who came to give her music-lessons. He expressed the opinion to father that Laura had great talent, but he never seemed to encourage it He smiled superciliously when she played, and when she had finished he purred. Laura always swore that he purred. He told her when she played wrong notes, and sometimes he played the piece to her himself. And Laura informed me:

"When he plays, all I can think of is pomade." I mooted a scheme by which we should lure him out into the yard one evening and then get Jingle to manhandle him. "Squeeze some of the oil out of him." Laura's eyes brightened at the suggestion. But we could never get Jingle to fall in with our plan, and when I taunted him with being afraid of the music teacher, and offered him my pocket-money for three weeks ahead, he only laughed.

IV

The feud between Laura and myself over the question of the spiders lasted some days. It was not till the second day that we could even discuss the matter coherently. Then, when Laura was in bed, and I had come in to fetch a clean collar for the morning (for some reason or other my collars and handkerchiefs were always kept in her room), she suddenly said:

"Why did you do it?"

"What?"

"Putting the flies in the spider's web."

"P'saugh! It's nothing! It's quite natural. The spider would get them anyway."

"It isn't natural. It's only natural when he catches them himself."

"But this one hadn't got a fly."

"Well, it was no business of yours."

I then had a brilliant inspiration.

"What do you think's the worst?" I said. "To starve to death slowly, or to be killed quickly?"

"Why?"

"It's just as cruel to starve the spider as to kill the fly. A fly's no good anyway."

"You don't know anything about it"

"Not only that: Mr. Tilden, our mathematical master, told us that a spider isn't really cruel. When he catches a fly he gives it a bite which 'sphyxiates it for forty-eight hours. So that by the time it comes-to, it's dead!"

"Rubbish! How can it come-to, if it's dead?"

"It depends upon whether the spider has eaten it or not. Of course, if he's eaten it, all its worries are over."

Laura sat up in bed. I could see her dark eyes peering at me across the room.

"Suppose," she said breathlessly, "he's only partly eaten it!"

"Then," I answered, "it doesn't come-to; it only comes one."

Having uttered this brilliant and cynical witticism, I thought it advisable to dash from the room.

Three mornings later, when I went into the garden, I found Laura bending over a small bush. She was so absorbed she did not hear me approach.

"What's up?" I asked.

"He's turning it over and over and biting it," she said huskily. "He's killing it, and—I threw it in!"

"Well, that's all right."

She turned away, and her face was quite colourless. Her hands were clenched.

"What's the matter?" I asked.

"I feel sick."

"Well, go and be sick."

Then Laura rushed at me again and hit my ear.

Yon would hardly believe it, but the next morning I found Laura there again. She had caught and put in a daddy-long-legs and two flies.

So, you see, when I was only ten years old, I knew all about women.

CHAPTER II

A CROWDED LIFE

Life in my father's house was rich and crowded. Every hour there was movement, anticipation, Ji colour. I had my niches and shrines, and the ambit of my existence was fringed with breathless romance. Laura and I, although we fought and quarrelled, were intensely intimate. Laura had the faculty of exciting me. When she entered the room I was conscious of warm and brilliant colour, although she might be wearing a black frock and her face might be pale. I loved to watch her, and stepmother, and my father, and all the busy people coming and going. They had so much to give me. Their experiences peeped at me across rose-coloured spaces. The garden, the spiders, the tool-shed. Jingle, the great brewers' drays in the yard, stepmother carrying up a pile of clean linen, Laura practising scales, a corner of the playroom with the pale sun making patterns on the floor, dinner and the great dish-covers, father rather flustered and in a hurry . . . someone coming in to ask a question, Grace singing in the kitchen, school again . . . bewildering but rather adventurous, something new always happening. Home to tea, Laura with a washed face, positively shining. Stepmother a little agitated, some people coming in to supper—the Mowlams. Pa, ma, and Evie— very old friends; perhaps Uncle Stephen. A terrible man, Uncle Stephen. I dreaded him and worshipped him. He was father's brother, but not a scrap like father. He was tall, wiry, hard. He had almost white hair and a dark moustache, possibly dyed; a clean-cut, bony face, and he wore circular-rimmed glasses, which gave him a fierce, concentrated expression. He did dumb-bells, and punched a ball, and shot pigeons. He lived at Netting Hill and kept a large stationer's shop. But all his instincts were towards sport and keeping fit.

He had a curious-shaped piece of land at the back of his house, which he had completely netted in so that he could have a cricket-practice pitch. It was a narrow strip, broken half-way by the projection of a railway funnel. There was no grass on it. It was just mud. Every week or so he made me go out and play cricket with him. I dreaded it, but I was too frightened to refuse. I could never make up my mind which terrified me most, his bowling or his batting. He bowled frightfully fast. He took a long run, but owing to the projection of the funnel you couldn't see him when he started, but you heard him. Suddenly he appeared round the bend, rushing at you at a fearful rate, his eyes blazing, and as he delivered this ball he emitted a kind of growl like a savage dog. The ball always seemed to come straight at my head or legs. And if I drew back an inch he bawled out: "Stand up to 'em, boy! Stand up to 'em!" When he batted it was no better. He used to drive the ball straight back at me with terrific force, and it seemed impossible to escape in that netted-in cage. I used to try and bowl wides so that he couldn't get at them, but he nearly always did, and if they didn't come straight back and hit me on the chest, they flew all round the netting, struck a wall somewhere, and eventually caught me on the back of the head. While I was rubbing myself he would exclaim:

"Pitch 'em up, boy! Pitch 'em up!" I used to return home covered with cuts and bruises. I felt lucky to escape with my life.

II

Of course Laura soon discovered my post of observation in the passage, where we could look into the private bar, but she never found it so absorbing as I did. She got impatient. The fair halo above the head of May gave her no satisfaction. The glittering mahogany and glass, the cunning arrangement of taps and levers and sinks stirred no response in her bosom. The conversation of the brilliant personalities who came to worship at the shrine of good-fellowship left her cold. But these things stirred me profoundly. In the first place, I realised that the social system was divided into three definite classes—the lower, the middle, and the upper. It must be so, for as on the railway there is a first, second, and third class, so in my father's house there was a public, a private, and a saloon bar. By going back into a passage you could get into either, but once established there you were completely cut off from the other two. You could sometimes observe or be observed by them, but thanks to the ingenious scheme of little glass shutters you could always shut off anyone's view of you. Presumably the manners and customs of the human species are regulated in the same way. The bishop and the bargee, the wife of the bishop and the wife of the bargee, all have their little glass shutters, although, like the other animals, they come to the same stream to drink at sundown. I observed, moreover, that the bars were places of spiritual mystery. Curious little movements and cross-currents, a kind of masonry, were always in evidence. Men came in in groups, and whispered together. There was a deliberate telepathic connection with certain units and the gods and goddesses on the other side of the bar. A corpulent, red-faced individual would pant his way in and hand a brown paper parcel across to Olive, remarking wheezily:

"Three-thirty."

Olive would take the parcel without the slightest evidence of understanding, and reply:

"Ah, right, Charlie."

He would then toddle out, but at the door he would perhaps meet another very similar person. Without any word of greeting they would return to the bar, and the second man would say:

"A bass and a mild-and-bitter, Olive."

They would drink their refreshment as though it were positively distasteful, fiddling about with their moustaches to keep them out of the beer. Then the first man would tap the other on the upper expanse of his stomach, and whisper. The second would twirl his dripping moustache, and look utterly lugubrious. At last he would reply in a thick voice:

"Nothing is like it used to be."

This would seem to satisfy the other man, and he would hand him an envelope and they would go out. I observed that this freemasonry pervaded the day, but late in the evening it spread out into open discussion and broad generalities. Men talked eloquently and forcibly about politics, trade, and fighting. As the hour grew late their voices appeared to merge into a long, continuous drone, the art of listening vanished, the lower, middle, and upper classes vanished; it was just one voice, like the voice of a drowning man a long way off, comfortably indifferent to his fate.

Perhaps I was sleepy on these occasions. I ought to have been in bed, but the rich variety of this life fascinated me, and there was always a chance of father calling out:

"Now, gentlemen; order, please!" Or even more pertinently:

"Jingle!"

It was always satisfying to observe the homage paid to father. The gentlemen invariably called him "Mr. Purbeck, sir," and they always listened to him as he leaned across the bar and emphasised some point by beating the air with his fat first finger.

Mrs. Beddoes was called Mrs. Beddoes, although I once heard a young man refer to her as Mrs. Bed-fellows. Olive and May were called a variety of nicknames, too bewildering to remember. May was my adored ones pert, self-contained, and, alas! inaccessible to me and too accessible to everyone else. The men all adored her, and she was just as pleasant to the lower and middle classes as she was to the upper.

This is where Olive differed perceptibly. Her bright, queer, expressionless eyes always seemed to float above the heads of the customers and to be fixed upon the entrance door of the saloon bar. There was something tragic, provocative, expectant about her. She served the upper classes watchfully, the middle classes disdainfully, and the lower classes with unconcealed disgust.

III

The evenings which the Mowlams spent with us were always rather starched and unsatisfactory. They were special friends of stepmother, and Laura and I could never see what she could find in them. Mr. Mowlam had some sort of position in a piano-factory in Kentish Town. He was a peculiarly disappointing man. He had a really beautiful head, with snow-white hair. A fine, classical head, with sharp features and clear grey eyes, and yet I really think he was one of the most stupid men I have ever met. I could never account for him at all. He had all the presence of an evangelist, a reformer, a seer. And yet the only thing he was really interested in was pedigree rabbits. He kept a lot of these ridiculous animals in hutches made out of packing-cases in a yard in Kentish Town, and he used to loan them out for breeding purposes. At supper time he would regale us with tedious and unnecessary details about the profits derived from the amours of the all-too-fertile does, or the dubious history of some black buck called Dodo. On any other subject he leered knowingly and clicked his tongue, suggesting that he knew all about it, but he wasn't going to say.

Mrs. Mowlam was a big woman, very broad and heavily-built. She had a kind, motherly face, and would have been quite pleasant if she had not been so pliable with regard to persuasion to song. She had no great opinion of her voice, and indeed she had no cause to have. It was always Mr. Mowlam who said:

"Now, Annie, give us a song."

And stepmother always kindly added:

"Yes, Annie, do."

Annie did not really want to sing, and no one in the room really wanted to hear her. Looking back on it, one realises that the whole thing could easily have been avoided, which simply goes to emphasise the extraordinary stupidity of Mr. Mowlam. She had a tiny little high, plaintive voice, and always sang little ballads with words of this description:

"I'm a merry little fly,
Stranger quite to care and sorrow.
As my life is short, I try
Every hour fresh bliss to borrow."

Even father revolted at the physical inappropriateness of this song, and remarked one morning at breakfast that the singer was more like "a merry little hippopotamus"—a remark which caused Laura and me to be late for school, but which nevertheless brightened the day considerably. It cannot be said that Evie Mowlam was a friend of ours, either. She was in the early thirties, and she patronised us. The upper part of her face was almost as beautiful as her father's, clear, transparent, and sensitively modelled. Her nose was well shaped and rather large, and then her chin seemed to race away from the whole proposition and leave a row of splendid teeth dangling in the air. As Laura said, "She never seems to be not grinning." She was overpoweringly affectionate, vehement about trifles, discursive, and unconvincing.

Laura and I were perhaps a little prejudiced about Mrs. Mowlam's singing, because it was apt to clash with our own performances. For you must know that we were both at the reciting age, and we required even less persuasion than our lady visitor. I specialised in Shakespeare, and squeezed in between the furniture, which was always impeding my gestures, I used to recite the quarrel scene between Brutus and Cassius, Mark Antony's oration over the body of Caesar, and Hamlet's monologue on death. Laura considered Shakespeare hackneyed, but she also espoused the tragic muse. She let herself in on Eugene Aram, Curfew Shall Not Ring To-night, and a piece which she considered her masterpiece, which began, "I am not mad! I am not mad!" We once attempted Hubert and Arthur together, but found it quite impossible, because a point would come when, catching each other's eye, one of us would laugh. It seemed quite easy to be Hamlet or Caesar all on one's own, but to stand there by the folding-doors and have Laura in a plaid skirt, with the familiar pigtail tied in a red bow, suddenly turn to me and say: "Good morrow, little Prince!" was too much for anyone.

It is doubtful whether the Mowlams derived any enjoyment from our performances, any more than we did from Mrs. Mowlam's singing, but they were decently polite. It was father who was the stupid one in this case. He would say:

"Now, Laura, what's it to be? This way for the early doors! Annie, come and sit here in the stalls with me. Move up, Fred. Now then, who's going to begin? Tom?"

And he would commence clapping just like people do in a theatre. And Laura and I would flush with excitement, and push each other about. And there is no doubt that father enjoyed us enormously. I watched his face whilst Laura was performing. He was really feeling it all. His eyes were glued upon her, his lips mutely responding to the action of hers. When we had finished he would turn to the others and say:

"By Jove! Did you ever hear anything like it?"

It is very interesting, this un-analytical admiration that the majority of parents have for the performances of their children. It must be some sort of by-product of the instinct of self-preservation. I am quite convinced that neither Laura nor I had any but the most ordinary talent for reciting, and yet father—who was not in other ways an uncritical man—seemed to be completely mesmerised by our performances. He was amazed, entranced, and went about telling everyone of the riot of genius he had helped to bring into the world. And naturally we both believed it.

IV

It was father who eventually discovered me peeping through the skylight into the bars. He said:

"What are you doing there, Tom?"

I looked foolish, and replied:

"Oh, just having a look through."

For a moment he flushed angrily; then he came up and took the steps away. He said nothing, but I saw him standing there with a curious, perplexed expression on his face, as though some entirely novel aspect of life had been presented to him. For some time after that I avoided the passage; a rich corner of my life was cut out. On the stairs I could hear the drone of the voices, but I dare not resume my observations. And then there occurred a most unfortunate event. I had gone to bed. It was Saturday night; no school tomorrow. I was very excited, and I could not sleep. After a time I realised that father would be safely downstairs, serving. Saturday was always a busy night. I crept downstairs and fetched the steps from a lavatory where I knew father had put them. Very gingerly I opened them out and mounted them. The bars were crowded. One could hear the snap, snap, snap of the brass cranks where May was drawing off glasses of beer. Everyone was serving as rapidly as possible, the air was blue with tobacco-smoke. Above the din of conversation could be heard the constant jingle of coins and people tapping on the counter and calling out for drinks. It was all very exciting. Just below my window was a kind of terrace of bottles. Occasionally one of the servers made a dash towards it and I had to be careful to duck out of sight. I do not know how long I lurked there, watching and listening to this engaging drama, where all the actors seemed entrusted with important parts, but the most important part—the actor-manager—was obviously my father. It was he whose individuality seemed to fill the stage, and I felt very proud . . . "Purbeck's Paradise."

Someone in the saloon bar—among the aristocracy—was raising his voice in a thick rumble. Quite clearly above lie general confusion I heard a long string of unprintable oaths. Immediately there came a crash upon the counter which cut the whole flow of talk in two. There was a dead silence, and then the thunder of my father's voice:

"Now then, there! That will do. Hi! you, clear out of the bar!"

The drama was id movement. The actors were snapping up their cues. The old emotions were let loose. The chorus was resumed, but more indistinctly. The important action of the piece was yet to be developed. Alas! from my position I could not see the villain, the rumbler, the outcast of the decencies. But I could hear a kind of dim, subdued counter-rumble, and the hissed exhortations of his supporters, and I could see the hero glowering across the bar, gloriously commanding. And in the background, grinning as usual, and wiping his hands upon a towel, the alert and sinuous Jingle. It was the briefest of comedies. The waves of sound resumed their normal roar. The partisans of disruption apparently chose the wiser course, and hustled their champion from the lists. The hero enjoyed a momentary intoxication of having "gripped them" on an opening night to a full house. Then, swinging on his heel, he turned to the terrace to collect a bottle. It was not where he expected. His face was still flushed with anger. He glanced up suddenly and loomed right into, my eyes!

I darted back, but I knew I had been too late, I scrambled down the steps and tried to carry them away. A sudden fear of my father came over me. I was in a frenzy to escape. I had a momentary prevision that he would strike me, and he had never struck me . . . never, never. And if he did, I should be so ashamed. But he was angry. I had never seen him so angry.

I felt the strong, firm grip of his hand on the upper part of my arm. The steps were taken from me. I wanted to cry, and I could not speak. At the end of the passage was a dim hall, illuminated by one gas burner. I remember noticing a dingy print of Queen Victoria in a lace cap, a relentless presentation of the proprieties. My father was carrying the steps away. His voice seemed strained and distant.

"I told you not to do that, Tom."

I shivered against the wall, not knowing how to act. Suddenly he put the steps down, and came over to me and gripped my shoulder.

"I don't want you to do that, boy."

That was all he said. It was not an order, and certainly not a menace. It was husky, tearful, almost despairing. I whispered breathlessly: "All right," and went upstairs. As I turned the corner I saw his profile, the steps held in front of him. He looked tired, pathetic, curiously alone. I wanted to go back and ask his pardon, but I could not bring myself to do it. When I got into bed I lay awake staring at the darkness, and after a time I cried a little, because my father was lonely. He was alone, and I was alone. Everybody. ... I could go in and see Laura, but she would not understand. She, too, is alone. How lonely everyone is! All separately walking along in the darkness . . . alone, alone, alone.

Someone is tapping on my door. Father? No, of course that is Laura. She always taps like that. She comes in ghost-like—but abrupt. That is like Laura—an abrupt ghost. Some new excitement. What does she want?

She sits on my bed and dangles her legs.

"Tom! " mysteriously and portentously. "I've just got an awful idea!"

"What is it?"

"Eve is like a white rabbit"

"Rubbish!"

"No. Think of her. The way she looks and eats. It stands to reason. If a man is always thinking about white rabbits, he has a daughter like one. They're teaching us that now at school. It's frightfully interesting. I've forgotten what they call it"

"Oh, go to bed!"

"Sulky!"

Laura slaps me and goes out. What a fool she is! An abrupt, foolish ghost wandering through the night—alone.

Glorious daylight dispels all these visions. Everything is just the same. The smell of coffee and bacon; father vigorously polishing his brown boots in the yard, cheerful and friendly. The Sunday newspapers folded neatly on the white cloth. Ming—our tabby—curled up on the window-sill, her paws curved inwards and her narrow slits of eyes expressing furtive ecstasy.

Strange that the important news should come to me three weeks later from the mouth of my Uncle Stephen. At the end of one of our dreaded games of cricket, he said suddenly:

"Well, my lad, so you're going to boarding-school!"

I was not going to be such a fool as to profess ignorance. He massaged his nostrils vigorously and added:

"You'll have to stand up to them there. You develop that off-drive and you'll be all right."

Just as I was leaving, he stopped me and said: "When you first go to school, Tom, the boys will all ask you what your father is. You take my advice and say he's an hotel proprietor. Don't tell them he's a publican."

Anyone who has been to a public school will appreciate the almost incalculable value of Uncle Stephen's advice.

CHAPTER III

THE LIMITED MONARCHY

The four and a half years which I spent at Leydhurst College was an experience which appears now to be completely divorced from all association with the rest of my life. While it lasted it seemed a self-contained eternity. When it was over, it dwindled to a brief, incisive episode, a curious little boxed-in paraphrase of life. Whereas in my father's house all was movement and rich colour, at Leydhurst everything was static and of only one colour, a cold, bright, sunny yellow. Everything appeared determined beforehand, fixed and finished. One had to get into it, adapt oneself; it never came out to help one. There was nothing you could do for which there was not a formula, a code, a standard, or a cure. Cut off from the rest of the world by fields and hedges, it aped the mannerisms of a limited monarchy without a foreign policy. It had a domestic policy—of an unrelenting, reactionary kind—and it had its courts of justice, its police, its pomp, its self-satisfied egregiousness of citizenship, its state religion, and its unbreakable tradition of manners. Almost at once, too, I discovered that it had its three bars. This fact surprised me, for I had been informed so often that "all that sort of nonsense gets knocked out of a boy in a public school." I found just the contrary to be the case. "All that sort of nonsense" is openly encouraged by the boys themselves, by the masters, and by the Procrustean laws. A boy is commonly written down "a cad," not for the reason of any moral, physical, or intellectual lapse, but because some slip in the conventions betrays the fact that he has strayed into the saloon bar, whereas his proper place is the public bar. It may be through wearing the wrong-shaped collar, or brushing his hair in an unusual manner, or failing to catch the exact intonation of the popular accent, or some intangible abuse of fashion; but whatever it is, the law is inexorable. Moreover, whereas in my father's house the laws of the bars were liberal in their construction, and elastic in their interpretation, at Leydhurst they were enforced with acid cruelty. God never invented anything crueller or more primitive than the average public-school boy. He has not the merciful 'sphyxiating bite of the spider, but he has all the luxurious cruelties of a cat. He enjoys torturing his victim. He finds out all the raw edges of its sensibility and he nags away at them.

He is taught to believe that his school stands for something—something connected vaguely with the glory of England, the singing of "Onward, Christian Soldiers," and the almost sublime ambition to come out top of the cricket averages. For the rest, everything is futile and effeminate, consequently to be tortured and ragged out of existence.

His preceptors are always dinning into his ears phrases about honour, loyalty, independence, and truth. He considers honour an affair of sticking up for the people in his own bar; he feels loyalty to be safe with the vision of his father going to the city in a top-hat and paying his rates and taxes; he mistakes egoism for independence, and he has no use at all for truth. Ambition is satisfied by being like everybody else, only more so.

At Leydhurst most of the boys were what I might call "private bar" boys, but there were quite a good few saloons, and a generous sprinkling of the "unspeakable publics," always referred to as cads. There was only one possible loophole for the cad to escape into the more select bars, and that was by virtue of his muscles. A real "blood" was tolerated anywhere, partly through the fear which he inspired and partly through the awe and respect which a public performer always commands, be he an actor or a football-blue.

II

I do not propose to enlarge upon the impressions of my school-life, but I must pay a handsome tribute to the sagacity of Uncle Stephen in giving me the advice he did on the eve of my departure.

I was one of about fifteen new boys, and during the first week we were all subjected to an interminable cross-examination. Every old boy, bigger than oneself, came up to one and said, "What's your name?" and then, "What's your father?" and usually a string of other questions. If the boy was smaller than you, you naturally told him to go to hell, but if he was bigger, you either had to answer or get your head clumped, or involve yourself in unknown terrors in the days to come. The questions were designed primarily to discover which bar you aspired to. I must say at once that my reply of "an hotel proprietor" was entirely satisfactory. I realised later on how valuable this answer was, for another new boy came whose father was a publican, and he said so. The gibes and general contumely which this brought upon his head overwhelmed him for the rest of his school-days. He was flung mercilessly into the most sawdusty corner of the public bar, labelled "that little cad Tompkins," and subjected to continuous ironic questionings about the price of gin.

Somehow the term "an hotel proprietor" bore an entirely different complexion. My father might only be a shareholder in one of those big hotels on the Embankment, or he might own one of the sunny-terraced places on the south coast. Anyway, a proprietor only proprieted. He didn't even necessarily work. He must attend board meetings in a top-hat. He might be rich.

I found myself quite easily in the saloon bar, the more especially as I was fitted out with the best of clothing, and father kept me liberally supplied with pocket-money.

Nevertheless, the whole of my first term was a torture. I was utterly wretched and homesick. I yearned for Laura and stepmother. How ghastly is all this isolating of the sexes. The army, the navy, and the schools . . . they all have that bleak unreality of Leydhurst. Men and women, boys and girls, they should always be accessible to each other. Women are no better or worse than men, but they shroud them with their unfathomable mysteries. The design included them, and when they are left out the pattern of everything becomes distorted. A community of isolated men pursues the chimera of qualities which it terms—manliness, a quality which has nothing to recommend it at all. And so it forms false standards, puffs out its chest, bullies, conspires, hates, and makes wars, and panders to its stultified licentiousness.

The limited monarch who ruled over this establishment was an individual as far removed from my conception of a satisfactory social being as anything I had ever seen. He was intensely affable and patronising. A thin, elderly man, with a refined narrow face, always smiling and anxious. He had taken various degrees at Cambridge, including that of Doctor of Divinity. His smile was a sickly, defensive posture without any sympathetic appeal. It appeared to be the nervous outcome of his anxiety to impress the school trustees that he was observing the orthodox conditions of his appointment; towards the masters an expression of the kindly good-humour in which he took his position in this third-rate school when his talents obviously were worthy of a nobler institution; towards the boys the expression of a super-saloon-bar lounger who is rather ashamed of being seen there and suddenly catches the eye of the small boy who takes home his landlady's washing. The interminable services in the chapel nearly drove me distracted. Everything was droned, intoned, and conducted on the line of least resistance. The fat mathematical master talking sleepily about the anger of God . . . someone's turn to read the Lessons—old James, the "Stinks" master, snuffily spouting . . . as though he were quoting from a seed catalogue. No one convinced about anything, everyone doing it because the barbarian festival is an interesting heritage that every well-conducted limited monarchy ought to retain. "Am I mad? Or are they all mad?" would sometimes flash through my mind. Then Mr. Speen up in the organ-loft would pull out a stop, and the school would really let itself go.

"Onward, Christian sol-hol-ol-jer-ers,
Marching as to er-war-er,
With the cross of Jee-zus
Going on before-er."

This appalling tune can only appeal to the worst passions of the mob. It is perverted romanticism. I could see its effect on the faces of the boys. I knew its effect upon myself. We loved it while it lasted. It intoxicated me with thoughts of Laura, the gay lights in my father's saloon . . . the world before me, with its doors to all the mysteries unopened. Savage impulses stirred in me, an indolent condensation of the senses. I felt gloriously self-centred, important, superior. But how slowly it all moved. Would the term never end? If only I weren't a new boy!

III

The Easter vacation was the briefest, but oh, how glorious and free! How I envied Laura, now a student at the Royal Academy of Music in Tenterden Street. How full and thrilling her life appeared! Growing up . . . her long legs filling out, her leather music case, her pigtail caught up and tied with a red bow on the nape of her neck, her checks fuller and fatter, her eyes more animated than ever; frightfully busy and consumed with the important development of her career. Yes, career! . . . career, that was Laura's new magnet. Wonderful stories about professors and fellow-students, and playing at "the Fortnightlies" ... the importance of it all, overpowering. And her freedom of movement, her dazzling freedom of choosing ribbons and selecting stockings, no walls of Jericho to fall on her if she blew the wrong blast on the trumpet. And people, always fresh and interesting people, passing through her life, touching her, surprising her and passing on. And my father, childishly glad to have me home, pretending not to be proud to have a public-school boy for a son. And in the afternoon I walk with him (an innovation this), and the streets are full of hansom-cabs, and bicycles, and gloriously beautiful women, and I am again in touch with the eternal verities. Every woman I meet appears to contain the embryo of an entirely new set of human experiences. I, too, am growing up. Leydhurst is forgotten. Suddenly the deep voice of my father says:

"Are you happy at school, Tom?"

He does not look at me, and we march stolidly along.

"Father," I reply, and I realise that this is one of the first effects of my immersion into the Leydhurst principle of "manliness." There must be something in a system which inspires one to lie so cheerfully. Then there comes a curious, eerie, uncomfortable suspicion creeping up my spine. It concerns my father. I'm not sure that he would fit into the Leydhurst scheme of things. If he came down on Speech Day, what would the boys think of him? It had never occurred to me before to doubt my father. He is just himself. They could never appreciate all the fine shades of his character. His sense of honour, his loyalty, his independence, his truthfulness. He might wear the wrong clothes! he might drop an h or a g! or he might say something which showed that he was not an hotel proprietor, but a publican! He might come down in brown gaiters and square-toed boots! Appalling! I began to realise that Leydhurst was casting its spell over me.

IV

Indeed, it did not take long for this metamorphosis to take place. In the course of a few terms I was as much of a prig as the best of them. I was as securely tied up as the daddy-long-legs in the spider's web. I wrote a lying letter to my father persuading him not to come down on Speech Day, although I was yearning to see him. I gave some rambling reason; I forget exactly what it was. The summer term slipped by fairly pleasantly. There was sunshine and cricket, and I had learnt from Uncle Stephen to "stand up to 'em." I made facile friendships, learnt how to avoid being bullied, discovered a soul in an assistant master, and was a popular figure in the tuck-shop, being always in a position to stand treat.

During the whole of my four and a half years the Head only spoke to me once—apart from the usual business of scholastic life. On that occasion I was standing in the corridor of the quadrangle and he came past. He glanced at me and smiled pleasantly, and said:

"Ah, Purbeck!"

It struck me at the time as being very decent of the old chap. It implied that he recognised me and did not take me for Simpkins junior, also that I was not doing anything at the moment to annoy him, like standing on my head or putting out my tongue. But when I look back upon it, it does not impress me as suggesting excessive interest, when I realise that it represents the complete record of our intercourse.

But there was a second master, who for a long time was my form-master, who was of a more sympathetic disposition. Like most of the other masters, he rang the changes on tweed suits and the cloth of the Church.—the Reverend James Parke Tidsall. He was a middle-aged man with a laboriously over-modelled face, sallow in colour. It seemed to be all lumps and projections. He looked like a man who had suffered untold anguish and lived through it, or untold temptations and mastered them; and every time he triumphed in this way a piece of his face stuck out further. In the process his eyes had been left right back in his head, peering through his shaggy eyebrows like those of a bear in a cage. But they were kindly, penetrating, interested.

He ignored me for two terms, and then one day something I said in class seemed to amuse him. I was bidden to tea. He had a pleasant, ironic way of inviting your opinion upon some vast generality, as though he were trying to extract some measure of relief from the tedious routine of school-life. He would say:

"Well, Purbeck, what do you make of life?" or "Now, Purbeck, if you were in power, tell me what your foreign policy would be?"

He asked me endless and intimate questions about my home-life, beginning with the inevitable:

"Tell me, Purbeck, what is your father?"

To this I replied airily, "Oh, he owns hotels, sir." (Disgusting little snob!)

"Excellent! An excellent and essentially paternal profession for a father. A kind of fidus Achates to the wanderer and outcast. And you! Do you propose also to minister to the material comforts of mankind?"

He was the only one who seemed to connect the limited monarchy in any way with the friction of the world. He was the only cabinet minister with a foreign policy. I remember very vividly a remark he made to me during my last term. He said:

"Well, Purbeck, what are you going to do in the world? You'll never get on by just being a nice boy."

Naturally I had no concerted programme to set before the Rev. James Parke Tidsall, but so completely impregnated was I then with the Leydhurst spirit that I replied nonchalantly:

"Oh, I don't know, sir. The pater has an idea of my going up to Oxford, and taking up law."

A cold-blooded lie! I never called him "the pater." He had never breathed a word about Oxford, and I had as un-legal a mind as any boy in the school. But "the law" sounded well. In the best Leydhurstian manner. And all the time I was thinking:

"What a queer thing to say about being a nice boy!"

It sounded so dismally weak and damning. Had I only the limitations of the nice boy, and nothing else? I didn't at all want to be a nice boy. In fact, I wasn't. I wouldn't be. I glowered against the wall, and felt unhappy. The eyes of Mr. Tidsall were watching me quizzically. Suddenly, some queer spirit of revolt broke out in me. I cut in savagely with:

"What I'd like to do myself is to keep a pub like my father does, and hand out pots of beer" . . .

The eyes of Mr. Tidsall completely vanished among the projections on his face; hundreds of little lines ran hither and thither like streams trickling down the valleys between the hills. He put his arm round my shoulder and led me into the corridor (for the bell was ringing for chapel).

"It is just as I suspected," he said.

Good! He'd suspected it; then he could tell them, and be damned to them.

"Mr. Goodrich and I were discussing you the other day. He had an idea you were destined for the Church, but I said, 'No, I know quite well what Purbeck will become.'"

All right, then; get on with it. Say a pub keeper, or a potman . . . quick!

"Only I am still a little indeterminate in which branch it will be.'"

What do you mean? Father's only got one branch. That's in Camden Town.

"'But,' I said, 'I am quite convinced that Purbeck will manifest surprising ability in one of the arts.'"

He grinned his departure into the passage to the vestry. As I stood amongst the group of boys in the chapel, chanting more or less in unison:

'O all ye little hills and sheep,
Bless ye the Lord:
Praise Him and magnify
Him for ever."

it suddenly occurred to me, "He must have thought I was acting." It was very difficult to arrive at truth in this place. What was the old saying about Truth in Wine? Perhaps so. . . . Perhaps in my father's house there was more truth than there was in this chapel.

Under the influence of drink men were apt to say exactly what came into their heads. My father himself drank sometimes, but never to excess.

"For the Lord is a great God and a great King above all gods. In His hands are all the corners of the world, and the hills and the sheep are His also."

I would like to have this service conducted just once with everybody drunk. Especially the Head, and that thin, vinegary little wife of his with a down on her upper lip. I would like to see Tidsall and Goodrich, and all the other masters, garrulously drunk and discussing the truth of the whole thing. Old James, the "Stinks" master, a Scotsman and no fool, explaining precisely what he meant by "the anger of God." How grand it would all be! Grand and inspiring! And Mr. Speen up in the organ-loft, leaning over the balustrade and telling the Head exactly what he thought of him, in his own language (Speen was a Welshman). And suddenly above it all a fearful crash, and my father's voice ringing out:

"Silence, gentlemen!"

CHAPTER IV

LAURA'S AFFAIR

Laura came into my room to brush her hair. It was a pleasant intimation that old customs need I not be discarded because she was now a woman of the world and I a man who had left school the previous day. I was in bed, too excited to get up; too busy with various anticipations. The winter sun illumined the cosy companionableness of the whole room: the green-tiled washstand, the buff-coloured walls, the photograph of Henry Irving as Hamlet nonchalantly holding the skull of Yorick, my school things piled up carelessly by the fireplace like passengers waiting at a railway-station, and, above all, the face of Laura reflected in the mirror in front of the window, intensely familiar and queerly unfamiliar. Her mobile face, olive, foreign-looking, broadly modelled above the brow, her dark, animated eyes and full red lips. She swung her head first one side, then the other, as she brushed out the great tresses of her blue-black hair . . . absorbingly interesting. She talked breathlessly, but I was almost too consumed with the vision of her to listen properly. How beautiful she was growing! At least, no, not exactly beautiful; but you had to look at her. She gripped you. There was always something going on about her.

"She is like a musical instrument herself," I thought.

"You can play on her."

I knew all about Laura and her glorious life. She wrote me breathless letters to school fairly regularly, but always with the "frantic haste" side emphasised. When she went to the Academy they soon found out that her second study—the fiddle—should really be the first study, so the piano had had to play second fiddle, as it were. She was very much in earnest, worked like a Trojan, and had undeniable talent. She was launched. The Career, with a very, very big capital C, was already in progress. She had played at the Fortnightlies and at a public concert at Blackheath; and she drove about London in hansom-cabs with young men. Magnificent! And yet there was something more than this about Laura which fascinated me. She was so very much a woman and so completely incomprehensible. It was largely this incomprehensibility which intrigued me, I think. It seemed to link me to all the potentialities of romance. As I watched her the memory of Leydhurst dwindled to a sound like a toneless repetition of a proposition in Euclid ... as though one had spent years proving something that had been proved already, and wasn't really worth proving when you had done it.

A middle-aged lady named Mrs. Snell, and a great friend of stepmother's, once said: "Laura is one of these temperamental women. That is to say, she's always either irritable or amorous."

On the surface there was a horrid element of truth in that statement. No one could be more charming than Laura, acutely sympathetic, affectionate and gay. On the other hand, no one could be more trying or unreasonable. She magnified trifles, worked herself into a frenzy over quite hypothetical grievances, was easily jealous, and could at times be positively cruel.

II

I do not know what she had been saying, but I found her sitting on my bed. She was still busy with her hair. Suddenly she said:

"Did the boys ever say anything about it?"

"What?"

"Dad's business."

I felt an odd feeling of shame creep over me. I replied:

"No. They didn't know—exactly."

She gave me one of her quick looks and said:

"You never told them?"

"No—I—I didn't tell them."

Some tremendous emotion was passing over her face. She jammed hairpins into a dangerous position in her mouth and spluttered through them:

"I didn't either, but—they found out It's disgusting."

I felt peculiarly guilty. Laura and I were both guilty, and both rather mean.

"After all," I said rather lamely, "it's nothing to be ashamed of."

She stood up and exclaimed quite fiercely:

"Isn't it! You wait till you start doing things!"

She shook out her hair again vigorously. Then she added:

"Do you know, it's been perfectly beastly! I know what they all think. When anyone—wants to bring me home in a cab, I—never let them come to the door. I get off in the Camden Road. I make some excuse. But all the same, they know. I can tell by the way they look at me. I've heard some of the girls snigger, and refer to beer."

It was obviously up to me to defend my father's position. I had never given the ethical side of the problem much consideration. I had simply felt unreasonably ashamed, like Laura—a shame prompted mostly by the thought of what others would think. I sat up in bed and said:

"As you know, dad conducts his business as decently as any tradesman in Camden Town. Anyone will tell you. It's caddish of us to criticise. He earns the money that keeps us. There's nothing wrong with the business when it's decently conducted. It's simply the abuse that's bad. It's just the same with a butcher or a grocer. If people go and eat too much you can't blame the butcher or the grocer."

"I know! I know all about that," replied Laura. "At the same time, it's beastly! Especially when you're trying to do things. You come up against it all the time."

She began rolling up her hair at a furious pace.

"You needn't pretend," she went on. "You've found it out already. Why did you always write and choke dad off coming down to you on Speech Days?"

This was an unpleasant thrust. A bold insinuation that I not only denied my father's business, but that I repudiated my father himself. It was a fact I would never acknowledge, even to myself. How disgusting Laura was!

"I only thought it would bore him," I ventured.

Laura laughed, implying that she knew that I knew that I was lying. Why was Laura always so annoying in this way? She always lived in the instant. I had been away for all this time, and directly I got home she butted in at once with all this unpleasant innuendo. I wanted to begin at the beginning. One might go away for five years, and Laura would meet you at the station on your return, and you would perhaps find her having a row with a porter. And she would continue the row and be full of the details of it for half an hour, as though it were a more important event than your return. You had to know her very well to know that of course she didn't really think so. You had to play her like a salmon. She would swing back after a time and would demand to know every little incident of your journey. And afterwards you would find that she had forgotten nothing that you told her. In fact, she would remember things you said, and bring them up in argument against you years after. Some little incidents you might relate which occurred to you as being trivial and humorous, and she would find them tragic and almost unbearable. Other episodes which appeared to you quite ordinary would supply her with an inexhaustible fund of mirth. Of course I couldn't repudiate the dad! At least, not exactly. It was only the slow realisation that the two ingredients wouldn't mix. I thought much more of the dad than I did of the school. Only I was not strong enough to stand up against the school atmosphere. Father wasn't cultivated, of course. ... I remembered one day after my first year making some reference to Darwin. Father had immediately fired up.

"Darwin! Fiddlesticks! Don't talk to me about Darwin. What I say is, if a man came from a monkey, why shouldn't a cock-sparrow have come from an elephant?"

Quite unanswerable, but it wouldn't do, you know. Fancy the Rev. James Parke Tidsall overhearing such a remark I ... It wouldn't do at all. It was very gradual, this process of discovering the danger of a little knowledge. And here was Laura taunting me with her "trying to do things." Of course I meant to try and do things. Laura wasn't going to have it all her own way. I said spitefully:

"Well, cheese it! I'm going to get up."

In a flash the mood of Laura swung to the opposite pole. She struck an attitude, holding the brush above her head, her eyes dancing with merriment.

"I haven't told you the news!" she exclaimed.

"What's that?"

"The Zulu pudding has got a young man."

She burst into laughter and rolled me over on the bed, and I laughed too. Then, picking up my trousers, she threw them at me and rushed out of the room. How fine this life was! How adorable was Laura!

III

I stood looking out of the play-room window. At least, it was no longer now the play-room. It was Laura's "studio." AH our old toys were buried away in boxes. Here she came to practise the fiddle by the hour. It was right away from the rest of the house. The floor was covered with cork-lino. In the comer was a sewing-machine covered up with a wooden lid of some reddish-brown wood. A brass music-stand by the gas-fire held some open sheets of music. Bach! Music was piled up on the floor and on a small bamboo table. There was a heavy leather-upholstered chair and two stools. Odd collections of trunks and bed-fittings tried to hide themselves behind a serge curtain. Cecil Aldin's dogs had been taken down and were superseded by two reproductions of Raphaels. It was partly Laura's room and partly a place of transition. Not a very satisfactory combination. Laura had not come home from the Academy. I was waiting for tea. A fine rain was driving into the darkening streets. Just opposite, a hurdy-gurdy was grinding out a perfectly heart-breaking dirge. The gas-fire hummed. London could be very melancholy.

I enjoyed my periods of melancholy in the same way that I enjoyed a London fog. It was a mysterious condition out of which anything might suddenly appear. I loved the mournful tune of the hurdy-gurdy, thick, treacly, opaque . . . and downstairs in the parlour the gas would be lighted, the tea-cups shining, probably buttered buns. . . . Laura full of exciting tidings, stepmother mildly tremulous, father contagious—blinking round the room, pretending not to be excited too. All very familiar and very dear, to be viewed at various and abrupt angles. A church spire asserted itself vaguely across a vista of chimney-pots. Always beautiful, buildings stretching skywards. Like Oxford, perhaps. Strange I should have said that to the Rev. Parke Tidsall. "Oxford and the law." It was the most Leydhursty attitude of me, the upward thrust of the limited monarchy. . . . Oxford, a dream like going back to the Middle Ages and eating iced meringues, ragging one's way through a Consistory of parchment prelates, being a hero in The Boy's Own Paper serial: the vision gripped me in my most pliable mood. My most vivid friend at Leydhurst, Martyn, really was going up to Oxford, probably the law, possibly politics. But Martyn had it all, all that Oxford would demand of him. I could see him slipping into the toga of the pleasant, cynical reverence for the "ghosts of England's greatness "... a born theorist, crushed by this weight of masonry and taking it all "like a gentleman." I hadn't got it. Oxford was too romantic for me. ... I should go mad! My scale of social values was still imperfectly adjusted. Had Oxford its three bars?

At the Grammar School Laura and I triumphed by the sheer weight of our following. Our new satchels and boots, our barmaids and prize-fighters and Zulu puddings put them all to rout Our position appeared impregnable. Leydhurst and the Royal Academy of Music shifted the focus to a disturbing angle. Certain, things wouldn't do. Certain things weren't done. One might drink his liquor, but one doesn't shake hands with the landlord. Cake for tea and the pantomime at Christmas is not wealth. Should the paintwork of a parlour be picked out in two shades of green? Nay, does one have a parlour at all? How maddening it all was! Poor Laura! she had felt it most bitterly.

Perhaps she had been to places where things were ordered differently, been criticised, ostracised, suffered endless misgivings.

As I stood there, I suffered a sudden realisation of a very definite fact. Something about the sewing-machine in its red-wood case brought it home to me. Father was not really rich. He was only rich in the Grammar School sense. The gilt mirrors in the drawing-room, the superabundance of heavy furniture in the parlour, the plush curtains, the wax fruit, and "The Death of Wolfe"—all an illusion and a snare. The realisation did not distress me. In some peculiar way I felt relieved. Oxford was a mirage—stone fingers pointing at the sky—just another limited monarchy, or perhaps a collection of limited monarchies. What was it people meant by "the Oxford manner"? It must mean that if you once went there you could never eradicate the taint. Even Leydhurst cast its spell, impressed you with a more or less permanent attitude, but Oxford would permeate you. There could be no escape. At the age of sixty you would not be yourself, but an automaton moving up and down "in the Oxford manner." To live, one must always be escaping. I can hear Laura. She is laughing on the floor below, her face bright and pink with the cold wind, her black furs tucked tight beneath her chin. She will have a lot to say. Father is moving heavily on the stairs and laughing, too. His voice comes booming up:

"Tom!"

"Yes, dad?"

"What was it the King of North Carolina said to the—"

Thank God!

IV

Was there ever anything so persistent as Laura's first lover? I think he excited me more than he did Laura herself. I'm not sure that he was absolutely her first lover, but he was the first to break through the cordon of our reserves and carry "The Duchess of Pless" by assault. He was a fellow-student at the Royal Academy, and his name was Anton Zuk. I could only piece his story together from my own observations, and from various confessions which Laura was good enough to give me. His mother was French and his father was a Czech. His father had been killed in a duel over some affair connected with a Polish dancer. His mother had served a term of imprisonment for throwing vitriol over the wife of a Government official. Neither of the love-affairs were in any way connected. When released, she had brought the boy Anton to England. He was then fifteen. Both he and his mother detested England. "They could think of nothing bad enough to say of the place or the people, but they had continued to live here for ten years. His mother had a certain amount of money, and they lived in a fiat in Netting Hill. As a musician he had no technique at all, but he was a kind of musical maniac. He had a small, sweet tone, and after he had played he was speechless with emotion for several minutes. One felt he was going to be ill. His face went a kind of greeny colour, his lips trembled, and his eyes quivered dangerously. His hatred and contempt for all other musicians was almost painful. If you mentioned their names, he would have a hiss like a snake. At the fortnightly concerts he hissed the other students. He hissed his professor when he criticised him. He had a small black moustache which he jerked up round his nose on such occasions, exposing a line of brilliantly white teeth.

His mother encouraged these manifestations. He would play some quite ordinary little air, dragging it out, smudging the passages, and over-sentimentalising it, and accompanying the whole performance with loud snortings and gasps. When he had finished he would put his violin down and stand there like a tottering statue. His mother would rush across the room and throw her arms round his neck, and weep, murmuring passionately:

"Oh, ma mie . . . ma mie . . . adorable!"

One day at the Academy, Laura was practising in one of the rooms whilst waiting for her professor. She had, as a matter of fact, gone to the wrong room. The professor had not turned up; she continued to enjoy herself. She said she played very well. When she had finished she was about to put her violin back in its case, when she observed a small man tip-toeing across the room. It was Anton Zuk. She knew him by sight. She said:

"Hullo!"

The room was getting dark. He made no reply, but as he advanced she noticed that his eyes were shining. He stretched out both hands to her and almost involuntarily she placed hers in his, to find in less than a minute that they were saturated with tears and kisses.

"At last! At last!" was all He said.

She said that the experience produced in her an odd sense of mystified elation. She could not make up her mind whether she wanted to kiss him on the lips or to box his ears. She did neither, but stood there powerless. He continued to hold her hands, but looking wildly into her eyes, he murmured:

"Tom . . . you, I adore you. I have watched you. You are the only one. An artist, a musician. All your soul. . . . God! how beautiful you are!"

What could Laura be expected to do? She was twenty. It was the first time anyone had told her she was "an artist, a musician." The first time anyone had singled her out and told her she was beautiful. The whole thing was too good to be thrown away. Her own romantic impulses were profoundly stirred. She drew her hands away at last and replied feebly:

"Oh, do you think so?"

The outer fortifications had fallen. She put up a stiff fight to defend the approaches to "The Duchess of Pless." She manoeuvred with him over teas and lunches. She skirmished with him in passages and corridors. She marooned him in Regent's Park„ and completely side-tracked him in the Camden Road.

One day she unburdened her soul to him. In reply to his protestations, she said:

"I can't ask you home, Anton. My father keeps a public-house."

For a moment he appeared to tremble, then, seizing her hands feverishly, he whispered:

"I will wash it all away with my tears."

The vision of Anton Zuk washing away such a solid institution as "The Duchess of Pless" with his tears might have stirred her risibility, only that she felt a little shocked and offended. What did he mean? It wasn't at all the right kind of reply. As a matter of fact, Herr Zuk did not properly understand the meaning of a "public-house." It came out afterwards, in the course of a fevered attempt at reconciliation, that he thought "a public-house" was a kind of house of ill-fame. The revelation did not amend matters, but it produced storms of emotion, cross-currents of misunderstanding; it taxed the maternal resources of Laura. All her pity for him welled up. She enjoyed it enormously.

And one Sunday evening, quite unbidden, he called. He had tracked her to her lair. The visit was not a success. Uncle Stephen was there, and two old friends of father's, a Mr. and Mrs. Pennycuick, also connected with the licensing trade. Anton sulked in the corner, never taking his eyes off Laura except to bare his teeth at the company. Mr. Pennycuick, a large, impersonal man with a red, mobile face and a highly-coloured waistcoat held together with hundreds of leather buttons, once rounded him up and gave him a long dissertation on music-hall comedians in the 'seventies. It came about through hearing that Anton was a musician. He stood it for nearly fifteen minutes, then he turned abruptly away. A little later on he vanished without saying a word.

When he had gone, father showed his disapproval by a sullen gloom.

Uncle Stephen butted in with:

"Who is this garlic-eating little mountebank you had here?"

Mrs. Pennycuick sniggered and said:

"Really! I thought these foreigners were supposed to have manners? Really!"

The thing might have fizzled out except for this opposition. Laura naturally took his side. She said he was a genius—a great artist; none of us could understand him. She flounced out of the room and went to bed without supper.

The next day she walked with him in Regent's Park. He observed her sympathetic mien, and crowded in all his advantages.

"It is horrible . . . horrible, this life of yours," he growled. "These people—s'ss—that fat man. Who are they all? Laura, you must come away with me. I will save you from them—s'ss! God how I love you. You have beauty, intelligence, a soul. You should live where only beauty moves softly. Some little place we will have just to ourselves. You and I. And at night I will draw the great curtain, and you shall play to me—the Lalo, as you did this afternoon. And I will sit so, with my eyes closed, crushing out the memory of everything except you . . . you, slowly swaying to the rhythm of my lover."

He gripped her hand and added: "To-morrow you shall know everything."

There was something intriguing in this idea. Laura had always wanted to know everything. It sounded dangerous, and Laura was never known to flinch at danger.

They met on a bridge over Regent's Park Canal. His face was deadly white, and he was restless and mysterious. Suddenly he snatched a book from his breast pocket. It was an old Bible in Czech characters.

"Look," he said. "This was my father's Bible. He carried it with him on his campaigns. See my love for you."

He opened it and tore out a handful of pages—the whole of the Book of Deuteronomy—and flung them over the railing. A light wind scattered them over the surface of the canal.

"So I would tear out all that is sacred in me to serve you. These sheets, like the blood from my heart, shall mingle with the waters of the river. On and on they shall go till they reach the great sea. And St. Aloysius will find them. He is my patron saint. He will understand my message."

"But this isn't a river, this is only a canal. It doesn't run into the sea at all!"

Poor Laura! I don't know whether he ever kissed her, but I know he bit her once in a paroxysm of love or hate. The scar was on the angle of her jaw for weeks. He was always hanging about the road when she went out. He sent her enormous bouquets of orchids and boxes of sweets tied up with scented ribbons. He sneaked into the house at odd times, and once went into the bar. Unfortunately, not knowing the ropes of the establishment, he went into the public bar, drank two glasses of beer, and nearly got thrown out by Jingle for having a row with a navvy. He sent her long poems in French, broke his violin over his knee in a fit of humility at her superior playing, threatened her with a revolver and two knives; appeared one day with a gash above his heart. He had tried to stab himself but fainted before the fell deed was accomplished. He made love, swore, cursed, whined, and threatened in five European languages and one Asiatic. What was Laura to make of it? Was ever woman in this manner wooed? Was ever woman in this manner won? The answer is probably yes.

It was father who cut the Gordian knot of this erotic persecution. I know, because I happened to observe the whole performance. Anton had called, and Laura was out. I watched the top of his head as he walked reluctantly downstairs. At the foot of the stairs was father He looked ugly, very thick and square in his tweed knickerbockers and brown gaiters and square-toed boots, still glistening with the early-morning gloss. His face was rather red and his eyes protruded, as they did when anything excited him. His hair stuck out, and he was bristling like an Irish terrier watching a rabbit hole. He spoke quite calmly, but with a note of acid finality:

"Look here, if I find you hanging about my gal any more, I'll give you a damn good hiding."

CHAPTER V

BACKGROUNDS

Suckling and Gradidge, two other clerks, and I sat on high stools, balancing the quarterly accounts. Mr. Barnard, the managing director of Messrs. Braysfelt & Stene, the wall-paper manufacturers in High Street, Marylebone, had impressed upon us the necessity of getting the work finished by Saturday. This was Thursday afternoon. An exhausted sun crept down the flank of the high building in the court and cast wistful patterns on our desks and ledgers. A quarter past five—another hour and a quarter to go. What an important companion is a clock when you are employed on uncongenial work! He is either your friend or your enemy. He has two friendly hours—lunchtime and knocking-off time. Otherwise you do your best not to gaze upon his face, and yet your eye is always wandering thither, and then he is your enemy. A good plan is to persuade yourself that it is much earlier than it is, then if you look up he gives you a pleasant smile. But woe unto you if you worry him I He frowns, and frowns, and sulks—sometimes he appears to stop altogether. I was in a bad mood. My clock detested and tortured me. Something about the sunlight stirred memories of Leydhurst. Not such a bad place, after all, the limited monarchy. The habit of cricket, and sport, and rags takes a lot of eradicating from the blood. The schoolboy in a city office . . . cruel! The transit should be more gradual. What sort of school had Suckling been to? I never liked to ask him. He was much older than I. He might have been born and bred in this place. He had a clear-cut bird-like face, with glasses, and his long broad fingers were interminably stained with red and black ink. He seldom smiled, but was always pleasant and good tempered. His life appeared to satisfy him. Not so Gradidge, who was a glutton for work but always in a state of revolt about some little thing. A North countryman, clear-headed, ambitious, and frankly a materialist, but with a mild sympathy for other things. He was only dissatisfied because he was not making more money. Strange that it should have come to this. Not Oxford and the law, or even one of the arts, as Mr. Tidsall hinted, but—just going on being a nice boy!

I know I had been a nice boy in a fateful interview with dad. Some parents have a genius for concealing their feelings, and male parents have a special side-line genius for lying low about their business affairs with the family. Neither Laura nor I had the faintest idea what father's position was: whether we ought to be prodigal, or whether we ought to be economical. He gave us everything we wanted, but kept the reins well in his own hand. Laura was now twenty-one, and explained to me that other girls at the E.A. had an allowance. Father would not do that. He never denied her a penny, but she had to come and ask for it. And then, a month after my leaving school, occurred that embarrassing interview.

I can see father now, pushing his way about the furniture in the parlour, rather red in the face, blowing his nose an unnecessary number of times. Something, it appeared, had gone wrong. One of his partners had defaulted—an awful muddle about some shares. All news to me. This was the first I had heard of partners. I had always looked upon "The Duchess of Pless" as a benevolent autocracy. Father was frightfully upset—obviously worried. He had had other hopes for me. (Oxford?) Now he feared I should have to buckle down. It was very regrettable. Oh no, not really—serious. We could all go on the same. Laura must continue her studies. She would complete her course soon. Only ... he had hoped something better. I must choose a career. We should all have to hedge a little.

A career! Under the circumstances how could I hit upon the choice of one of the idle and quite unnecessary arts? I felt a wave of chivalry and commercial ambition sweep over me. It would be my mission to save my father's house.

"How would it do if I helped you, dad?"

What a nice boy I was! But my father shook his head dubiously. No, the licensing trade was not one he would recommend to—me. If I thought of entering a commercial house, it could easily be arranged. Chartered accountancy, insurance, ship-broking, all good, remunerative professions to a young and energetic man. As my father fidgeted with the arm of the horsehair chair I realised that he knew nothing about me except that I was a nice boy. I knew even less about him, except that he was my father. Love blinds one. Children to parents are an embarrassing joy, seen through an emotional mist. He looked so helpless and unget-at-able. My heart bled with pity for him. Again he spoke:

"Things will mend, I hope. I'm sure they will. My friend Barnard, the wall-paper man, said he could do with a lad to learn the business . . . could start straight away on a low salary. I want you to do what you like, Tom."

II

I was thrilled, but disappointed. Quite soon, whatever else happened, I should be encountering new experiences, rubbing shoulders with fellow-strugglers, seeing new faces, earning my living, starting out on that long trail to the Mecca of what we call—independence. But—a wall-paper factory did not appear very alluring. It had not the human appeal of my father's splendid bars. Wall-papers were a background. It was the actors themselves who moved me. I wriggled from one leg to another, and answered:

"That would be fine."

The spring found me learning the wall-paper tirade as a junior clerk. I was taken over the factory and shown the various processes of sizing, printing, flocking, gilding, and folding. The old building seemed to rock with the eternal rumble of rollers and machinery. Doors banged. Boys, with their faces splashed with whitening, rushed hither and thither. Men in white linen overalls performed dexterous feats of conversion upon lengths of white paper with the aid of sticks and rollers and machines. It fascinated me to watch the pattern grow. One, two, three, sometimes as many as seventeen printings, and behold! rich bunches of flowers and vines ready for my lady's boudoir. It seemed incredible that there could be enough bare walls to support all this illusion. I began to love the smell of size. Every trade has its smell which to the craftsman is as inspiring as salt to a sailor. But down in the dingy offices among the account books and ledgers my soul dried up. It was there I began to understand about the clock.

Still only—twenty past five. Another hour and ten minutes. Damn Suckling! Why doesn't he scream or sing? It is summer time . . . July. The fields at Leydhurst will be green and cool. Perhaps there's a school match to-day. Long and Biddle coming out to bat. The boys cheering. A starling twittering above the pavilion. . . .

What are all these figures? We added them up three times. Twice they were different—the first time I've forgotten. I was always bad at figures. "Maths." proved my Sedan in the Metric: I must make an effort £47 15s 3d. No, it's never been that before. What a queer-shaped head Gradidge has. Like a ram his forehead bulges out, but there's no back to it. Has Gradidge people? A mother? A sister? Of course he's married! He's always talking about "the missus," as one might talk of "the Press" or "the Government." Whatever sort of woman would she be? A decent chap, but how horrible to be married to him! Everything would become tight, formed, inelastic. As he gets older the way will narrow and narrow. I mustn't do that. The woman I marry . . . apple-blossoms against a sky heavy with heat-mist, king cups and clover diapering the green meadows, a skylark singing of lovers who have passed, the air tender with unborn memories . . . why unborn? Because I know all about them before they happen—these episodes. I shall only live them all again. Her eyes melting before the fire of mine, the fragrance of her body ... is it all unknown to me because I have not met her? She is coming across the meadows, alert and watchful; her little chin is raised in expectation, her cheeks dimple, the apple-blossom nods approval; sunburnt mirth sparkles from her eyes, she stretches out her arms . . .

Hullo! It's half -past six.

III

Laura suffered from a popular womanly illusion. Which is, that if a thing is reasonable it ought to be done, and done at once and unquestioningly. This has never been man's way. He knows too much about logic to employ any of the dangerous stuff. He equivocates and buries his head in the sand.

Reason has never been a very powerful factor in shaping human affairs. Love, greed, and the Roman Catholic Church, even the daily Press, have all done more.

Laura had nothing of the conspirator about her. If she wanted a thing, she yelled for it instantly. If denied it, she wanted to know why, and the reason had to be pretty convincing. If she thought it right and reasonable that she should have it, she fought for it as relentlessly and with the same unscrupulous methods that she employed when she fought me in the garden about the spiders.

One evening she tracked me to my room, and began by saying:

"I've made up my mind."

I knew this meant trouble of some sort, so I emitted a grunt of lukewarm enquiry.

"I've been thinking about it a lot. And I'm not going to stand it any longer. It's ruining my career."

"What is?"

"Living at home. I'm going to get rooms out—probably somewhere near Baker Street or the Park. Of course I shall come home for the week-end and at odd times. But I'm going to have my own place. I'm getting on. Jakes' have got me several engagements for next season, and I'm going to teach. If dad doesn't like to help me out with the rent, he can do the other thing."

I said, "But the old chap will be very upset."

Laura's eyes flashed. "I can't help that. He'll get over it. I don't see why I should have my whole career spoilt just to humour a whim of his."

"Well, it's not exactly a whim."

"What isn't?"

"Living with your own people."

"Yes, it is. There's no reason for it at all."

She kicked one of my slippers across the carpet, and exploded:

"Lord! How I hate these beastly bars! The smell of beer and tobacco, the crowds of half-drunken

"You don't go in there."

"No, but you're conscious of them all the time. And you pass outside and see them. And everybody knows you're connected with the beastly place. A pub! A filthy pub! And last week-end I spent with the Copleys at Tring. Bare walls, chintz, and old furniture . . . taste, everybody moving softly, talking of interesting things, a silence I never knew existed, like a deep velvet curtain against which everything seems beautiful. I'm sorry, old boy, if I seem selfish. But I don't see why I shouldn't make a start. As a matter of fact, I don't see why you shouldn't. You'll never get on, going backwards and forwards between this pub and the wall-paper factory."

"It's all very well" I began, and then I could not exactly determine what was all very well. The matter required enormous consideration. I hadn't Laura's set conviction that "getting on" was the Alpha and Omega of life. I hesitated and said:

"When are you going?"

"On Monday."

IV

Father's attitude in the matter surprised me. It was an eventuality which had never occurred to him, but he took it very well. He was obviously a little disconcerted, disappointed perhaps, but he laughed and exclaimed:

"Oh-ho-ho! So that's it, is it?"

I saw him standing in the yard, smoking, and thinking it over for nearly an hour. Then he took a 'bus to Slocombe Street, Marylebone, where Laura had taken her rooms. He took a long look at the landlady, without making any comment; then he examined the drains. Being apparently satisfied in both cases, he paid a month's rent in advance. He allowed her to take any furniture she wanted from the house, and he bought her a felt for her bedroom. The rooms looked quite pretty when Laura had finished with them, with grey walls and white paint and one or two brilliant-coloured cushions. She explained to me that as she got on she was going to buy old furniture, and to return father's piece by piece.

"I mean to have a four-post bed," she said, "and old oak in the living-room, with Japanese prints and Persian tiles, and a bust of Beethoven."

"What about a few original Van Dykes and Raphaels?" I enquired.

Laura didn't take my humour in good part She flushed and said:

"Oh! you—you never believe in anything."

She was intensely in earnest about it all. She looked upon these rooms in Slocombe Street as the threshold to the Kingdom of Fame. With the gas-ring in the tiny kitchen, curtains to make, a hat to trim, pupils coming at three o'clock, a visit to her agent in the morning, then practice, practice, practice—no time for anything. A breathless life. The clock had not the horrors for her that it had for me. Always late, always rushed, she sent the hours skedaddling like ninepins.

It was unfortunate that the very week she took her departure father was laid up with rheumatism in the eyes. It was a complaint which frequently visited him. He could do nothing but stay; in bed, or sit up in the parlour with a bandage round his head. After supper, stepmother and I took it in turns to read to him—articles out of the Morning Advertiser or the serial story running in Lloyds' News. It was August, and London was close and enervating. One night I went up to the parlour. Father was sitting alone in the dark. I shut the door quietly. How queer he looked in the dim light, the bandage shutting him off from the world. What was he thinking about? Someone across the street was singing a ribald song. One could hear down below the dim murmur of the bar, the occasional popping of corks. How melancholy it seemed without Laura. What a little cat she was. Father turned and heard me.

"Is that you, Mary?"

"No, dad. It's me."

"Oh! Light the lamp, will you, boy?"

"Yes, dad."

The green shade illumined the maze of furniture. I drew the curtains.

"Shall I read to you, dad?"

"Oh! . . . thanks. Yes, you might read me a bit from the paper."

I take up the paper. I skim the headings and the political news. Yes, stepmother has read him the details of the Whitechapel murder. I read a long report of the Distillers' Commission . . . interminable. What is it all about? My thoughts are roaming while I read. What is Laura doing? What is it really like at the Copleys's Chintz and old furniture, people moving softly and talking of interesting things. . . . How I envy Laura, her pluck, her enterprise, her splendid egoism.

"What do you think, dad?"

He does not answer. I tip-toe across the room. Father is asleep, or dreaming of something quite different, too. The Distillers' Commission had been too much even for him. I lower the lights and creep out of the room. Downstairs the bars are gaily lighted. I boldly enter. I am allowed to do this occasionally, now that I am a man of the world. That is, if I have a reason. To-night I want to see the evening paper. It is in any case sufficient excuse. The saloon is nearly empty, but the public and private are full of animation. I get out of the way and pretend to read. The majestic figure of Mrs. Beddoes sways backwards and forwards, carrying tankards of ale. May has left, and a dark girl with a provocative giggle has taken her place. Olive still watches for the prince to enter. She is absently listening to a young man who is telling her some story in a shrill wheeze of how "he did the old bird in." In the private bar are two men having an animated debate. One is a forlorn individual who might be a funeral mute. The other is a thick-set man with side-whiskers. He keeps tapping the other on the top waistcoat-button and saying, "Look here. Small." Tie makes a gurgle as though his argument were suspended above the other's head, ready to drop and crush him. I am suddenly alive to the nature of this remarkable discussion. They are arguing as to whether Jesus Christ would have been a Liberal or a Conservative. The thick-set man is getting the best of it, for the reason that he has a greater capacity for not listening.

"You can say what you like. Small," he insists, "the teachings of Jesus Christ go to show that He was a true-blue Tory. He said, 'The poor ye have with ye always, but Me ye have not always.' What does this mean? It might have been cut out of a leading article in the Standard or the Morning Post Then He said, 'I come not to bring peace but a sword.' What's that? Militarism."

"Yes, but, my dear fellow—"

"Listen to me, Small. Talking about the sword like that showed He was a militarist. Then He said, 'Render unto Caesar the things which are Caesar's.' In other words—support the Constitution. That showed He was a financier. Turning water into wine showed He was in with the brewers. By God! He might have sat in Lord Salisbury's Cabinet."

"Yes, but what about the Sermon on the Mount?"

"Listen to me, Small . . ."

I could listen all night. Father would not approve of this profane discussion. He would order it to cease. But how daring? It was just what I had dreamed might take place in the chapel at Leydhurst. Was the thick-set man sincere? Possibly. Or he may have only been experimenting in his own mind. Some small corner of it became suddenly alive and luminous. Man is the hunter, eternally seeking quarry. Why shouldn't he experiment? Old James, the "Stinks" master, would probably talk like this in his cups—perhaps more logically and convincingly, but still experimentally. What are we all doing? We can't stew in a chapel, repeating things we are not allowed to question. My heart warms to these companionable fellows. Is there truth in the cup? Not only truth, but adventure, tolerance, and a kind of high, romantic courage?

Laura a hostess, serving tea in her own "place." I a guest. In fact, one of several guests. Five of us, and the other four musicians. Septimus Coyne, one of the young British composers, flaccid and rather shiny, with a scrumply down upon his chin which you don't know whether to be intentional or not; Angus Colum, a heavily-built boy with a flat top to his head, leaning forward on his knees and turning his head from side to side, as he grins at the various speakers with an expression which seems to say: "Music's the only thing worth talking about, and even that is rather piffle." He is a violinist, and so is Daisy Weir, a thin, straight' girl whose head is too large for her, and comes forward. She speaks rapidly and emphasises her points by shaking her curls at the listener. The fourth musician is Mary Copley.

In truth, I find my social debut disturbing. I am not a success. They talk music the whole afternoon. Both the men ignore me, except Coyne, who once asks if I have ever had nettlerash. When I say no, he seems disappointed and settles down into a kind of coma. The room is growing darker. Once I rise and go and look out of the window. The street is deserted, except for a lamplighter crossing backwards and forwards. Above the roofs of the houses a star surprises me in the colourless sky. Someone is standing close behind me, and a voice says:

"Don't you love it . . . all this?"

As I turn and look at her, I am profoundly conscious of what she means. It is as though an angel were snatching me from my vision of failure. I rise to the highest pinnacles. She is—I don't know what she is, but I know what she is thinking. Do I love it, all this? This contact with youth blissfully intent on life, watching alertly . . . the melancholy mien of the dying day, the autumn with its tang of wakefulness and hope, the lamplighter? All my emotions are arrested, held and quickened. I do not know what her face is like. It is all in half-shadows, and her deep eyes are questioning me it is just at that angle I shall always see her, as though coming towards me, drawing me, then holding me suspended. Yes, yes, I love it all. But it is you, the contact of this autumn night with you and your disturbing sense of having lived it all before, and yet the blinding surprise, amazement, unexpectedness of you.

CHAPTER VI

ODD SOCKS

There was an awful to do about socks on the day of our wedding. Mary took over the management of me shortly after we were engaged. She thought about all the little things. She wedded herself to my domestic life. It is indeed an excellent plan. One slides into married life, without that abrupt plunge which often proves so chilling. In the first place, I was initiated into the true significance of Woodstack. Woodstack is the name of a small town in Surrey, but it came to represent something infinitely more important. It was a tradition, a cult, a revelation, an entirely new experience. The people who lived at Woodstack lived in a world as remote from the people who frequented "The Duchess of Pless" as the Caspian Sea is remote from one of the Highgate ponds. At Woodstack one could not believe that "The Duchess of Pless" existed. The whole key of my mental outlook became transposed.

I spent a whole year listening, and being surprised. I was madly jealous of all these people who frequented the Copleys' house. They all seemed so clever, and sophisticated, and intimate, and comfortable. I only escaped exposing my Philistine upbringing by remaining silent. I believe I must have almost acquired the reputation of being one of these "strong, silent men." It is a reputation easy to acquire. If you remain silent and keep on frowning people are apt to take the strength for granted.

I frowned because I was angry with myself. I was not entirely ignorant of the matters discussed, but I was feeling my way, and seldom had the courage to express an individual opinion upon these important abstract things. I envied the young man who said that "Schumann bored him to tears." I would have given anything to have been able to make such a colossal pronouncement. I envied a thin girl who said there was absolutely nothing in the Royal Academy worth looking at, and that an interior by Peter de Hoogh in the National Gallery was worth all the Turners put together. I envied Laura. Except for music, she knew very little more than I did, but she was absolutely emphatic She fitted into this atmosphere with complete success. The fact that she was a really talented violinist excused a lot, but she was always willing to give an opinion upon literature or painting or any other subject with an uncompromising conviction, and to argue about it. She did not care what anybody thought. They could like her or dislike her, but they couldn't ignore her. And for the most part Woodstack liked her. Mary, and her mother, and her brother Giles adored Laura. She was becoming, if not a beautiful in any case a very striking woman, with her dark hair and eyes, and her pale, expressive face, always alight with some fury of movement.

Unfortunately for me, the majority of the Woodstack people were musicians, and music was a subject upon which I was profoundly ignorant I soon found, however, that even the musical profession had its three bars. There were the half-dozen giants at the top, about whom there was very little divergence of opinion; then came the rank and file of serious musicians who disagreed about everything; and finally, right away in a class by themselves, came the ballad-singers.

I think, of all classes of the community that I have ever encountered, ballad-singers are the most ignorant. They know nothing outside their own job and very little about that. They have all the egoism of the actor without his naivete and quick sympathy. There was one who used occasionally to visit the Copleys. Her name was Bessie Steyning. Her conversational limit was the phrase: "My dear, they simply loved it!"

She was very large and fair. She seemed to be all back and front—if you know what I mean. She had masses of magnificent fair hair swathed in black-velvet ribbons and sparkling with little gems; a clear, beautiful complexion needlessly powdered, and small, expressionless eyes. She manipulated one of those high soprano voices which are like burnished steel—clear, strong, and unrelentingly safe. You could hear her making a bee-line for the top C and you knew quite well she would get there safely, and at the same time you didn't care. She stood by the piano like a pudding. You felt that she looked upon her voice as an asset, like a bungalow up the river, or a set of sables; something she meant to get the highest rate of interest on, and at the same time make other women envious. Her whole conversation was designed to show that all the managers were running after her, that the public were wretched when she was not singing, that her fees were enormous, and that, indeed, her whole success was positively embarrassing.

II

Happily, the majority of the Copleys' musical friends belonged to what I might call "the private bar" class. They were not as trying as Bessie Steyning, but I did not get on with them very well. They had all Laura's self-opinionativeness without her candour. They were supercilious, furtive, and pettily jealous of each other.

The most congenial spirit I met there was a landscape painter called Yves Radic and he was half-mad, I think. He was my first, experience of an art-madman. He lived in a bam which he had converted into a studio, and he lived like an emperor, without an emperor's responsibilities and discomforts. He lived alone with his career. He was of French-Polish stock, and he had a small private income. He did his own housework and cooking: that is to say, he occasionally removed some of the heavier debris from his plates and dishes, or grilled fish and sausages over a spirit-stove. He was himself small and rather dirty, and the barn had the appearance of being in a transitional state between habitation by cattle or man. The floor and atmosphere suggested cattle; the bottles and canvases suggested man. There appeared to be hundreds of bottles. They stood in rows against the wall. A large circular table was piled up with half -used tubes of paint, papers, palettes, bottles of turpentine, oil, vinegar, beer, pieces, and vodka; whilst in the centre would repose half a ham, turning brown at the edges and collecting the dust. I believe he drank vodka as a concession to his ancestry rather than because he liked it. The room gave one the appearance of unbridled license.

But when I got to know Radic I found out that he was by no means a free man. He was a slave to an absolutely autocratic artistic conscience. He was fundamentally one of the most sincere people I had ever met His manners were appalling. I cannot think why he took to me, but he did. He asked me to go and see him. I could not get the hang of his work at first, but gradually it grew on me. His landscapes were very low-toned. At first they seemed to me to be almost monotone", then I discovered that they were indeed full of colour, but in a very restrained key. Tears afterwards I realised that they were founded rather on the manner of Daubigny and Pointelin, but I had not seen any of these artists' work at that time. He had a way of making me sit down, and then he would produce a canvas and hug it to himself, look across at me suspiciously, and fumble about with it and lick his lips. Then suddenly he would turn it round for my inspection, and glance quickly, almost fiercely, at my face for a verdict. I had a feeling that if I looked at it disapprovingly he might rush at me with a palette-knife. He was intensely in earnest All this solemn nonsense of social progress, all the hubbub of politics, all this insanity of business, and behaviour and manners, nay, even the banalities of love, and honour, and friendship might go hang. The only thing that mattered was Art. And not only Art, but his art, his own peculiar vision of a certain composition.

He was dirty and small, but he made Bessie Steyning appear contemptible. In all his opinions and actions he was extreme, but his painting was sane and sombre, conceived on a lofty plane, composed with a reverent regard for values. He had no moral sense. He would sometimes disappear for days, and come back and boast to me of his depravities. Socially he was an anarchist. He sneered at religion, and law, and custom; but I found him exhilarating. I have since met men somewhat like Radic, but never one who was so loyal to the sacred fire within him. He believed in painting a thing direct and leaving it. If it was not satisfactory he would do it again. I have known him paint a subject five times, and then destroy the result because it did not satisfy him.

He disturbed my conscience more than anyone I had so far met My own life seemed weak and pitiable in comparison. After all, what was I doing? I was simply living up to the dismal prophecy of the Rev. James Parke Tidsall. "A nice boy!" I had drifted completely. I had no definite impulses except to be pleasant and kind. Thanks to a quite fortuitous accident which I shall describe later, I had for the time being escaped the sordid drudgery of a life for which I was not fitted. I had a hundred and fifty pounds a year of my own, and I had launched out into romantic drama; not that I had any strong impulse to write romantic drama, but because it occurred to me that it might be pleasant In any case I thought it would be nice to try. Laura had her career, and it consumed her. But I realised that her frenzy was quite different from Radic's. Laura wanted to fiddle well, but even more compelling seemed to be her desire for success. She wanted to be acclaimed, and applauded, and written up in the Press, to be recognised as a virtuoso. Radio exhibited his pictures, but ignored everyone's opinion concerning them. He never read the newspapers. He bared his teeth at the mention of them. He sometimes sold his pictures, and this seemed to worry him exceedingly. He was haunted by the idea that someone would get hold of them who didn't appreciate them; would probably put them in a wrong light. He was rude to his clients, contemptuous of dealers, and indifferent to public opinion.

I found it necessary to point out this comparison to Mary. And what she said was:

"It's very different with painters. Their work lives on after them. A musician has to make his effect while he lives. He leaves nothing behind—unless he's a composer. It's quite natural for that dirty little genius to be indifferent, and for Laura to be ambitious for success."

Nothing could ever shake Mary's loyalty to Laura.

III

This took place at the time when I was living with Laura in Slocombe Street, and when we were beginning to get on each other's nerves. My romantic drama was a distinct fizzle. I gave it up haK-way through the third act I explained to Mary that it was really Laura's fault. I could not work in the same house with her. And Mary said:

"Nonsense! you could if you were keen enough."

Then I knew that that was true. I wasn't keen enough. There must be something else. I settled down to a course of hard reading. I joined Mudie's and borrowed books from the Copleys! I waded through hundreds of pages of Adam Smith's Wealth of Nations before I realised that it meant nothing to me at all. I read Kant and Comte and Herbert Spencer, and didn't understand them. It all seemed higgledy-piggledy. Meredith appeared to write about snobs, Hardy about people I didn't know, Stevenson about long-winded pirates. I went on and on. I was like that steward on the steamer in Maxim Gorky's autobiography, In the World, who believed that if he could only go on long enough reading books he would eventually come to the book. But I never could get to the book. I had exhausted Shakespeare at school, at the time when I believed that the last word had been said by Marcus Aurelius. Possibly I was right. In any case, I was at a difficult age.

What I really liked to do was to wander about the streets, and talk to cabmen and coffee-stall keepers, or to go over and see my father and casually stroll into the bar, and listen to conversations between Mr. Small and his friend.

My father took the defection of Laura and me very well. He was always pleased to see us. He seemed rather amused than otherwise. He was always proud to read about Laura's performances in the newspapers, but he never went to hear her in public, except on the occasion when she made her debut. And then he expressed the opinion that he did not care for music in a concert-hall. He preferred it in the parlour upstairs of "The Duchess of Pless," I went to see him two or three times a week, and Laura about once a fortnight. To our relief he never expressed any desire to meet the Copleys or any other of our friends. He seemed to appreciate the fact that we had drifted into a different set, and that it was quite natural and inevitable. Curiously enough, stepmother resented our departure more than he did. She hinted that it was unkind, and that we had gone away because we were ashamed of the establishment, and of our "swell friends" getting to know our connection with it. There was a horrid element of truth in this, and that was why I made a point of going whenever I could.

I enjoyed a glorious five days when I served in the bar. Father was very opposed to it, but he eventually gave way. He was laid up with a bad cold, and one of the barmaids had suddenly gone off without warning with a local bedstead manufacturer. They were very short-handed, and business was brisk. I found the experience very entertaining. I made several friends in each of the bars. No one impressed me more than Mr. Timble. He was the local undertaker. A large, florid man, always dressed in heavy mourning, he carried the atmosphere of his mournful profession with him whenever he went Every funeral seemed to affect him as though it were that of his dearest friend. He spoke in a deep, hushed voice. His pale, protruding eyes seemed ever on the verge of tears. He visited the bar several times a day, and I always expected him to herald his request for a whisky-and-soda with the usual formula: "In the midst of life we are in death." But he always bowed solemnly, and said:

"Well, young Mr. Purbeck, and how is your father?" When I had reported, he always continued:

"I have known your father for fourteen years. An honourable and upright man, sir; a man to be respected. I hope his son will be worthy of him, I'll take a small Scotch with a splash, please."

I have an idea that he took advantage of my father's absence. I don't believe father would have allowed him as many drinks as he ordered. He sometimes had as many as ten or twelve whiskies during the day. It did not appear to affect him very seriously, except that he became more humid and lugubrious, and perhaps a little more confiding. He told me of some of the difficulties of his profession, the unreliability of mutes who were given to insobriety and giggled on the hearse, the lack of imagination of well-to-do people over the possibilities of an impressive funeral, the ingratitude of next-of-kin, the vulgar ostentation of the poor, who always demanded plumes which they could not afford. I gathered that he had this in common with my father, that they both believed that there was a proper way to conduct everything: a government, a funeral, or a drink.

One evening he came into the bar in a great state of consternation. The only other person there was Mr. Peel, the estate agent. Mr. Timble bowed to me, and his lips quivered. He went through the usual formalities, but he drank his whisky at a gulp and ordered another. Then, drawing Mr. Peel and myself into a confiding group, he said:

"Gentlemen, I have had a most distressing experience. I have been in the funeral-furnishing trade for forty-three years, and I have never had a more distressing experience."

Mr. Peel, a foxy little. man, said, "Go on!"

"I had the case to-day of Mrs. Boddice, the widow of Charles Boddice, the corn-merchant. Poor thing! She was seventy-two, and she died from double pneumonia. She left eleven grown-up children. She had never lost a child in her life; an admirable woman."

"I remember 'er" said Mr. Peel. "She 'ad a slight moustache and used to keep a lot of little birds in cages."

Mr. Timble drank, and continued:

"It is a customary and proper thing, as you know, during a funeral procession, for gentlemen in the streets to remove their hats. It is a little point about which I am peculiarly sensitive. I always ride on the hearse myself, and I make a particular note of this observance. If it has been generally respected, I consider the funeral to have been a success. If it is only partially or spasmodically done, I consider it to be a failure. It appears to me that people are becoming more and more irreligious. The funeral of Mrs. Boddice this afternoon was treated with scant respect. I was not surprised that Mr. James Boddice, who was riding in the first carriage, was extremely indignant. It is almost what I might call part of the perquisites which one expects with a, funeral for which one has paid ten or fifteen pounds. At the comer of the Highgate Road the whole procession was held up in a few minutes by the traffic. At the comer were three loafers, leaning against a lamppost, talking and spitting. They ignored our—cortege. I quite sympathised then with Mr. James Boddice, who, unable to contain himself any longer, thrust his head out of the window and exclaimed: 'Hi, you there I Take off your 'ats!' And then, gentlemen, what do you think happened?"

"Go on!" said Mr. Peel, incredulous of whatever was coming.

"The three loafers turned round and looked at us. Then one of them suddenly took off his hat and cheered! Then the others followed suit, and as we proceeded up the hill these three ruffians cheered and cheered as though it was—a Lord Mayor's Show! Can you believe it? . . . Can you imagine it?"

"Go on!" said Peel.

Yes, I could imagine it, but I had to duck behind the shelves of bottles to focus the scene I could not allow Mr. Timble to see my face. He would never afterwards hold out any hope that I should be worthy of my father. It was positive torture. I hunted for some mysterious bottle for a long time. . . . What a scene! And why not? Why should the worthy corn merchant's widow be cheered at her wedding, when she had done nothing, and not get a hand at her funeral after an honourable life, the mother of eleven, and not losing one? Oh, James! James! what have you got to be indignant about? . . . I shall never be able to fill my father's shoes. What would they think of me at Woodstack if they saw me handing over two pints of mild-and-bitter to a cabman and his friend? Even Radic would disapprove. Not of the act itself, but of the waste of time. I ought to be doing something dynamic, moving, low-toned . . . immortal.

IV

I wrote to Mary about it, and she said, "Of course you must help your father, if he is in difficulties."

Mary was never wrong. She was always completely in tune. I can't—you may think it funny of me, but I can't—tell you of all the incidents which led up to our wedding. There are some things one doesn't talk about to one's dearest friends. After all, it is no business of yours. I would rather not talk about it. I would rather talk about those socks.

Mary had two hundred a year of her own, and Mrs. Copley offered us the lease of a small house in St. John's Wood as a wedding present. So we decided that three hundred and fifty was ample to marry on and there was no point in waiting. I had no career, and no ambitions. My only obsession at that time was to marry Mary. There is one thing I would like to say about us. I did not know till I met her how funny I was. To Mary I was a perfect scream. She was always doubling up with laughter over met

"You are a funny old thing!" she would say as she undid my tie and re-tied it She laughed when she showed me how to wash my hands and clean my fingernails. She laughed when she showed me how to walk, and put on a hat, and play tennis, and to rush and open a door for a lady when she was going out of the room. I must have been the funniest thing that ever lived.

We were married at Woodstack, in the village church. It was what the Copleys called a quite informal wedding. I only got there in time by the skin of my teeth. The fact was, I went down from town, and as I was rather late I thought I would get a shave at Waterloo station. I allowed myself twenty minutes for this, but as it happened, there were two other men waiting, and only one barber, A boy was having his hair cut when I went in, and the barber was just finishing. I was in a fever of agitation. The first man had a shave and was disposed of in five minutes. I reckoned that if the other man only took the same time I should just have time for my shave, with five minutes over to catch the train. But the second man seemed to have an annoying stubbly growth that took a long time and the barber was of the oily, conversational type. The seconds were ticking away. Curse him! He was droning on about some ridiculous murder case at Walthamstow, his sharp, pointed nose sticking up in the air. How I hated the man! Five minutes were already up. Six minutes. Six and a half—now!

"I think I'll have a shampoo, please."

Tears started to my eyes.

"My God, sir!" I said. "Are you obliged to have a shampoo? It doesn't seem at all necessary. I'm in a frightful hurry."

The man looked round at me, and the barber dropped a towel. How could I possibly explain? I said: "Oh, go to the devil, then!" and I dashed out of the saloon.

Father was waiting for me on the train, in a great state of excitement, thinking I was not coming. He had been there for fifty minutes. He usually got to a station an hour before his train was due to start.

I arrived at Woodstack unshorn. A cab was waiting for us. The ceremony was due in half an hour. We told the driver to drive to the village barber's. When we got there we found that he had shut up his shop and gone to London to buy a bicycle.

"What the devil does a barber want with a bicycle?" I said savagely to his wife. I was quite unreasonable. The only thing to do was to go to the Copleys' and borrow Giles' razor. And then father came out with one of his annoying superstitions. It wouldn't do at all. A bridegroom must never see the bride on the wedding day till he meets her at the church. I gave it up.

"Very well, then," I said. "I'll get married dirty."

I got married dirty, and Mary seemed to think that this was screamingly funny, too, especially when the first thing I had to do after the ceremony was to borrow Giles' razor and have a shave.

It was father's first meeting with the Copleys, and he came through the ordeal very well. He was the only man who appeared in a frock-coat and top-hat, with a white button-hole. I was married in a tweed suit and Mary in a navy blue travelling coat and skirt. There were about fifteen or twenty people at the reception. Neither stepmother nor Uncle Stephen was able to come, but Laura might have been the hostess. She had on a wonderful light blue frock, with a picture hat trimmed with daisies. I think father was rather prepared for the Woodstack crowd. Many things must have surprised him, but he did not show it. No one was in proper wedding garb. There was no champagne, only hock and tea. There were no speeches. Everyone was pleasant, informal, rather high-spirited, and anxious to avoid any display of emotion. It must have been different from that when he was a young man. He was very quiet and formal. What was he thinking of it all? Once I heard him addressing a little speech to Mrs. Copley. I could not catch what he said, but I was pleased to see her face light up with surprised pleasure. He kissed Mary, and said, "Well, God bless you, little girl!" Quite a success, the old man. . . .

"A perfect old dear!" Mary told me in the train.

It was an hour later, in the train, that the climax arrived. Mary suddenly said: "What have you got on?" and she lifted up the leg of one of my trousers.

"What do you mean?" I said.

"Those are not the socks I sent you. They were black, with a light blue clock."

"Well!" I answered, and I looked down and beheld a woolly brown sock. "Oh!" I murmured, and I pulled up the leg of my other trouser. Then Mary collapsed, and I was obliged to laugh too. The other sock was black with a light blue clock.

"I must have muddled them up," I stuttered.

"Muddled them up! Oh, you old booby!"

"I don't think 'booby' is a right word to employ to your husband."

But Mary was completely finished. She rocked backwards and forwards. It was extremely difficult to snatch a piece of her fugitive face to kiss.

When she eventually recovered she said that at Okehampton she would really have to see what I had packed. We stayed the night at an hotel there. I had packed a goodly number of things, including a bath thermometer and some dirty collars, but no socks at all.

"It's quite time you had someone to look after you," she said. "To-morrow morning we shall have to go shopping."

But, strangely enough, on the morrow even Mary seemed absent-minded. We both forgot all about the socks. We drove out to an inn right away on Dartmoor, and then we remembered. There were no shops within five miles of our inn. I spent the first week of my honeymoon wearing one brown woolly sock and one black one with a light blue clock. A trivial incident, perhaps, but it is queer how sometimes a trivial incident, about socks, for instance, may have an important bearing on one's whole life.

CHAPTER VII

CHANCE

Nurse Dipper was a privileged person. An old friend of the Copley family, old in face and young in body, very alert and business-like. She picked up my hat and thrust it into my hand.

"Now then," she said, "we want to get rid of you. You go for a good sharp walk, and come back in about an hour and a half. It'll be all right. Don't worry."

The door snapped to, and I was out alone in the rain. I raced away into the night like a criminal escaping from justice. I was pursued by a demon hissing into my ear that I was running away, that I was a coward. I wanted to go back and I wanted to go on. I must cover so many miles. The only light in this dark sea of fear and remorse was that I must do precisely what the nurse told me. I looked at my watch under a street lamp. A quarter to eleven. I had got to go on walking till twelve-fifteen. At twelve-fifteen to the second I should slip my latchkey into the door. To be told what? . . . Horrid little visions danced before my eyes. I could see myself in the hall, the drawn face of Nurse Dipper, perhaps stepmother. . . . Who would break the news to me? What fools, cowards, and egoists are men. We take everything we want, and when the price has got to be paid we are not there. On and on I rushed . . . We are spendthrifts, defaulting bankrupts. It is all so easy, natural, pleasant, so morally defensible. We are so secure in our citadel of sense-discretion. I wanted to get to the river, or somewhere where there was open space, and there appeared to be nothing but narrow streets, muffled figures, loiterers, 'buses, and policemen.

And they all appeared far away and unreal. What was real was that room, with Mary lying in her anguish. Perhaps at this very moment that tall doctor who had arrived with the peculiar-shaped bag . . . And I could do nothing; I was turned out in the rain, like a dog. How cruel is this arbitrament of fate! To those we love we bring unspeakable suffering, which we can neither share in nor assuage. We do it consciously. She endures it consciously, allowing that nothing is produced without suffering. The history of life is a story of epochs of travail, following one after another. Nature is like a process of preparing banquets, and clearing up after them, and then preparing for another one.

She is like a housewife, knowing that everything she does will have to be done again. Directly the housewife dusts a table, the dust begins to collect again. Directly she cooks a meal, someone devours it, and she has to begin to think of the next. She is surrounded by destroyers, people who are always undoing whatever she has accomplished. And she knows she dare not stop.

A horse-tram came leisurely round the comer, with bells tinkling—I must be somewhere in Camden Town—the horses trotting indifferently. Horses! Strange, at that tragic hour, I should be consumed with another and most unlikely vision; A horse-race! . . . If it had not been for a horse-race I should probably not have been there at that moment. Someone had described it to me. The previous year, a race—I think it was the Cesarewitch—had been contested by a field of fourteen horses, but it was considered a foregone conclusion.

The favourite, "Mohair," was considered a certainly. I have never been to a horse-race in my life, and I had certainly never heard of "Mohair" or any other horse. But this race I had seen again and again in imagination.

And on this night the ridiculous spectacle danced vividly before me.

"Mohair" broke away and had a clear field. The horse exceeded the wildest expectations of its backers. The whole thing appeared to be over. The crowd were only becoming interested in seeing which of the others would come in second and third. They were bunched together indescribably. Entering the flat, "Mohair" suddenly crossed its legs and fell. There was a yell of excitement. The jockeys, seeing what had happened, urged their beasts on frenziedly. Near the winning post three appeared to detach themselves from the rest. There was a confusion of black necks, and of blue, yellow, and claret-coloured silk. No one was quite certain of the result. But when the flag went up it appeared that the race had been won by a horse named "Baionnette," a rank outsider. What has all this got to do with me? ... It may appear a singularly inappropriate memory to have crossed my mind on that fateful evening to me. In some ways it undoubtedly was. But it had happened that my Uncle Stephen was at that race, and he had backed "Baionnette" for a hundred pounds. His reasons for backing this particular horse were obscure. He had just inherited a small legacy, and he announced his intention to give up horse-racing entirely. The Cesarewitch was to be his last plunge, and he told us that he had set aside "a certain sum for a certain purpose." This certain purpose was revealed later. When the settling-up came. Uncle Stephen had netted over six thousand pounds over the race.

I shall never forget the night when he came to break the news to us. He telegraphed to Laura to be at "The Duchess of Pless" at nine o'clock, on very important business. He came into the parlour, tugging feverishly at his heavy black moustache. He was pretending to be very self-restrained, but he was patently in a great state of excitement. His eyes glowed, and he could not sit down. I think he had been drinking rather more than was good for him, but he was quite lucid and coherent. He came straight to the point. He said:

"Laura and Tom, I have always wanted to do something for you. And now I'm glad to say I have my chance. I don't believe in leaving people money when you die, if you can do anything for them before. It's when you're starting on your career that it's valuable. I propose to settle three thousand pounds on each of you kids."

II

The receipt of this news was almost unnerving. Laura gave a cry and threw her arms round his neck and kissed him. While so occupied, I was instantly torn between two emotions—the wild thrill of excitement shared with Laura, and a peculiar apprehension regarding my father. Stepmother and I both looked at him. He was very solemn. When Laura had completed her manifestation of love—which, by the way, was unique of its kind, for she always voted Uncle Stephen "an old stick"—father said:

"What do you mean, Stephen?"

Then uncle told us about the horse-race, and Laura clapped her hands and said: "How ripping!" But father shook his head and said:

"It's very kind, Steve; very kind. But no good comes of . . . money like that."

And Uncle Stephen threw back his head and laughed.

"Take it or leave it," he said.

Laura's eyes flashed. "I know I'm jolly well going to take it," she exclaimed. "It means recitals, orchestral concerts, Berlin, Frankfort, Vienna—everything. Everything! It makes all the difference to your career."

I could not escape a momentary and surprising vision of Laura playing at an orchestral concert in Vienna because "Baionnette" had pushed past the post in front of another horse by the tip of his nose.

Of course, no one could prevent Laura taking the money. She was of age. But neither of the brothers appeared directly concerned with her. There was an indecisive duel of the eyes. A brief fragmentary argument on betting between them.

"It's chance. It's all chance. Everything is chance," said Uncle Stephen.

"No, no. There's honest dealing. There's fair dealing. It's supply and demand."

"Isn't it often just chance who comes into your bar, and what they spend?"

"They come because they get good value."

"Isn't it chance that one man is born a millionaire and another a crossing-sweeper?"

"No, no; it's heredity."

"Who's going to say? Isn't it a gamble on the Stock Exchange? Isn't it often a fool who will make ten thousand a year, and a clever man two hundred? Back your fancy, I say, and go in and win. If you lose, take it like a sportsman."

Suddenly turning to me, he said:

"What do you say, Tom?"

I replied, "I think you're right, uncle."

It was an awful moment. I knew I was betraying my father. I believed that he was right, and I believed that Uncle Stephen was right. But undoubtedly my dominant feeling was personal ambition. I had been an unsuccessful clerk in a wall-paper business for over a year, and here was salvation. I wanted the money. I wanted to escape. I wanted to marry Mary. I was like Laura, only I had not my plan so definitely mapped out. Suddenly I had an inspiration.

"After all, guv'nor," I said, "horse-racing is recognised by the State."

My father gave me a surprised look. I knew what he was thinking, "Is the State the arbiter of my conscience?" but he said nothing. He fumbled his way through the furniture and shrugged his shoulders, as though he were casting us off. Stepmother followed him indecisively. She was bewildered by the news. At the same time she could not quite understand father's attitude. One cannot reject a fortune so easily. She was sorry for everybody, and anxious for a compromise

"Well, well, Stephen," she said in her tremulous voice, "I'm sure it's very kind of you. The children must be very grateful. Jim is tired. You must come and talk it over again soon."

We all seemed to fall apart. Each of us was consumed with the individual significance of the news. Uncle Stephen was enjoying it most, for he knew that we should accept. Laura had forgotten about us all, even her benefactor. Her eyes were dancing with the anticipation of a thousand nights of triumph. And I, too, fell into a reverie of selfish delights.

III

I need hardly say that my thoughts had flown instantly to Mary. I, too, forgot my benefactor. Within the space of a few seconds my whole outlook on life shifted on to a different plana I was going up and up. All the black apprehensions of those previous years vanished. With Laura I had been to the Copley's I had walked with Mary in the trim garden. I had sat with her under the cedar tree, and watched the son setting on the Surrey hills. I had slept in a white panelled room with chintz curtains. I had spent days amongst old furniture and good pictures, living with people who moved softly and spoke in gentle voices. And the realisation of the sordid contrast of my father's bars had almost paralysed my will. This was a different world entirely, and one I was not schooled to. I began to understand Laura and her references to the "filthy pub." What had appeared to me before to be rich and wonderfully moving became suddenly drab and depressing. It could never be the same again. But my prospects of moving up into this more alluring world seemed utterly remote. I would never dare to make love to Mary, although she filled my waking dreams. She was an intangible goddess sent to torment me. I was a clerk in a wall-paper firm, and my father was a publican. My prospects were negligible. I had not even ambition. I must put it all away. And then suddenly ..."Baionnette" won by a nose! If "Mohair" hadn't fallen—if one of the other horses had made the slightest extra exertion—everything would be as it was. But now? Blindly I had groped my way to Uncle Stephen and pressed his hand.

"That's all right, my boy," he said. "Come over on Sunday morning. We'll have a knees-up."

Laura and I were in revolt. We behaved disgustingly. There was no quarrel with my father, no word of recrimination. But within a month I had left "The Duchess of Pless" and had gone to share a maisonette with Laura in Baker Street We spent two hundred pounds on furnishing it. It was a kind of miniature Copleys'. We went Copley-mad. We bought chintz and cretonne, and an oak gate-leg table, and rush-seated chairs. I threw up my situation in the wall-paper firm and began to write a romantic drama. The whole thing was like a dream. We entertained students, went to theatres and picture-galleries, dined out at restaurants, and made Woodstack, the Copleys' house, the focus of all our activities.

IV

As I raced along on that fateful night in the life of Mary and myself, all these events danced before my mind, dominated by the ridiculous spectacle of a horse thrusting forward its nose. The child who was now being born probably owed its very existence to this fortuitous circumstance. Uncle Stephen was right. It is all chance. Every one of us is the plaything of a long line of gamblers. The upsetting of a cup five hundred years ago, a letter written in the Middle Ages, the lucky thrust of a claw in primordial times, and lo! you and I are born. Father, who polished his brown boots, and sold good beer, and sang hymns on Sunday morning, believed in a God who ordered things reasonably, and he was quite wrong. Laura and I had found him out, and our attitudes could never again be reconciled. Not that we loved him the less, but we saw him as he was. Fate ordained that we should go on and leave him behind.

The tussle of Laura and me to live together lasted nearly a year, and it ended disastrously. I cannot say to what extent the change in me was due to the change in my fortunes, but I do know that at that time—I was twenty-three—I was suddenly conscious of a tremendous psychological upheaval. I gained confidence in myself. I began to think and act independently. I was less shy in meeting people I "discovered" writers who moved me profoundly. I became ambitious. And my ambitions and outlook were constantly clashing with Laura's. Laura, indeed, was impossible to live with, She worried me to death. We agreed on all main issues. We rejoiced in each other's society. Indeed, we were very fond of each other. It was over the little things that the trouble came.

She was always practising, and the maisonette was not large enough for me to escape from the sound of her fiddle. The scales, and arpeggios, and repetitions, and double-stoppings got on my nerves. I had to listen. She was always upbraiding me for my untidy habits. She was always losing her latch-key, or her muff. She was always bursting in on me to tell me the details of some scandalous behaviour by some concert-manager. As I stated before, there was always "something doing" with Laura. I could not be in the same building without being conscious of her. Her personality was too pronounced to live with. Things that appeared to me to be of no consequence at all would be enlarged by her out of all proportion. At one moment she would be laughing, and then some little incident would lash her into a veritable fury. The most trivial thing would upset her for a whole morning. She enjoyed a fair measure of success in her profession, but the bitterness of it tortured her. She had not a man's sense of fatalism. She was always up in arms about something. She quarrelled with managers and agents and conductors. Her life appeared one eternal protest By which you must not imagine that she thought only of success. She was developing into a very fine artist, and with a woman's logic she could not understand why the whole world did not instantly proclaim her as such. She had no faculty for making the best of her difficulties in that most difficult and corrupt of professions.

And I felt that I was no comfort to her. She required constant attention and encouragement. "She ought to get a husband," I thought, and then I shuddered at the prospect. Laura was almost destined to make a bloomer of it, to marry the wrong man. And I, too, had my profession, and my ambitions, requiring constant attention and encouragement, and instinctively I turned to—Mary. A brother and sister can never do anything more than run on parallel lines. They watch each other racing along.

It was Mary who said to me:

"We shall have an awful business marrying Laura to the right man. She's such a volcano."

Mary was the most sensible person in the world. She was inevitable. I could think aloud in her presence, and my thoughts became pruned up, crystal-clear, fluid. When she was not with me I could almost talk with her. Although I always knew the quality of her mind, her statements always surprised me, as everything about her had the faculty of surprising me. Identical actions had the eternal aspect of novelty. I would be haunted by the tilt of her little chin, and when away from her anxious to verify the impression. When I saw her again the tilt would be the same, but it would still be surprising and unexpected. Mary would be as easy to live with as Laura had proved difficult. That, I suppose, is why I took her away and made her suffer....

I had heard her groan. I had heard her scream. Perhaps at that very moment she was . . . People were pouring out of a theatre. A large coloured poster depicted a scene from "The Queen in

Chancery." Mountebanks in fustian. A fat man asked me for a match. I gave him one, and stood there shivering. "Thank you so much. Good night." How trivial it all seemed. I could go back now. Time to go back. I had walked all this way rapidly, just in time to give that fool a match, and now I must go back. If he only knew! The god of chance again.

I dared not think of Mary. She held me by an unbreakable chain of episodes, necessities, passions. The communion of a year, and she held me like that Mending my socks, correcting my composition, selecting my ties, managing me, humouring me, surprising me, shaping me.

A woman walked the streets furtively a few paces ahead. She looked watchful but weary. A sudden mad desire for companionship with a suffering creature came over me. I overtook her and said:

"What a night! It's cold. Why don't you walk quicker and keep warm?"

She turned her lifeless face to me and answered:

"If I'd walked quicker you wouldn't have caught me up."

"I'm no good to you. I only wanted to talk."

"What's your game? Ain't you coming home with me?"

"No. I can't. I'm worried. My wife's expecting a baby. I've got to get back."

"You're a rum 'un, you are."

"She may die. I'm nearly off my head. Even now, at this moment, she may . . ."

"That's nothing, kid. I run that risk every day."

I stopped and looked at her. Drawing out half a sovereign, I handed it to her.

"Have a night off," I said. "You look tired. Just to wish me luck, do!"

She looked at me suspiciously, and then thrust it back.

"I don't want yer money."

"All right," I said. "Good luck." And I hurried on. In a minute or two she caught me up and touched my arm.

"Here, kid," she said; "I've changed my mind. Give me the half thick 'un."

I handed it to her in silence. She looked at it and dropped it into her bag. Then she gave my elbow a little push, as though starting me on my journey, and said in a lighter voice:

"That's all right, sonny. You're a good 'un. It's all in the game. Good luck to yer, and the woman, and the blinking kid!"

And she vanished round a comer.

All in the game! One may do everything possible, and fail. One may do nothing, and succeed. Had I done anything to deserve a "blinking kid"? It might go on and produce other "blinking kids." In the course of centuries I might be responsible for a whole race and a thousand people, as I was linked to some dim figure in the past, who was again linked to other dim figures.

On the other hand, I might die out, like the tail of a comet hurtling through space. It was all in the game. Was God a gambler, like Uncle Stephen? It is not difficult to breed, neither is it moral or immoral, organised, essential, or scientific. It is just casual, a chance. And yet the responsibility is unrealisable. A consumptive potter with an intemperate wife may have thirteen children. A Carlyle or a Shelley may have none. A magnificent woman may remain celibate till her death. One idle act may be the nucleus of a race or it may be the means of death. Leonardo da Vinci was probably the greatest man in all history: a painter, sculptor, architect, musician, poet, engineer, scientist, and philosopher—supreme at all these things—and he was the illegitimate son of a peasant woman. An accident! Tchaikovsky went mad. Heine was a chronic invalid. Dostoievsky was an epileptic Shakespeare's children were dunces. If there was a reasoned order at the back of this breeding business, it eluded me completely. The only happy people were people like my father, who struck a circle round their lives and walked within it. People who could stand foursquare to the winds of failure or success. Laura was unhappy. Mary—Mary was probably dying, a victim to the mad freak that "Baionnette" won by a nose!

And I—I should not be able to go on. There would be nowhere to pillow my thoughts; no guiding star on the lonely waters. I should drift about in a sea of melancholy amidst the uncharted isles of despair. . . .

I passed a coffee-stall gleaming with copper and white plates. Half a dozen indiscriminate specimens of the flotsam of the big city were enjoying its hospitality. I looked at my watch. It was just twelve, and the house was round the comer. I would obey the nurse. I would not return until twelve-fifteen. I went up to the proprietor and ordered a cup of coffee. A stout woman was eating sardines on toast. A sickly looking youth was whispering into her ear. On the other side an indescribably dirty old man, with bloodshot eyes and a ferocious beard, was holding forth to an individual whose face I could not see.

"I don't care what 'e is," he was exclaiming. "It isn't honourable. 'E never done the right thing by 'er." (Mumbles from the other man.) "I don't care about that. I don't think any more of a man because 'e wears gold sleeve-links and parts 'is 'air in the middle. What's a 'undred a year—or even a thousand a year—to a gal who can never be called respectable again!"

I wanted to say:

"You old prig! What does it matter, as long as she lives, as long as the child lives? What about Leonardo da Vinci?"

I gulped my coffee, and fled. Dishonourable, dishonourable, dishonourable! What has honour got to do with you, you old ruffian? Or me? Or with any of the big things? My case was honourable enough, as far as that went, but on that night I wouldn't have cared, anyway. Life! The great thing is to live. The great thing is for Mary to live. One can adjust afterwards. It was all chance.

The house was lighted up. I dropped my latchkey and fumbled against the door. It took me ages to find it again. I could not hear a sound. Again I pressed it in the lock and turned it. The light in the hall blinded me. There was the strong smell of antiseptic. My heart was beating rapidly. I groped my way into the light. Someone tripped across the hall with a case, and started, to go upstairs. She turned when she saw me. It was Nurse Dipper.

"You needn't look so scared," she said. "Everything is all right. You've got a dear little daughter."

My father came out of the drawing-room and held out his hand to me.

CHAPTER VIII

THE BECHER STUDIO

No one could possibly work in a house where there's a baby. In comparison, even Laura would seem passive. A baby seems to be labouring under some eternal injustice as though it said:

"I didn't want to come. But as you made me, you've damn well got to do exactly what I yell for."

When it is quiet it is even more insistent It is necessary then to leave one's work, and tip-toe upstairs and tap on the door, and say:

"Nurse, is Midge all right?" (Midge being a diminutive of Madeline.)

It might be choking, or having rickets, or dying in its sleep. On my writing-desk is a book on Infantile Diseases and Cures. It is a terrible book. I never thought that so much compressed peril could be got into such a small space. It brings out beads of perspiration on my temples. Work is out of the question. The trouble is, I can get no one with whom to share these nightmares. Mary has not read the book. I left it about for her to read. I thought she ought to read it, to be prepared. Once she picked it up and said:

"What's this?"

She glanced through half a page, and said, "Rubbish!"

Women are extraordinary. They have all sorts of innate senses and intuitions we wot not of. Mary does not seem to worry at all about Midge. She sings to it, makes funny noises, does all the necessary things. She overlooked me for some time. I hardly seemed to count. Then one day she said:

"I think, dear, you ought to have a room out to work in. This house is too small."

You must know that at that time I was a novelist. That is to say, I had begun to write an intensely realistic modem novel, in the Russian manner. It was Mary's idea that I should write a novel, and my idea to make it Russian. I took some cockney characters and made them talk for pages about their souls, like the Brothers Karamazoff. It wasn't very good.

There followed what might be called the Midge Period. For the first two years of our married life it was all Midge. I did eventually have a room out, but I was always darting home at unnecessary intervals, worrying about Midge, worrying about Mary. At the end of two years, Mary discovered that we were living above our income. This was very alarming. It seemed incredible that a huge sum like three hundred and fifty pounds shouldn't be sufficient to supply our simple requirements. It was obvious that I must abolish the Brothers Karamazoff and seek remunerative work. But this Mary would not listen to. She said:

"No. I know what it is. If you just go and take on some clerical job you will go down the sink. But if you hang on, trying to do something big, you will one day succeed."

One day! . . . We argued about it for weeks, and then, of course, Mary had her way. I continued with my room, and household expenses were cut down. But I felt uncomfortable. I threw the Brothers Karamazoff overboard and started another novel in a lighter key, and tried to write short stories.

At that time Laura had just returned from a successful tour in the United States. She had made some money, and was in very high spirits. She came and stayed with ns. She made me feel drab. She was so vivid, forceful. Her eyes were brighter than ever. Success was stamped all over her. And yet I was not sure that success was doing her any good.

"She will never quite be Laura again,' I thought. In a hundred little ways she dazzles me, and disappointed me. She was the big artist, conscious of her furs, and name, and réclame. Avid for praise, sensitive to criticism, on the alert for any opinion concerning herself, despising the unsuccessful. It was as though applause was still ringing in her ears, and she was hypnotised by it. She paid a kind of state visit to "The Duchess of Pless," kissed my father passionately, poured out the story of her triumphs into his ear, but was too occupied to ask after his affairs. And father beamed with pleasure.

"Well, well, well!" he said. "Becoming famous ... eh? Fine! fine!"

We had tea in the parlour, as of old, but nothing was said about the King of North Carolina or the King of South Carolina. Laura had made crowds of new friends, well-known conductors and artists, and wealthy patrons. She was very full of it I watched her looking round the stuffy little room, with its overcrowded Victorian furniture, and the wax fruit, and "The Death of Wolfe." She made no comment, but I could tell by her eyes that she had the measure of it They glittered critically.

"Laura is cruel," I thought, and then

"No; she isn't cruel. She's hypnotised, that's all."

II

I discovered that I was right, the following evening. Laura came into my room. She was a little unstrung.

She had been to a concert in the afternoon, and heard some big artist play Beethoven's E Flat Concerto. Her mind was barging about in all directions. I knew she was in one of her difficult moods. She was tired, sorry for herself, hungry for sympathy. She suddenly cried.

"What's the matter, old girl?" I said.

"Oh, I don't know. I was thinking of dad, I think."

"Dad! Why? He's all right"

"You go and see him pretty often, don't you, Tom?"

"Of course I do. Several times a week."

"While they were playing the slow movement, I suddenly began thinking about—mother. I don't think we've treated him very well, old boy; do you? . . . Lonely. He must be lonely sometimes, don't you think? Such a long time ago. The years seem to make barriers, don't they? One can't help him, quite like that. I try and think of him and mother when they were young like we are. It's all so far away. How beastly that we grow old and—get a sort of crust on."

"I think the guv'nor's quite happy, you know."

"Stepmother's a dear, but it can never be the same."

"I wasn't thinking of stepmother. I think he gets a lot of pleasure out of—little things."

Laura dabbed her eyes, and pecked me on the cheek.

"I must go more often. I must try and go every day. There's such a lot to do . . ."

Laura did indeed go the next evening, but she came back in a bad temper. A week later she went off to the South of France with a girl friend.

Mary visited my father regularly. She went at least once a week She took him some patent pipe-cleaners, gave him wrinkles about keeping the pewter bright, found him a new cook, when the fourth after "the Zulu pudding" had left, read to him when his eyes were bad, and sent him photographs of "the Midge."

Sometimes he and stepmother would come and dine with us at midday on Sunday. He was always very jovial and gay. Afterwards Mary and I would leave them alone in the drawing-room to have a nap, whilst she and I took the Midge out in a pram«

"Poor old dears!" Mary would say, and I would sigh in agreement.

The young are always pitying the old. It is for the most part a quite unnecessary attention. The old do not need it. As a matter of fact, when the young say and feel these things it is too often disguised pity for themselves, a too vivid anticipation. They do not realise that the "crust" is only a mantle of adjustment.

Those were golden days. Life seemed too crowded to do anything with. My hands were full of the precious stuff, and I could do nothing but idly watch the drift of it through my fingers. We made several friends, and indulged in the usual social suburban diversions. We spent week-ends at Woodstack, went for short excursions, visited the picture galleries, and looked in the shops. But we could never be away for long. There was the evening ceremony of bathing the Midge, an affair conducted with all the preparation and pomp of a Roman Te Deum.

If we went to a theatre it was necessary to creep into her room on our return and watch Madeline asleep. It is a curious thing that she was always Madeline to me when she was asleep, and the Midge when she was awake. Mary always kissed her downy skull, but she could do this without waking her up. For my part, I found it sufficient to hold my face very close to hers and smell her. She had a wonderful tickly smell that made one want to laugh. Mary said it was disgusting the way I did this—

like an animal. My defence was that at present we really had nothing more in common than our animal instincts. I hadn't observed any particular spiritual advance on Madeline's part. In reply to which Mary naturally told me not to be an idiot and to turn off the light in the hall.

My short stories were all returned from magazine' editors with the little printed slip of regrets. The novel in the lighter key made but desultory progress.

One day I took Mary to task about it. I said:

"Look here, darling; I don't believe it's any good. I'm nearly twenty-six, and I've done absolutely nothing. I'm interested in all this stuff, but it doesn't come off. I shall have to chuck it and try something else."

Mary puckered her brow, and thought for some seconds. Then she said:

"Well, I don't care what you do, darling. Only I won't have you taking on a job just for the sake of a job. It must be something which leads somewhere. It must have ambition at the back of it."

I kissed her with fervour. I was enormously relieved. I felt myself tingling with ambition.

III

I know quite well that at that time, if I had not been married to Mary, I should have gone and assisted my father at "The Duchess of Pless." And I think he would have liked to have me. He was becoming a little less brisk in his movements, and the days tired him. But I knew that to be a glorified potman would be unworthy of Mary. It led nowhere. Only, perhaps, to freedom and good-fellowship. . . . Queer, what a hold the atmosphere of that place had over me. I did not drink, myself, except occasionally a glass of port. But I liked to watch the people who came there, and listen to their talk. It was a kind of clearing-house of character. Very often in the evening, when we entertained intimate friends, I would give an imitation of Mr. Timble discoursing on the decadence of funeral etiquette, or old Mrs. Still analysing her sequence of husbands. I did not tell our guests that these were actual people who were themselves the guests of my father. I was still too much of a snob. I presented them as imaginary types. Our friends seemed to find them diverting. Uncle Stephen said that if I got a little more "biff-biff" into them, they would be worth doing in public This led to a discussion about going on the stage. Then visions of long tours away from Mary and Midge finally dissipated the idea. I was no further on. While Mary and I were discussing the ever-present subject one evening, our little ant-heap was disturbed by a bomb-shell from Laura. It arrived in the form of a long telegram from Edinburgh, announcing the fact that she was engaged to Edgar Beyfus, the concert agent and impresario.

"My God! it's the wrong man, of course!" I exclaimed.

"How do you know?" said Mary.

"I feel it in my bones."

"Don't be an ass. He may be quite all right. Do you know anything about him?"

"Never heard of the juggins. But why so sudden? Why an impresario? An impresario suggests someone to help her career, don't you see? Damn her career!"

"Tom, don't be so stupidly unreasonable."

"Well, can't you see it? He'll be a fat, influential Jew, with pots of money, who can pull the strings of concert-work all over Europe. Ton see if I'm not right!"

"I'm sure you're wrong. Laura's no fool. She'd never marry a man she didn't love."

"Wouldn't she! With Laura it's the career first, and love—also ran."

"You're mean and unkind, and I hate you."

I soon put that right; then I snatched my hat and went out. Laura, Laura, Laura! How awful! I could have wept. Laura never ought to marry. She was one of those people foredoomed to tragedy. I was convinced that this man was the wrong one. I walked up to Hampstead Heath, visualising him and cursing him. I thought no more about my career.

We heard no more from Laura for eight days. She never wrote letters if there was a telegraph-office handy. On the eighth day we received another telegram to say that she was back in London and that she was bringing him to see us that evening.

Edgar Beyfus was not at all like I had imagined. He was young, tall, rather good-looking, not a Jew. He had dark eyes, a dark moustache, and a pleasant smile. He was well-dressed but not over-dressed; and his manners were irreproachable. He always said the right thing, and he was very friendly to us. I was immensely relieved. We sat in our little drawing-room and talked till nearly twelve o'clock. It was a love-affair all right. One had only to note the way they kept looking at each other. Laura seemed quite different. She was gentler and more pliable. Her eyes swam in a mist of dreams. She hardly spoke about her career. She was tenderness itself. She asked after all our doings. I had never known her so sympathetic She went upstairs with Mary to see the baby. When she came down, her eyes were dancing.

"Isn't she a darling!" she said. "I kissed her on the ear, and it made me feel all cosy inside."

Then Edgar had to go up, and he expressed the sensation of feeling "all cosy inside." He admired our furniture, and the arrangement of the little rooms. He was perfectly charming.

"Thank God! Thank God!" I kept on thinking to myself. "He's all right He's quite a success. I shall like him."

When they went, I walked with them to the end of the road. We were all very merry. We fixed an appointment for the following week. Laura kissed me, and said:

"Good-bye, dear old boy."

It was an unusual endearment. When I got back, I found Mary kneeling in front of the fire, and looking very grave.

"Well?" I said. "That's all right, isn't it?"

She did not answer, and I repeated:

"Well?"

Without looking at me, she said:

"You were right, Tom."

"What do you mean?"

"He's the wrong man!"

Women are incredible.

IV

The following week I began my career as a scene painter. It came about through meeting a young man called Duncan Brice, at a friend's house. He was a jolly, rotund little person, and he told me he was working at the Becher Studios. The Becher Studios turned out to be a large scene-painting emporium in Paddington. He invited me to go and inspect them. The place immediately fascinated me. When I beheld an enormous woodlands glade all wet with size, I suddenly thought:

"Here is my job in life."

I had always had a certain aptitude for drawing, but never sufficiently pronounced to encourage me to give up everything to be a painter. But this was a profession of its own. I liked the smell of size, and the little scale models, and men in white blouses up on a scaffolding, splashing away with enormous brushes, the crude colours that looked so well a little way off, the sense of the theatre. I was introduced to Mr. Julius Becher himself, a large, genial man with the stump of a cigarette lost in his beard.

I reported the matter to Mary, and then I wrote to him. The end of it was, he agreed to let me go and work there. For the first six months I was to receive no salary, and at the end of that time he said he "would see."

I had not been so keen on anything for a long time. The prospect seemed to hold out the joy of painting without demanding that intense concentration and subtlety which I had not got, and the joy of the theatre without its nerve-strain and late hours. They were a most congenial company. Mr. Becher used to drink enormous quantities of beer. He kept a barrel in the corner of the studio, and the beer was supplied free to the staff. He had a great sense of solemn fun. He never smiled, but the men called him "uncle" and were always ragging him good-humouredly. He had a huge and powerful voice, and he was always striking ridiculous attitudes and declaiming fake Shakespeare. There was a small boy whom he called "Launcelot Gobbo," whose duty it was to keep his chief constantly supplied with liquid refreshment. He would suddenly stand up and mop his brow and exclaim:

"Boy! . . . Wassail!"

Launcelot Gobbo would immediately rush and fill a large pewter tankard with beer, and bring it to him. Then a conversation like this would follow:

"Ah! what is this leprous distilment?"

"Beer, my lord."

"Beer! Devil damn thee black, thou cream-faced loon! Didn't I tell thee to bring sack?"

"Sorry, sir."

"Bah I Let me taste the poison. (Drinks it at a gulp and points tragically at the door.) Go to! Get thee to a nunnery!"

"Yes, sir."

There was one man called Snayle, a cockney, with a wonderful falsetto voice. In our lunch-hour he would give extremely funny imitations of an Italian prima donna, with all the gestures and manners and tricks of the voice. Although for a long time I was not allowed to do anything but size canvases and mix buckets of colour, I found this life most interesting. Duncan Brice initiated me into a lot of the mysteries of the underside of life in the West End of London. It was a subject upon which he was no mean authority. He was an extremely clever draughtsman. If Mr. Becher left the studio for a few minutes, he would nip across the room and make a rough charcoal sketch of a nude woman right in the middle of a forest glade that the chief was working on. There would be a ringed sentence coming from her mouth: "Hullo, Uncle! What are you doing to-night?" When Mr. Becher returned the whole studio would watch him furtively. He would observe the drawing critically, with his head on one side. Then he would suddenly bawl out:

"Oh, my lights, and liver, and lungs! Oh, my lungs, and liver, and lights!"

Then he would pick up a straight-edge, and chase Duncan all over the room. Punishment having been inflicted, he would return, panting, and call out:

"Boy! . . . Wassail!"

It was surely the most disorderly and free-and-easy place of business that ever existed. Nevertheless, beneath it all, excellent work was accomplished. Julius Becher was considered one of the best scene-painters, with an absolute genius 'for the mechanical part He took a lot of trouble with me, and at the end of six months he said that I could "tell my mamma that I had been a good boy, and that he proposed to pay me fifteen shillings a week."

This was precisely the salary that I had enjoyed during my brief period as a clerk in the wall-paper firm. But what a difference! As Mary said—that led nowhere. But here I might one day become a force in the theatrical world. Like Mr. Becher I might hobnob with actor-managers and become a member of the Garrick Club. I might revolutionise stage-production. I was in a living movement.

V

Mary would never explain to me why she thought Laura had engaged herself to the wrong man. She was mysterious and obstinate about it, and I convinced myself that she was quite wrong. We did not see much of Laura for some time. She got an important engagement at the Gewandhaus at Leipsig, and went on a recital tour in Germany. When she returned she gave a recital at the St. James's Hall. I had not heard her play for a long time, and I was amazed at her improvement. She had often been accused by the critics of a certain restlessness and uncertainty of rhythm, but on this occasion she appeared to be a complete master of her moods. Edgar had given her a present of a Guarnerius, but this alone could not account for the increased richness of tone, the fine balance and breadth. I sat there and watched her frowning over the bow. She was dressed in black velvet, with a long chain of cornelians hanging to her waist. I felt proud, and a little jealous, and watchful, and mystified. Laura seemed far away from me, a goddess on Parnassus, communing with spirits too removed for me to understand. Mænads were dancing in star-like glades, the jagged profile of bare rocks rose up against the night sky, a woman was weeping . . . you could not know her story. The night was too bewilderingly beautiful. Tears and rapture, pity and passion, were they not all akin in these dark folds of colour and movement?

By the door Edgar Beyfus was standing. His eyes did not leave her face. Yes, of course, Mary was quite wrong. A good chap, Edgar. I could feel it in Laura's playing. She had found the golden key. She was no longer a girl pushing towards success. She was an artist communing. You cannot accomplish anything until you love. For love implies suffering. You cannot be big until you love and suffer—horribly.

In the artists' room afterwards I was the unintentional witness of a little incident which is always vividly impressed on my mind. There was a small room leading out of a larger. I hurried into the larger room to look for Laura. As I could not see her, I peeped into the smaller, just in time to see Laura kiss her fiancé. There were no half-measures about Laura. She seemed to be crying; then, as he entered the room ahead of me, she gave a little croon and, flinging her arms round him, she pressed her lips to his, and held him. It was a volcanic kiss, overwhelming.

We all went to supper at Fagani's. There was the usual gay reaction from the nervous strain of recital giving. Edgar ordered champagne. I have never known Laura in such a merry mood. We all laughed and chatted inconsequentially.

"Did I play well? Did you like my frock? Who was there? Weren't they a ripping audience?"

Laura darted at each of us. Mary and I both said we had never heard her play so well. Edgar said he never thought that even a Guarnerius could sound so glorious. Mary said her frock looked perfect. Laura ate a large quantity of macaroni and drank a considerable amount of champagne. Then she began again to talk excitedly of her career. She was going back to Germany in the spring; and there was a scheme afoot for visiting Russia.

Edgar smiled, and said, "What other plans have we?"

She looked at him, and laughed.

"Oh, you!" she said. "I know what you want. . . . You'll have to wait your chance."

And she crowned him with a sprig of parsley.

"Mary," I said, when we got home, "I'm annoyed with you. Why do you still persist in believing that Edgar is the wrong man? I think he's a ripping chap. I'm perfectly convinced that they are desperately in love I happened to see something. He wouldn't have given her that Guarnerius unless. . ."

Mary stifled a yawn, and shook her head.

"Damn it!" I said. "Do you still insist that Edgar's a mistake?"

"I'm more sure of it than ever," she answered, and began to undress.

Women . . . . But there! . . .

CHAPTER IX

THE DISSECTING-ROOM

Sunday night in "the dissecting-room." Giles called it the dissecting-room, because he said that Mary and her girlfriends used to meet there and dissect each others characters. It had probably been designed as a billiard-room. It was a lofty, bungalow kind of place, built on to Mxs. Copley's house; rather scratchily furnished with wicker chairs and ottomans, and an upright piano. It had always been consecrated to Giles and Mary, and their friends. It had a door leading on to the garden. The walls were brown wainscoting with a dark green canvas stretched above. I never liked this room. To-night, as I lay back on the ottoman, smoking, it filled me with an unaccountable sense of melancholy, and something worse . . . gusto picaresco. It was a good scene, though—a painter's effect. The faces clear-cut beneath the lamps, the room above lost in mystery, trails of blue tobacco-smoke drifting hither and thither. Why was I in such a silly mood? What was this dead-weight, like a premonition of evil? At the other end of the ottoman were Mary and a girl called Agnes Winter, giggling and listening to Radio, who was leaning forward and talking earnestly. In the centre of the room, close under the lamp, sat Mrs. Copley, stitching away at a piece of maroon-coloured embroidery. Her gentle face appeared concentrated on her work. She was not listening to Radic. In the further comer Giles and Angus sat facing each other over a chess-board, the board being supported by some mysterious piece of furniture covered with a blue-and-red check cloth.

I sat watching Radio, and only partially listening to him. He was vehement, as usual, and talking about "the good European." His small black tousled head kept thrusting forward like a ram, and he held one finger up and then flopped it down heavily on his leg and fumbled about with his knees. His queer transparent eyes flashed hither and thither, and his mouth broke into supercilious sneers. "Oh, yes, I believe you. . . . Men go into politics sincere, and in five minutes they are drinking tea with duchesses."—Mary thought this was very funny.—" An artist can be sincere, yes. Indeed, he is the only one, for he is alone. One man alone can be sincere. Two together can be sincere. Three go to pieces, and more than that, eat each other up. . . . When a man loses his will-to-express-regardless-of-all-consequences he loses everything. He becomes a debtor. What is it the politician says? 'I owe something to my party. I owe something to my constituents.' You see, he is already bargaining with his conscience. He is already compromising. Soon he becomes a beggar, yes, then a slave."

"Tell me, Radio, what do you mean by two people being sincere?"

"A man and a woman, yes . . . occasionally, when they love or when they . . . passion is always sincere. The good European destroys sincerity with his Royal Academy pictures and his temples of pity. He is like a dog running round in circles, trying to bite his own tail."

"What should he do, then? Run after other dogs and bite their tails?"

"Yes . . . preferably. If he values his type, he must think of himself"

How tiring Radio could be at times with his stale Nietzsche! And yet, of course, there was something in it. Perhaps we worried too much about each other. . . . What does Mrs. Copley look up like that for, as though she were listening? A dog barked somewhere at the front of the house. The electric bell rang. Another visitor. Well, why should I be agitated? All sorts of people drop into the Copleys' on a Sunday night.

A few moments drift by, during which one of the chess-players says, "Dash it! I didn't see that," and then comes the click of the dissecting-room door.

The door opens, and two girls with drawn, white faces enter the room. One is Daisy Weir and the other Eleanor Bowater. Curiously enough, they both glance at me first. I seem to expect this, and I jump up and go to them. Everyone is conscious of the sudden intrusion, like the rustle of the skirts of a tragedy. We seem to converge into a group under the lamp, everyone except the chess-players, who have looked up, but have not stirred. In spite of my anxiety I am peculiarly conscious of every little thing in the room.

Eleanor reaches me first, and puts her hand on my shoulder.

"It's all right . . . something awfully queer. Not really serious. . . ."

"What do you mean?"

"Laura. She burnt her violin this afternoon, at the Queen's Hall, during the concert."

"Burnt her violin!"

"I'm afraid it's awfully queer. But don't worry, old boy."

"Sit down, both of you."

It was Mary's hand which pulled me down on to the ottoman. Giles comes striding across the room, exclaiming:

"Good God! Not the Guarnerius!"

The two girls looked from one to another; then Eleanor said:

"You know it was the Harmonic Society concert this afternoon. Laura was playing the Vieuxtemps concerto. Sir Arthur Jeeves was conducting. She looked quite all right when she came on. She played gloriously. The whole thing went perfectly till she came to the slow movement. I don't know how it was, but both Daisy and I seemed to detect some change in her. She seemed nervous, abstracted. Once she nearly forgot to come in at the right moment. But she got through all right. At the end of the movement she peered into the audience with a queer look, and put her hand to her head. Sir Arthur began to tap with his baton, preparatory to the last movement, when she suddenly turned and walked deliberately off the platform.

"He looked rather surprised. Everyone imagined that something had gone wrong with her fiddle, although she certainly did not break a string. Sir Arthur waited, and spoke a few words to the leader. People began to whisper. The minutes went by. At last he walked off. He was absent nearly ten minutes. Daisy and I began to get into an awful state. At length he returned. He announced quite calmly that, owing to a sudden indisposition, Miss Purbeck would not be able to continue the concerto. The orchestra would play the next item. Of course Daisy and I rushed out and went to the back. We found her kneeling on the floor in the artists' room, staring at the fire. Mr. Loeb, the agent, was walking up and down the room, ejaculating: "My God! My God!" 'What is it?' I said. He pointed towards the fireplace. On the fender were the relics of a burnt fiddle. There was nothing left but a piece of the charred neck and the scroll with some gut still dangling. 'Laura,' I said, 'what has happened?' and I tried to kiss her. She thrust us both away. All she said was, 'I had to do it.' Mr. Loeb waved his arms in despair. 'She has destroyed it,' he said, 'of her own free will.' 'No, no,' said Daisy; 'it must have been an accident. It was an accident, wasn't it, Laura?' She only shook her head, and Mr. Loeb continued, 'She has destroyed the Guarnerius. She has destroyed her career.'"

II

When I heard Eleanor say this I gave a cry.

"Where is she?" I said. "I must go to her."

"There isn't another train up to town to-night," she answered. "And we don't know where she is. But I'm sure she's all right, Tom. She wasn't crying; nothing like that. She looked flushed, excited—peculiar, not really distressed. I think she must have been working too hard—a sudden nervous breakdown."

Daisy took up the narrative.

"There was an awful confusion, of course. Other people came round. Septimus Coyne was there. You know he is a tremendous admirer of Laura's."

"But where was Edgar?" I asked.

"I saw him once at the back of the hall. But he never came round when all this happened."

"He never came round!"

"No. As a matter of fact, Eleanor and I went round to try and find him. When we got back Laura had gone. The commissionaire said she had driven away alone in a cab. We thought she might be coming down here. We left Septimus still poking about. He will be down by the last train."

She stopped, and we all looked at each other. The matter seemed inexplicable. There was nothing to be said. We all wanted to know, and to question, and we did not know where to begin. Mrs. Copley's calm voice broke in:

"Was the instrument insured, darling?"

The comparative unimportance of this query cast a spell of relief. Giles, vigorously massaging his temples, said:

"Even if it were, mum, no company would pay up for a thing wilfully destroyed"

"What could have been the idea?"

"Laura said nothing more? You could get nothing more out of her?"

"No. Of course we meant to when we got back, but she'd gone. A lot of people began to collect, hall managers and people. The concert wasn't over. The commissionaire said she went off in a great hurry. She had a violin-case with her."

"She had a violin-case with her! That's rum," said Giles.

The room began to feel oppressive. I groped my way towards the door.

"Where are you going, dear?" said Mary.

"I must get up to London somehow. I must find her. I will walk up."

"My dear boy," said Eleanor; "it's twenty-two miles, and the night is dark and wet. You wouldn't know where to look when you got there. She may be down by the last train."

Mary pulled me back into the room.

"I'm sure it's all right," she said. I was conscious of them all looking at me. I felt that I ought to hold the master-key to this mystery—that I was in some peculiar way responsible. I felt ashamed, confused, distraught. I walked over to the chess-board, and pretended to observe the position of the game. The two players returned and resumed their seats. We all three stared at the ridiculous little men with unseeing eyes. The girls were whispering in the opposite corner. Mrs. Copley walked out of the room. Angus offered me a cigarette and I lighted it without thanking him. I heard Radic launching forth into a new tirade. I caught the phrase: "To be any good at all, art must be unbridled."

The two boys continued their game in silence. Then Giles, who had the game well in hand, made a preposterous mistake. He flushed angrily and exclaimed:

"Oh, what's the good?" Then he turned to me and said:

"I don't see why it should ruin her career—just a sudden indisposition."

I did not answer him, and he called out:

"Eleanor, who was there? Was the hall full?"

Eleanor came over, and spoke quietly.

"There were no critics. Sunday, you know. But the hall was packed. There would almost sure to be some newspaper people. In fact, Daisy says she saw old Threlfall of the Daily Quest—taking a 'busman's holiday, probably. Sir Arthur Jeeves seemed to take it quite calmly. Of course I don't know what transpired between him and Laura."

"Septimus ought to be here by now."

Mrs. Copley came into the room, followed by a maid with a tea-tray. While she was putting it down, the bell went. Mary shot from the room like an arrow from a bow. The rest of us stood watching the door. The maid was fussing with the tray and whispering to Mrs. Copley, who replied, as though it was a matter of great importance:

"Yes, some of the Garibaldi biscuits, Mama"

There was an interminable wait; then Coyne entered the room in his overcoat, followed by Mary. No Laura. Coyne looked tired and oily, as though he had been greasing his hair and then wiping his hands on his pale face. A slight expression of importance crept over his countenance as he looked round at us, like that of a successful performer about to play his own composition.

III

It took a long time to get rid of the maid, and then they made him take off his overcoat.

"It's awfully queer," was all he would say for a long time.

"Did you see her again?"

"No. I never saw her at all, except on the platform. I saw Beyfus at the back and I saw him go out of the hall when Laura went off after the slow movement."

"What could you tell from his face?"

"Nothing."

"Didn't he look scared?"

"I didn't notice anything special. He was just standing there looking calm, and he walked out."

"Did you find out whether he went round to the artists' room?"

"Yes. He didn't go there."

"What are your ideas? Why do you think she did it?"

"Well, it looks to me as though there had been some sort of rumpus. You know what Laura is. He must have done something. . . . She wanted to show that she had finished with him. It was he who had given her the Guarnerius. They say he paid seven hundred and fifty for it. It was her way of showing him that she'd done with him."

"But why, in God's name, do it in the middle of a concert? It's cutting off her nose to spite her face."

"You know what Laura is. She's impulsive. She saw him there in the hall, watching her. It was a sudden mood. She couldn't stand it any longer. Something to do with the mood of the music, probably, also Laura's an artist. She wouldn't think about the effect."

Radio suddenly clapped his hands and exclaimed, "Braval brava! Why should she? . . . Unbridled, eh? What did I say? To hell with the publicans!"

"Publicans" was unfortunate, but Radic meant well. Then Mary interjected:

"But you say he went out of the hall when Laura walked off. In that case he wouldn't know that she had burnt the fiddle."

"I saw him go out, but I don't know where he went to. He may have come back again through another door, or have gone to another part of the hall, or have been watching outside. I did not leave the hall till Jeeves had made the announcement. I darted about outside to try and find Beyfus. When I went round to the back Laura had gone. The commissionaire told me that a cab had been waiting for her for half an hour, and that she took away quite a lot of things, including a violin-case, a trunk, and the charred remnants of the Guarnerius."

"That's queer," remarked Giles. "That looks more like premeditation than impulse."

The maid re-entered with the Garibaldi biscuits, and we sat solemnly, considering the problem. "The only thing that's quite clear," I thought, "is that as a prophet I was right and Mary was wrong, but when it came to intuition she was right and I was wrong. Edgar Beyfus must be the wrong man. It's all to do with him. Good God, poor Laura! I hope she won't do anything mad."

"Of course," continued Septimus, "after the show I hung about and tried to pick up what I could, but I couldn't get hold of anything very useful. Everyone was asking questions and no one was answering them. There were some newspaper people there, I don't mind telling you. Jeeves was surrounded, but not very communicative. He had had a great success with the Dvorak at the end, and I think he'd forgotten about Laura. I heard him say, "Oh, yes, very unfortunate, very regrettable. I can tell you nothing mora' And Loeb was tearing his hair. "How I have worked for that girl!" he was saying. "For ten years I have worked and slaved, and she throws it all away in five minutes." As a matter of fact, it was he who was the fool. He completely lost his head. If he had kept quiet the thing need never have come out. Jeeves told nothing except the indisposition yarn, but Loeb was blurting out the whole story. Of course he hates Beyfus. Laura has been with Loeb all these years, and now she goes and gets engaged to Beyfus, which means that in future Beyfus will be her agent, and husband, and everything else."

"Do you think that possibly" began Daisy, with distended eyes. Then she stopped and remarked sententiously, "Of course, there are always wheels within wheels."

Giles turned to Angus and said:

"Colum, you've been in the musical profession years—what do you know of Loeb? . . . and what is thought of Beyfus?—in the profession, I mean, of course, as an impresario?"

Angus thrust forward and, speaking in his lazy voice, he said:

"Oh, I don't know. Loeb is an old Jew. I've always heard that he's pretty straight—a sound man, not very pushing."

"Yes. And Beyfus?"

Angus grinned round at the company apologetically, and shrugged his shoulders.

"Oh, I don't know. It's just what one hears. I have heard that Beyfus is just the opposite."

I turned to him sharply, and said:

"You mean to say that you've heard that Edgar Beyfus is young, not straight, not sound, but very pushing?"

Angus wriggled uncomfortably, and murmured:

"Oh, it's just what one hears. There may be nothing in it."

IV

Then a dramatic turn was given to events. The maid again entered the room, and said:

"Someone wishes to speak to Mr. Purbeck on the telephone, madam."

I dashed out into the hall, and Mary followed me. I snatched up the receiver and cried "Hullo!" There was no sound but the hum of the wires. I kept on repeating "Hullo! Hullo!" At length a voice said:

"Is that you, Tom?"

It was Laura's voice.

"Yes, yes. Is that you, Laura?"

"Don't be excited, old boy. I just wanted to tell you, you are not to worry about anything you hear about to-night. I am quite all right."

"But, Laura, Laura—"

"Hush! It's been all very difficult. Don't believe anything you hear or read. I'll write to you in a day or two. Good night, dear, and my love to you all."

"But, Laura, why did you . . . Laura, Laura! are you there? Hell! Laura! Laura!" There was no sound but the low drone of the wires.

Mary caught my arm and kissed me.

V

As we went back into the dissecting-room, Giles was saying:

"The more I hear about it, the more convinced I am that Laura has been used as a pawn in some game between Loeb and Beyfus. Loeb may have been acting. Of course, if she is going to Beyfus he won't care if her career is ruined. On the other hand. . . Hullo I any news?"

"Laura telephoned to say she's all right. That's all. Nothing else."

"Where did she telephone from?"

"I don't know. She rang off suddenly, or we were cut off. Perhaps she'll ring up again."

Radic was shaking his finger at Eleanor.

"Everyone is your enemy . . . don't forget that. You only reach perfection through a process of destruction. Steel through the furnace, eh? Creation through suffering. . . . What do these chess-players say? 'Oh, dash it! I didn't see that!' ... To be a good chess player, or a big artist, you must see more than the other fellow, eh?"

Giles threw another log on to the fire, and muttered:

"There's nothing more we can do."

I suddenly thought of father. Probably at that moment he was serving drinks across the bar at "The Duchess of Pless," talking to Mr. Timble, or upholding the dignity of his house. "Silence, gentlemen!" Father—he would never be able to understand it, whatever the solution. To-morrow he would probably read about it in the newspapers: "Sensational Incident at the Queen's Hall. Violinist Destroys her Violin." An immoral act. A flagrantly immoral act Whether she wanted the violin or not, she destroyed a beautiful thing that could not be replaced. She might have given it away, or given it back to him. But that, of course, would not be like Laura. She would act abruptly, and think afterwards. Her voice had sounded unruffled, though, as though she was not unhappy. It was kind of her to ring up. We were "not to worry." That meant that she was not going to—do anything rash. I had been frightened of this. I always felt that Laura might do anything. Our mother was Spanish. ... I wish I had known more about our mother. Doubtless in her life she had—done precipitate things, and thought afterwards. I began dreaming of that romantic country, with its dark passions and slumbering tragedies.

Giles got out a pack of cards and began to play patience feverishly. We were all silent, when suddenly Radic came out with a most amazing suggestion. Rocking on his haunches on the ottoman, he said:

"You say. Miss Weir, that there was nothing left of the violin but the charred scroll, eh?"

"Yes, the scroll and a piece of the neck, with some strings dangling. Just a wreck."

"How do you know, then, that it was the Guarnerius?"

We sat there contemplating this remarkable insinuation. I think we all took it in different ways.

Then I turned to him and. said:

"What on earth do you mean, Radic? Do you think Laura would lie about it?"

"I haven't heard yet that Laura said that it was the Guarnerius. All she said was 'she had to do it'"

"But, surely, you?"

"Listen, old boy. I would not believe Laura capable of any deception, no. But there are too many chevaliers d'industrie in this. All these professions where success is the first consideration . . ."

"But what possible good can it do, if it ruins her career?"

"It may ruin her career, or it may make her career. Se non è vero, è hen trovato. It all depends on how the situation is—what you call it?—handled. One may try to ruin and the other to make. Two nice men, perhaps."

"But, in that case, Laura would have been a party to it. I refuse to believe".

My mind went whirling round and round. I seemed to hear Radic talking a long way off above the crackling of the logs:

"There is always the pull that way. A little more and one is over the edge before one knows it. There is a first cause, and then the story is complicated by things outside. The chevalier d'Industrie . . . capable of anything. . . . Oh, yes, believe me ... I know him—this good European."

CHAPTER X

THE CUBAN ASSASSIN

Only two of the morning papers had any mention of the incident, but the afternoon papers came out with flaming headlines and with Laura's portrait. The popular headline was, "Remarkable Incident at the Queen's Hall. Well-known Lady Violinist Destroys a Thousand-guinea Violin." Some hinted that Miss Laura Purbeck had had an accident, others that she had had a sudden mental aberration, due to a nervous breakdown. They all agreed that the matter was a mystery, and had not yet been cleared up. It was disclosed that she had left on the midnight train for Manchester, where she was to play on Tuesday afternoon. Sir Arthur Jeeves was reputed to have said that "he was not quite clear what had happened. Miss Purbeck seemed completely unstrung when he entered the artists' room. He only had a few words with her. From her manner he felt convinced she would not be able to continue, although she could easily have obtained another violin. Indeed, she had another one with her. He could not keep the public waiting. When the concert was over, she had gone." On Tuesday nearly every paper in England seemed to have Laura's portrait, with a long article about her, and an interview quoted from the representative of a news-agency who had run her to earth in a Manchester hotel. It was headed, "Miss Purbeck's Remarkable Story," and it ran somewhat as follows:

"Our representative, who found Miss Purbeck considerably recovered from the nervous strain of her experience at the Queen's Hall, was told a strange and romantic story. She appeared quite willing, indeed anxious, to relieve herself of an oppressive burden and to offer explanations and apologies for the unfortunate contretemps of Sunday evening. We will quote her own words: 'The Guarnerius was given me by my fiancé, Mr. Edgar Beyfus, on the 27th of last month. It was, as you know, a beautiful instrument and quite historic I first played on it in public on the 10th of this month, at Bath, and there was no untoward incident. On the following night, however, I was playing at Bristol. After the concert several people came round to see me—it is quite customary—and one gentleman sent in his card, on which was inscribed Senor Julio Gonzales, Thinking he was probably a musician of some sort, I gave permission for him to come in. He was a tall, dark, sallow-looking man, and he informed me that he was a Cuban. I don't know how it was, but he frightened me. I didn't like his eyes. They were sinister and penetrating. After paying the usual compliments about my playing, he picked up my violin. "This is a beautiful instrument," he said, and he looked at me closely. I replied that of course I knew it was, and I began to wonder what he was after. Drawing me a little on one side, he suddenly whispered, "Miss Purbeck, I do not wish to disturb you, but there is a curse on this violin!" I asked him what he meant, and he answered, "Thirty years ago this violin belonged to certain members of my family. To all of them who played it there came tragedy." I am not a superstitious person, and I was inclined to laugh at this portentous statement, but the man somehow gripped me. I could not help feeling that he was in earnest. In a few whispered statements he told me three appalling tragedies that had happened to different members of the Gonzales family during the time they owned the violin. It was horrible. Other people came up and interrupted us, but as he went he muttered, "I warn you. I warn you. I warn you." It all seemed very foolish, and I tried to dismiss it from my mind, but a few days later, being in London, I happened to mention the matter to my fiancé. As you know, nearly all these old violins have a pedigree, and Mr. Beyfus laughed and said he would look it up. Sure enough, we found that the Guarnerius had been in the possession of the Gonzales family thirty years ago, and they had held it for twelve years—just as he had said. Even then we should have been disposed to laugh the matter over, only that another uncomfortable incident recurred to our minds. We remembered that the Gonzales sold it to an American gentleman in London named Mr. Bonzard Smith, a very wealthy man who bought it for his daughter in Boston. He expected the girl over in the, spring. A few weeks later she was killed in a sleigh accident. Of the last owners from whom Mr. Beyfus bought it we knew nothing, but naturally the whole thing got on my nerves a little. I was too busy, however, to worry seriously. I determined that I must dismiss it from my mind if I was to play well. A week later I was playing the Vieuxtemps concerto at Glasgow with the municipal orchestra. I had practically forgotten all about my Cuban friend. I had played through two movements when, just as I was commencing the third, I caught sight of him at the back of the hall. He was grinning at me malevolently. I do not know how I got through that movement. I nearly fainted. But I did manage to struggle through. I'm not surprised, by the way, that the Glasgow Herald slated it. I was trembling like a leaf. When the concert was over I expected him to come round, but he did not appear. It seemed worse that he did not appear than if he had appeared. Was he following me about? And why?

"'My next engagement was at Nottingham, a few days later. I was becoming quite unstrung by the affair. I telegraphed to Mr. Beyfus and he came at once. I explained it to him, and he posted several men about the hall. If Gonzales had appeared they were going to warn him. But he did not appear. Neither did he appear at my recital at Bedford. I was beginning to think that it was pure coincidence. My next engagement was the Harmonic Concert at the Queen's Hall. I was playing the same concerto that I had played in Glasgow. For a time the importance of the occasion, the sympathetic attention of the audience, above all the music itself, so absorbed me that I lost all association of idea with the Glasgow incident. But suddenly, during the slow movement, the recollection of it occurred to me. I had to struggle to keep my mind on the theme. When the movement was finished I almost involuntarily glanced at that part of the hall where Gonzales had been sitting at Glasgow. To my horror I suddenly looked right into his eyes. He was sitting about ten rows back, and he was grinning. I felt paralysed with fear. I gripped my violin tight, as though I expected someone to snatch it away. I heard Sir Arthur Jeeves tapping with his baton preparatory to the opening of the third movement. And then I realised that I could not go on. I suppose I lost my head. I ought to have said a word to Sir Arthur, but instead of that I walked straight off the platform. I raced down to the artists' room. A large fire was burning in the grate, a clear red fire. My hands seemed frozen and numb. Instinctively I thrust them forward over the fire, hardly realising that I was still holding the violin. And then the awful thing happened. The violin slipped from my grasp and dropped right upon the red part of the fire. I gave a cry. If my nerves had not immediately given way I had plenty of time to snatch the instrument away before it was damaged beyond repair. But when I saw the flames lick round the body of my beautiful fiddle I was simply hypnotised by the tragedy. I heard the gut snap and I saw the body of it blazing away. I believe I laughed and cried at the same time. I suppose I was quite hysterical. In one way I experienced a curious sense of relief, as though the spell which the stranger had put over me had been broken. On the other hand I seemed to see all my hopes and ambitions vanishing into smoke. How could I possibly account for it? I don't know how long I knelt there, watching my fiddle bum, before Sir Arthur came into the room. "What is the matter? What is the matter. Miss Purbeck?" he said. I really can't remember what I answered. I believe I said, "Yes, yes, I'm coming," and I snatched the charred remnant from the fire as though I proposed to continue playing on it. Sir Arthur was very kind. I suppose I cried then. He said I was ill. I must lie down. In any case, he could not keep the public waiting any longer. He went away. I did not feel that I could face the ordeal of a kind of public inquisition, so directly he had gone back to the platform I got the commissionaire to get me a cab and I drove away to my flat, and then caught the midnight train to Manchester. I brought my old fiddle with me. I am only hoping that the public will understand and forgive me. I am now wondering, is this Cuban going to haunt my life, or now that the fiddle is destroyed, will he vanish altogether?'"

At Laura's recital at Manchester on Tuesday afternoon there was not a vacant seat.

II

The following night I visited my father at "The Duchess of Pless." To my surprise, all the bars were crowded. Everyone seemed to be reading or examining the evening newspapers. There was the loud hum of conversation. My father, looking flushed and excited, was hurrying hither and thither. When he caught sight of me, he exclaimed:

"Hullo, Tom! What's all this about Laura?"

"I know nothing except what I've read," I answered.

"It'll a nice thing, isn't it? I must say, it's a nice thing"—reaching down a bottle. "Why couldn't she tell us about this scoundrel? I'd have done something. I'd have settled him—this Cuban assassin!" He served two gentlemen with rum, and I heard him repeating, "Cuban assassin!" Trade was very brisk. I overheard the constant repetition, "Of course it is—old Purbeck's daughter!" Discussions were in force about fate, and destiny, and things that had been accursed. Old Timble was holding forth on the romance of the Hope diamond. Father appeared agitated, but I could not help thinking that he was rather pleased with the publicity. And once he whispered to me, "Well, I'm glad the damn thing was burnt."

A keen-faced man, named Hatchett, who ran a small easy-hire furnishing business in the High Street, leant across the bar and said:

"If you ask me, Mr. Purbeck, sir, my opinion is that the motive was robbery. He wanted to frighten the girl, then he was either going to steal the violin or offer her a nominal sum for it."

My father shrugged his shoulders. It might be so. He had been to Cuba—a treacherous race—mostly assassins. He did not like to forego the idea that the violin really was cursed. It satisfied his superstitious beliefs. Things were cursed. There was no getting away from it. There were a lot of mysteries we didn't understand. He had once sat down thirteen to table. During the following year one of the party had died from heart disease. There you were!

During a slight lull later on, my father beckoned me into the little room at the back.

"What do you think of this Edgar Beyfus?" he said.

"I know nothing against him," I answered.

"Ah! but—do you know anything for him?"

"He seems all right They say he's a clever, decent sort of chap. One of the coming men in the concert world."

"Ah!"

"I think you can rely on him looking after her all right"

Then my father did a surprising thing. He offered me a glass of port, and had one himself. "He wrote to me and asked my consent, you know," he explained, holding the port up to the light". By the same poet Laura wrote. You know what Laura is. A lot of—well, gush. Then she put it in such a way that it meant that whether I gave my consent or not, it wouldn't make any difference."

He laughed, and sipped the port like a connoisseur.

"I've never seen the fellow. He was to call on me but he's never been."

"Ah! he ought to have been. I think you will like him. This is good port, dad."

"Yes, it's the real thing, isn't it? Have some more, if you like."

"Thanks very much."

Two glasses of port went to my head. I said:

"This is going to be a big thing for Laura, dad. I thought it might ruin her career. Instead of that, I believe it will make her. Everybody in England is talking about her. She is destined to be great. At Manchester yesterday they sold out. I believe she'll be all the rage."

My father's eyes glowed quietly. Was I under an illusion when I fancied that he, too, had been drinking—a little more than customary? He was seldom so chatty and familiar with me. The din from the bars seemed to increase. I can't quite remember what I said, but I know I became a little sentimental. Father's brilliant daughter, my brilliant sister—and I had no jealousy of her. I was rather proud, that was all. It seemed so queer when I thought of the days when she and I used to play in the yard at the bade I was always the waverer, but Laura never had any misgivings. Since she was a kid, she meant to be great. Like many great people, she was perhaps a little unscrupulous. One couldn't help that. It was just—Laura. If she was abrupt and inconsiderate at times one had to forgive her. Fundamentally she wasn't only an ambitious woman. She paid for her mistakes in her conscience. She was really far kinder and more sympathetic than I. She was ambitious, of course. . . .

Father listened, and nodded, and his eyes roamed. He tapped the bowl of his pipe against the mantelshelf.

"It's all right up to a point," he ejaculated once. A loud high giggle came from the saloon bar, and then a man's voice bawling out something very loud. He pushed by me, and I heard the door snap to. Above the cries in the bar I suddenly heard that boom of authority:

"Silence, gentlemen!"

III

Laura's wedding, which took place a month later, was a very different affair from mine. It was done in style at a fashionable church, with a reception at a smart West End hotel. There were crowds of guests. Marj and I hardly knew anyone. Father wandered about the room with a red face, looking as though he wanted to fight someone. Uncle Stephen appeared in a brand new, badly-fitting tail-coat. He drank too much champagne, and had to be snubbed by Laura for overfamiliarity. This was not "Baionnette's day." Well known artists and newspaper people were in evidence, for Laura was becoming famous. The incident of the Cuban assassin had given a tremendous fillip to her popularity. Everywhere where she had played during the month the halls had been crowded. Many people went out of a morbid curiosity to see whether the villain would be there, or whether there would be a scene. At Hull a sallow little man with a black moustache was suddenly credited with being the man. A crowd waited for him afterwards and assaulted him. He was nearly thrown into the river, and only escaped through the intervention of the police. He turned out to be a little Austrian barber, with a passion for Bach, who had never heard of the Cuban assassin and was completely bewildered by his sudden unpopularity. He thought the world had gone crazy.

This incident also attracted considerable notice in the Press, and the little barber was surprised to find his photograph in the newspapers, above an article beginning: "There was very nearly a tragic sequel to the remarkable experience of Miss Laura Purbeck, the well-known violinist," etc.

Laura herself was more elusive than ever. It was impossible to get hold of her and cross-examine her about the details. She was always "simply frantically busy" or "rushed off her feet." On the only occasions when Mary and I saw her, Edgar was with her and usually other people. She appeared to be in a tremendous state of excitement like a person drunk with life. Only once in the passage of a restaurant, did I get a few words alone with her, and then she squeezed my arm and said:

"Dear old boy, I'm so happy."

I wanted her to come and spend an evening alone with us, and she promised that she would, but at the last moment she telegraphed that it was impossible. When we tackled her with the abruptness of the wedding arrangements, she laughed and explained that she was shortly going on a tour in Holland and Germany, and that if she married and took Edgar it would save taking a maid. Edgar said that this was quite true, and that he was taking lessons in needle-work, and studying the construction of lingerie.

"I see what you mean by his being the wrong man," I said to Mary one day. "He always flirts with her. If you love anybody very much you don't flirt with them—except, perhaps, sometimes when you are alone."

"Edgar is quite the wrong sort of person for Laura," answered my wife. "He'll feed all that side of her which craves for success and glamour, and starve the rest."

"There's never been anyone yet who has influenced her at all. She has done just what she thought she would. It's queer how different we are. I am like clay in the hands of the potter," I said, kissing my wife's hair. Then she held my cheeks between her hands and looked at my eyes quizzically.

"You're a funny old thing!" she said.

IV

I was now earning one hundred and fifty pounds a year as a scene-painter. I felt very important I was a married man, with a house and a child and responsibilities. The years had slipped by almost unnoticed. We no longer bathed Midge. Madeline performed that operation by herself. She began to talk and to have ideas of her own. I bored the men at the studio with a repetition of her remarks and stories. During my work I would suddenly stop and dream of her. I could almost feel her little arms round my neck, and hear the merry ripple of her voice. She was already like Mary, not only in looks, but in that mothering, managing way of doing things. Another Mary to lighten the dark spaces of the world. And I would sigh, and dream, and dream, till suddenly the voice of Mr. Becher would boom across the room:

"On such a night, when the sweet wind did gently kiss the trees, and they did make no noise Boy! . . . Take wassail to Mr. Purbeck; he is sighing his love towards the Grecian tent, where Cressid lay that night"

Was I completely happy? I couldn't tell. Sometimes a wave of restless ambition would sweep over me, the kind of ambition that Laura had, and then the voices would become mute under the sheer beauty and tranquillity of the hour. Life seemed sufficient unto itself. Why should I be ambitious? I was fully conscious that my career, so-called, was a poor thing compared with Laura's. Here was I, nearly thirty, utterly unknown and undistinguished, earning a meagre wage, with no particular prospects. Indeed, the prospects were not as bright as they had promised to be. The scene-painting world was passing through a difficult time, owing to the encroachments of the upholsterer. People no longer wrote plays which demanded forest glades, or cornfields crimson with poppies. Nearly all our sets were interiors. "The morning room at Lady Blanksyde's." Just white panelling to be ruled out to scale, and the furniture man did the rest. Had it not been for pantomime, we should have had little play for our fancy. No one is interested in the personality of the man who rules out the panelling in Lady Blanksyde's morning room. But Laura—Laura would probably know the real Lady Blanksyde herself. She would play in her drawing-room, feel quite at home at her country-house party, assume it as her right to be flirted with by Lady Blanksyde's guests. On the other hand, the little house in the Plane Tree Grove, with its gas going wrong, and the geyser which leaked, and all the petty household troubles. And Mary suddenly discovering a streak of grey hair, and Madeline's voice: "Daddy, daddy, when are you going to bring me home that big, big Noah's Ark?"

Would I change all this with Laura? Sometimes yes. Sometimes no. Mostly no. Oh, yes, assuredly no. Laura disturbed me, but she did not make me envious. A far more disconcerting element was Radic. Radic, the madman, who did one thing well and with a fine frenzy. I felt somehow ashamed of meeting Radic. I knew that he despised my profession. He would sneer and show his yellow teeth like a jackal. "Painting for business! Bah! These chevaliers d'Industrie!"

Sometimes I wondered whether there was anything in life to be sought for but happiness. And generally I persuaded myself that there was not. I was wildly happy . . . only on occasions would come that sudden vague emptiness, as though some deep chord in my nature was craving expression ... as though I was only marking time.

V

When Laura returned from the Continent, a change in her became apparent. She seemed more developed, more florid. More brilliant than ever to look at, she indulged in effects which are usually denoted by the word "striking." On the platform she wore crimson carnations in her hair and a band of black velvet. Her frocks were barbaric. In her playing her tone was just as full and mellow, but she had developed tricks of exaggerating the rubato, of playing about with the time to get dramatic effects, of over-sentimentalising. Moreover, in her whole attitude there was more abandon. She swayed from the hips, and acted the music with her f aca She came on to the platform with the assurance of a star performer, and selected pieces which showed off her virtuosity. Concert-director Edgar Beyfus took a suite of offices in Hanover Square, furnished with Chippendale and Persian rugs. He employed some half-dozen immaculately-dressed young clerks. Telephones and typewriters clanged discords in the outer offices. Newspaper advertisements began to speak of coming world-activities. The name of Laura Purbeck was never out of his lists. She was now referred to as "the great English virtuoso." Cunningly arranged quotations from the Dutch and German newspapers gave the impression that a new comet had appeared in the musical heavens. Needless to say, this orgy of exploitation had its reaction. The soberer London journals detest a fanfare. They criticised her in no measured terms. But their criticism in no wise affected her popular success. The glamour of the romance about the Cuban assassin still hung around her, and the glamour of her recent marriage fanned the flames. Everything about Laura was abrupt Abruptly she had leapt into fame, and equally abruptly the older musical societies and conductors dropped her. She became a popular draw at ballad-concerts, where her rendering of a trifle like the Humoresque of Dvorak would never fail to bring down the house. The angle of her musical outlook seemed to have changed abruptly. She was no longer the restless and dissatisfied student groping for beauty, uncertain, mysterious, reverent. She was a mistress of her moods. Whenever we saw her she was always in the. highest spirits. One night I said to Mary:

"If only she would cry! I would like her to come to me one day and—like she did in the old days—suddenly be uncertain of herself, not understand herself, but just be natural and have a good cry. It can't be right to be so satisfied."

A few days later they came and told me that Radic was dead. He had died suddenly in a nursing-home, after an operation on the throat. The news moved me profoundly. My poor old madman! He was just twenty-seven—a comet indeed. He had scrambled through his untidy life under the momentum of an almost undefined impulse. Old warring currents stirred in his past. Who could tell the bitterness and the anguish that went to his making? He never spoke of his mother or of his people, but he sometimes talked feelingly of his country. Small, unhealthy, bitter, greedy, cynical, and lascivious, and yet under the folds of this tragic entity there stirred something big. I liked him because he was transparent. The world to him was just a ridiculous place. If he had found it different, he, too, might have been different. He was remorseless in his sincerity. Doubtless, in the years to come, people would observe a low-toned landscape hanging on a wall, and they would say, "By Jove! that's a fine thing. Who did that?" And then I could see the sallow face of my friend peering across the ages suspiciously. He would be licking his lips and fidgeting, as he muttered, "You fool! What do you know about it?"

Most vividly came back to me the memory of that day when I told Radic the story about the Cuban. He never read the newspapers, so he had heard nothing about it. He listened to all I had to say, fidgeting with a palette as he did so. He grinned, and uttered little clucks of derision. When I had finished he remarked:

"Well, that was one up on Beyfus, anyway." Then he squeezed out a long wriggle of flake-white, and added:

"I was certain it wasn't the Guarnerius they burned. That proves it"

I protested that he was wrong in that respect. Laura would never have consented to such a criminal action. Suddenly Radic put the palette down and caught hold of my waistcoat-button.

"Purbeck," he said, "if the world was composed of more fools like you, and less knaves like Beyfus—I'd start all over again. Yes, believe me. I'd go to church, and wear clean collars. I'd read the newspapers. I'd believe in God."

CHAPTER XI

ANNA

Anna was barely twenty when she became attached to Mr. Becher's studio. She occupied a small room off the passage, where she did all the accounts and the typewriting. She was the subject of endless but quite innocuous mirth by all the members of the staff. Mr. Becher called her Rosalind, Duncan called her the Queen Bee. We all had our pet names for her, but we were very circumspect and proper in our attitude towards her. Anna did not encourage frivolity. She was reserved, competent, and a little matronly. I have never known anyone so changeable in appearance. She seemed to be a hundred different women, and each one with an aspect of her own. I was always having to peep into her room to see whether she was anyone fresh. Her face was rather heavily modelled for her age, and her figure developed and yet slim. At her best she was undoubtedly a very pretty girl. At her worst a very interesting and appealing child. She had masses of light-brown hair, and a clear, warm complexion. Her movements were brisk; her expressions slow and watchful. She appeared to take no notice of anyone, and yet to be ever on the alert. She had queer blue-grey eyes that hardly' ever looked at you, except occasionally to give you a quick, penetrating glance. It was difficult to get her to talk. She was very shy, but self-contained. This very reserve piqued your interest. You felt that she had a depth of feeling, of passion perhaps, as yet unawakened. Her voice was low, musical, and refined. She spoke to us, not as though she disliked us, but as though she thought we were just amusing little people she was observing from the heights of Parnassus. We did not count very much, one way or the other. One day Mr. Becher remarked:

"That girl will drive me mad. When I go in there to dictate a letter I feel like a schoolboy addressing the Sphinx. I want to be young and make love to her, just to see what happens. She has everything. Dido and Æneas, Paolo and Francesca, Lady Macbeth, Rosalind, Mary Magdalene, Becky Sharp, Catherine of Russia, Boadicea, the smell of Parma violets, the tears of Beethoven, laughter, Zephyr with Aurora playing when he met her once a-maying, and so on, and so forth. She's a kind of embryo of all these things. I wish one of you boys would make love to her and tell me all about it"

These remarks were only addressed to Duncan and myself, and I knew, as a matter of fact, that it was superfluous to give Duncan this advice, for I had already observed his advances. Duncan was like a male bird in the mating season. His feathers were at their glossiest when Anna entered the room. His rich colouring appeared to express his virility. His voice, when he addressed her, assumed a mellow timbre like a warm caress. He gave a superb exhibition of modulated empressement. He said nothing excessive, only in his manner and the tones of his voice did he betray the erotic craftsman. There was something positively disgusting in the way that he went to work. And he was such a good-looking boy.

"If Anna stands up to this," I thought, "she will be a very remarkable little—typist!"

Duncan pursued her during the whole of one winter without achieving any success at all. Anna would have nothing to do with him.

"She's not my quarry, old man," he said to me one day. "She's certainly going to be someone's, but I've drawn a blank."

"You are a beast," I replied. "Why don't you leave her alone? You know you're just fooling. You've no idea of marrying her."

"I don't know," he said. "I hadn't at first. It's awfully rum. But I'm simply getting crazy on that girl. I believe I would marry her if I had a chance."

In the middle of the afternoon, a few days later, Duncan suddenly came to me and asked me to come out to the yard at the back. He looked very red in the face and crestfallen.

"I've had a hell of a time, old man," he said, when we were alone. "I lost my head. I went in there. She was standing up, leaning over some papers. I went up and put my arms around her, and kissed her on the cheeks and lips. My God, it was awful! She flew at me like a panther. She struck me in the face. She snatched up a ruler. I've never seen such a face—blazing. I just bolted. I'm afraid there'll be a row. She'll tell the guv'nor, or resign, or lie in wait and kill me."

II

I told him that it served him right. At the same time, we didn't want a rumpus, so I suggested that I should go and apologise for him, and say that he simply lost his head, and he was very sorry. Duncan agreed, and I immediately went to her room. She was seated at the typewriter. Her eyes were very bright and her cheeks flushed. She looked uncommonly pretty. I stood by the door and said:

"Excuse me, Miss Kempner, Mr. Brice has asked me to come and offer you his apologies. He had been out to lunch with some chaps. They had a bottle of wine. He's awfully sorry he made such a fool of himself. He lost his head. He promises not to do anything of the sort again, if you will forgive him."

For nearly ten seconds her eyes were fixed on mina I felt her looking right through me, to see whether I was speaking the truth or whether I was laughing at her. It seemed an eternity. At last she lowered her eyes and said:

"All right."

She shrugged her shoulders, as though the whole thing was beneath contempt. She fiddled about with the machine. As I was going out of the door she looked up at me again, and I could not take my eyes from hers. Something nearly approaching a smile lightened her face. I managed to gasp:

"It's very good of you."

She looked down, and the noisy machine began to click.

This little incident appeared to establish a bond between Anna and myself. On several occasions I found her watching me with a queer, deep anxiety. I felt enormously flattered. I was the only one of the staff that she trusted, with, perhaps, the exception of Mr. Becher, whom everyone treated like a child. On one or two occasions she even ventured to address a remark to me about the work, and I was careful to show that I had no intention of taking advantage of this little attention. She never referred again to the incident with Duncan, and she did not treat him with any special show of animosity. The little tigress in her was appeased, and I felt glad that I had had a small share in the appeasement. During the lunch-hour I sometimes found her reading in the outer office, and I would go and have a few words with her about books. I realised the importance of being very gradual in my advances. She interested me, and I wanted to draw her out I pictured one day taking her home and introducing her to Mary. Mary would be sure to find a mine of interest in Anna. She would help her, introduce her to our friends, perhaps to just the right friend. The girl seemed out of place in this Paddington office.

I don't know what I expected, but I was rather disappointed in her choice of literature. She was a voracious reader, but Marie Corelli seemed to be her ideal. Marie Corelli, Edna Lyall, H. Seton Merriman, Mrs. Humphry Ward, and other people whose names I had never heard of. I think I expected to find her reading Alfred de Musset, or Cervantes, or at least Tolstoy. But it didn't matter. She was primitive, unformed. Mr. Becher was right. She was the embryo of every feminine past, present, and future possibility.

I learnt, after a time, that she lived with her mother and two sisters in a fiat near Paddington Recreation Ground, about ten minutes' walk from the studio. Her mother was the widow of a north-country dentist. They had at one time been quite well off. One of her sisters managed a penny bazaar; the other was studying calisthenics with the idea of becoming an instructress; whilst a third sister had married a clergyman and lived at Southend. Anna herself had attended a well-known ladies' college in Yorkshire; when she was only fourteen her father died, and the family had to retrench. I got all this information out of her piecemeal. Sometimes, if we happened to leave the studio at the same time, I would walk with her to the comer of her road. I found her a sympathetic listener to my stories about Madeline. Her eyes lighted up and she really laughed. It was a great joy to me as I walked down in the morning and recalled some particularly bright saying of Madeline's, to think to myself, "I must tell Anna that. She will enjoy it." The men had been somewhat chilling about my daughter's exploits and repartee, and it made a great difference to feel that at last I had someone to confide to.

February and March that year were depressing months, windy and wet, and the country was suffering from what is known as a wave of economic unrest Mary developed varicose veins in her left leg and was obliged to remain indoors. Madeline had a series of colds which kept her from school. Mrs. Copley lost a lot of money, owing to the failure of a copra company in which she had shares. My father had a return of rheumatism in the eyes. Uncle Stephen had broken out into betting again, and been unsuccessful. No one seemed to be having a good time except Laura, who now occupied an imposing flat in Mayfair, and kept two servants and three chows, and took cabs everywhere.

Our house began to show splotches of damp, and the builder said it required underpinning, an operation which would cost sixty-five pounds, and which the landlord refused to have anything to do with. I was not making enough money, and I could not ask Mr. Becher for an increase. The scene-painting world was not flourishing.

Suddenly I began to be assailed by that fatal vision which looks at life in perspective. We should be getting old. I had accomplished nothing. I could not even repair the wall-paper sagging in the hall. Mary thought I was "a funny old thing." The men thought I was "a queer old chap." The Rev. Parke Tidsall had hinted that I should never get on because I was nothing but "just a nice boy."

The only person in whose eyes I seemed to loom as something large and significant was Anna Kempner. With her I felt important, a living force, an exceptional being.

Things being slack, Mr. Becher said one day that we could all leave off at four o'clock. I walked home with Anna, and just as I was leaving her, she looked at me timidly, and said:

"Would you care to come home to tea with mother?"

I answered that I should be delighted. Mrs. Kempner was a solidly-built old lady, with a pleasant manner. She shook hands and said:

"I'm very pleased to meet you, Mr. Purbeck. I've heard a lot about you. My daughter tells me how clever you are."

Clever! I blushed to the roots of my hair and stammered dissent Anna thought I was clever! No one had ever accused me of being clever before. What on earth was I clever at? But it must be true, because Anna thought so. I glowed with pride. I admired the room and Mrs. Kempner's taste in decoration. We talked for some time, and then the calisthenic sister came it. She was taller than Anna, a strong, fresh-complexioned girl, but equally reserved. As I sat in the company of these three women I could not help being impressed by their healthy full-bloodedness. The room was very clean, the window open, and a warm March wind fanned the lace curtains. It was like being out in the open, and yet being warm and comfortable. They were very simple and easy to talk to. In Mrs. Kempner and the sister there was something Amazonian. Anna had the physique, but she was softer, rounder, more feline. A magpie in a cage uttered shrill notes of discord. The others did not seem to notice it.

I tried to describe the room afterwards to Mary. I did not really admire Mrs. Kempner's taste in furnishing, but the room had a peculiar hypnotic effect on me. The furniture was rather like the furniture father had in the parlour at "The Duchess of Pless" but there was much less of it, and everything was mercilessly polished. The wall-paper was in white stripes and the lace curtains were caught up with a crimson sash. On the tea-table was a pot of red berries. It was a bright, undistinguished room, and yet, as the March wind crept through the open window and the magpie screamed, I felt that I was being translated to some unexpected and transcendental state of being. I wanted to talk, and I did talk. I talked better than I'd ever talked before. And Anna kept on looking at me, and giving quick little glances at her mother and sister. When I told Mary this, she laughed, and said:

"You are a funny old thing!"

And I could see nothing funny about it at all.

After that it became quite a habit. On two or three days a week I would go home to tea with Anna. It was very convenient and pleasant. And then, one day at the beginning of April, I asked her to tea on a Sunday to meet Mary. I felt tremendously excited about this event. I felt that it was of the utmost importance that Mary should like Anna. It was a bright spring day and we had tea in the dining-room. I don't know how it was, but the meeting was not a success. We were all at our worst. Anna was very shy, almost taciturn. Mary did most of the talking, and that was mostly about shopping, and frocks, and actors. All my brilliance had vanished. I could say nothing. I did nothing but fidget and look from one to the other, and pray for inspiration. And then Madeline came in, and she was in one of her perverse moods. She had been very upset because Mary would not let her go and play with some boys in a disused railway-yard, and she was inclined to be peevish.

I was quite relieved when it became time for Anna to go. I saw her on to a 'bus. When I got back I asked Mary anxiously what she thought of her.

"Oh," she said, "she seems quite nice . . . rather quiet, perhaps."

Oh, damn!

IV

The heavy scowl of London broke into a smile at the approach of spring. Fresh flowers pushed their way through the soot-begrimed earth in our garden. The black trees developed surprising patterns of pink and white. Window-boxes, gay with tulips and marguerites, symbolised the rejuvenescence of exhausted humanity. Women put away their furs and fought at bargain sales for the spoils of sartorial genius. Young men broke out into coloured socks and ties, walked down to business and asked their guv'nors for a rise, got refused, and didn't care. What did it matter? The old earth had been saving up for this moment all the winter. There would always be a girl on the 'bus to ogle on the way home. Any day might produce a millennium. At its worst, it couldn't avoid a romance. Duncan announced that he formally handed Anna over to me. He had other irons in the fire. He hummed from morning till night, like a bee above the clover.

Of course, I expected that. I knew the men would begin to make innuendoes about Anna and me. They were a decent lot of chaps, but their standard of morality was not very high. Old Jouquet, who painted figure-panels and wouldn't drink beer, was a coarse old beast. He treated my assertion that my affection for Anna was purely fraternal or paternal as being a splendid jest.

Duncan said to him one day, "I bet you've been round some comers in your time, Jouk."

"My boy," he answered, "I've done everything possible. I haven't it on my conscience that I have ever missed a single opportunity."

And he clucked his tongue like a well-satisfied gourmand.

Anna was certainly becoming very necessary to me. I spent, of course, the greater part of my waking time at the studio. I left home in the morning at half-past eight, and I arrived back in the evening somewhat exhausted. Mary said I was getting dull. She sometimes remarked, "You are not listening to what I say." And when I answered, "Yes, I am, darling," she would say quickly, "Then what did I say?" And then, of course, I didn't know. It was deplorable. I had to pull myself together.

One day Duncan and I had to call at a West End theatre to take particulars of some scenery that was to be adapted. We finished our work rather sooner than we expected.

"As we are here," said Duncan, "we'll go and have lunch somewhere decent."

I felt in the mood for some mild dissipation, so we Went to the Trocadero. Down in the grill-room a band was playing. Duncan, in his lordly way, ordered a large bottle of Beaune. We did ourselves very well. We became extremely garrulous. He made me several intimate confessions. I was a dull dog in comparison, but the wine went to my head. I kept on thinking of Laura, then of Anna. This was Laura's life. Music, and thrills, and wine, and good things, everything heated . . . exhilarating. Life, life—what was that thing they were playing? ... A Spanish dance. Dark-eyed women in mantillas, swaying in a rose-tinted room, with the violet night outside; love and passion. Why do some people inherit all these things, take them as their birth-right, whilst others . . .? After all, what is anything in comparison with this? The primal appeal of the life-force . . . The only thing that counts.

Looking past Duncan I suddenly saw Anna, not in actuality but in a kind of fury of my imagination. An amazing and significant fact concerning her seemed to grip my will and hold me spellbound. I wanted to say to Duncan:

"She's saving them for her lover."

And then I could not explain it to him. I had noticed so often, but had learnt nothing from it till that moment Anna never kissed anyone—not even her mother. She had a curious way of holding out the point of her jaw for the other person to kiss. She did it with Mary. She did it with her sisters. She even did it with her mother. It was as though she was under a vow. All the message of those full, strong lips was being hoarded for someone. All her reserve was the sluice-gates of a mighty dam. She was passion personified. She was concentrating on a subconscious purpose. She was hoarding. She was atavistic. And then my colleague, with his: "She's going to be someone's quarry."

A feeling of spiritual shock came to me. I was stunned. I could not hear what Duncan was saying. He was talking about a chorus-girl he had met at the seaside. It seemed trivial and ridiculous. I wanted to scream across the table at him:

"Can't you see, you fool, she's saving them for her lover? That's why she scratched you."

Duncan ordered a liqueur, and I drank it. The band was playing something Hungarian now, but it was all on the same theme:

"She's saving them for her lover."

V

The madness which assailed me after this episode is a thing I cannot analyse. When we got back to the studio I had to rush and peep at her in her room, to see whether she was still there, or whether she was even yet another woman—perhaps Cleopatra, or Dido, or Pallas Athene. Yes, I should certainly have placed her among the myths that afternoon: possibly the Lady of Shalot; the typewriter would make an excellent loom. She looked up and said:

"Well?"

I answered: "Oh, I thought perhaps uncle was in here," and I darted away.

Problems and questionings piled one upon another.

"Why should one man have so much?"

I avoided her. I did not go home to tea with her. I pretended to myself that the solution did not concern me. I warded it off for a whole week, fully knowing the answer. And then, one night in bed, the ironic voice said:

"It is all yours for the asking."

I felt almost relieved to acknowledge this to myself. At last I was under no illusion. All that remained was to keep myself in hand, to retain my sense of proportion. It could not be difficult. I hurried home in the evenings. I was busy making Madeline a miniature theatre. . . .

Ten days went by, during which I did not speak to Anna unless it was about some matter concerning the work. Then, one afternoon, she met me in the passage. She rested her hand on my arm, and said:

"Will you come home to tea to-day, Mr. Purbeck?"

I was surprised. I thought she must know that I was trying to avoid her. I stammered and said, "Yes, with pleasure."

I did not see how I could refuse; besides—what harm could there be? Her mother and sister, and the harsh-toned magpie, and the bright crockery—all very, very—safe.

It was a warm evening, and we walked in silence to the door of the flat. Anna opened the door with her latchkey. I put down my hat and we entered the drawing-room. It was empty. Anna left me for a few minutes; then she returned with a loose wrapper over her shoulders. She came straight up to me and said:

"They are all out No one will be back for two hours."

Then she closed her eyes and held up her lips to me.

Neither of us spoke a word. I do not think that for the whole time I was there—nearly an hour and a half—we exchanged a single sentence. Even when I left I could not get my voice. I was too ashamed to say good-bye.

VI

I went through agonies of elation and remorse. I don't think that at any time I lost sight of one central fact—I did not love Anna, not in the big way, not in the way I loved Mary. But she was a madness which coloured my life. Had it not been for that abrupt conception of her as a girl "saving her lips for her lover" I might have been less foolish. As it was, she was a torment—and a torment I could not share with Mary. In her presence I was day in the hands of the potter. Her kisses maddened me. It could not go on. We arranged chance meetings. Once I told Mary I was going to the theatre with Duncan, and I took Anna up on Hampstead Heath. At other times I went home to tea with her when her mother and sister were out.

"All these years she has been saving her lips for me."

I could not escape the obsession of this central idea. I felt all my moral fibre loosening. I began to drink, in order to escape. One evening I held her in my arms. We were in a dark passage of the flats. I whispered:

"Anna, will you come away with me for a weekend quietly?"

She clung to me and said, "Yes."

We had been working late, and I had drunk a lot of port I laughed savagely and pinched her. I wanted to hurt her.

"You darling!" I said. "Then, listen. We will go down to Felixstowe on Saturday. There is quite a decent hotel there. No one will know us. I tell you what we'll do. We'll go down separately. We'll occupy separate bedrooms . . . adjoining, do you see? I got the tip from Duncan. It works better. In case anything came out afterwards, don't you understand? . . . nothing could be proved. Separate names, separate bags, everything . . . mustn't run risks."

She nodded gravely.

I could hardly breathe. In the night I decided to countermand the whole thing. I could not sleep. On the morrow, Mary said:

"You are looking very pale, darling. You look as though you want a change."

It seemed almost like the finger of fate. Instantaneously I went back on my nocturnal resolution.

"It is funny," I said, "that you should have said that. Duncan wanted me to go down to Felixstowe with him for the week-end. Do you think it would be all right?"

"Of course, darling."

Dash it! if she hadn't been so sweet about it, how much easier it would have been! If she had only been suspicious or hostile, or even diffident—but that warm-hearted "Of course, darling!" How I hated myself!

The daffodils were clustering in masses in the park. The starlings were busy among the sprouting shrubs. The world seemed quivering with sentient movement. The days drifted by. After all . . .

On Saturday the face of London changed again. It had that sullen stare which is surely foreign to any other city. The skies were an unbroken pall of leaden grey, as though it had always rained, and it always meant to rain for ever and ever. Irresolution was my reigning goddess. The fact that I had given way to the idea in thought seemed to discard all my better promptings in deed. Even if I didn't go—my mind was bitten with the acid of a feral impulse.

"I shall get drunk," I thought. "And then it won't seem so awful."

I hugged the thought all the morning. I hated myself sober. Anna gave me her slow smile.

"The train is 4.15, you said?"

"Yes, 4.15 from Liverpool Street."

I lunched with Duncan and drank an enormous quantity of beer. I went home about three o'clock to collect my bag. The rain was still coming down in torrents. I could not look at Mary. In the drawing room a fire was burning brightly. The tea was laid on a silver tray by the Chesterfield. Madeline would be in later . . .

"I've packed your bag, darling."

"Oh, thanks."

"What a disgusting day! I'm afraid you are wet I've put out some socks for you. You had better change at once."

"Thanks; I will."

I crept upstairs. I was tingling all over. My bag was packed and neatly strapped. The room seined dark. I could not focus anything. Absently I changed my socks. The rain came in squalls against the window. I switched on the light. Some impulse made me glance down at my feet. As I did so, I felt my heart beat rapidly. I stared at the socks on my feet as though I was looking at a ghost. One was a brown woolly one, the other was a black one with a light blue clock. They were identical with the ones—I had worn on ... on our honeymoon—Mary's and mine. . . .

When I went down to the drawing-room the firelight was playing on her face and on the arms of the chintz-covered chair. Otherwise the room was in deep shadow. An unfamiliar noise greeted my ears. Mary was weeping.

I believe I wept, too, then.

I went down on my knees. . . .

I never went to Felixstowe.

CHAPTEK XII

SUCCESS HAS ITS PRICE

One night early in June we dined with Laura and Edgar at their Mayfair flat. The other guests were a Mr. and Mrs. Burwell and a young German pianist named Freitel. Mr. Burwell was a well-nurtured, elderly gentleman who was rather deaf. Having plenty of money, he had devoted his whole life to travelling about the earth slaughtering animals. He had killed caribou in Iceland, bears in Siberia, lions in Africa, and cheetahs up in the Himalayas. He had inherited the fortune which allowed him to indulge in this orgy of bloodshed from an uncle who owned a drapery establishment in the West End, employing several thousand anaemic girls. His wife was a fair-haired woman with a long neck bound up with a quadruple line of pearls. She whinnied when you spoke to her. Freitel was an earnest, thoughtful looking boy in horn spectacles. He spoke better English than I have ever heard spoken by an Englishman. He talked slowly, cleaning up each word as he went along, looking ahead, building up sentences which dazzled you with their logic and construction and length. His sentences were like verbal sky-scrapers.

Laura was wearing a gorgeous frock of old-gold satin with touches of green, and a jade necklace. I thought she looked pale and rather on edge. She was inclined to be snappy when we arrived. She pulled Mary up over one of her pet stories about Madeline. She was quite rude to Mrs. Burwell because she whinnied at the wrong moment when Freitel was developing an argument It was a curiously strained dinner-party. We all seemed uncertain why we were asked to meet each other. I was subtly aware that all the time there was some undercurrent of dissension going on between Edgar and Laura. We all seemed to be pawns in the game. This was particularly true of Freitel. I could not tell whether Edgar had invited him, or Laura, but one was playing him off against the other. When he spoke they exchanged challenging glances.

Edgar did most of the talking, in his quick, level tones. He was equally charming to everybody. He even talked about moose and caribou and wild duck and twelve-bore guns as though he knew something about it. He nearly elicited a complete sentence out of Mrs. Burwell, but it ended in a neigh. He was interested to hear that I had left Mr. Becher's studio and had gone into partnership with a young man named Jevons. He flattered Mary about her frock. He paid his wife pretty compliments. He drew out Freitel. If the dinner-party was not a success, it could certainly not be attributed to our host.

When the champagne arrived, Laura seemed gradually to melt to a more genial mood. Mr. Burwell's bloody tales, which before had disgusted her, now only made her laugh. The dinner was excellent— it goes without saying. Two neat maids waited swiftly and dexterously. I could not help being intrigued by the remarkable contrast between Mr. Burwell and Freitel, who both sat opposite me. Burwell, with his comfortable urbanity, ensconced in the familiar security of a good dinner, letting fall sayings like, "By Gad! Beyfus, seven guns and a bag of three hundred," and the studious detachment of Freitel, a little shy in his surroundings, unwilling to accept either food or statement without the most minute consideration. I once detected him smelling a piece of pheasant on his fork, not as though he harboured any suspicion of secret treachery by his host, but as though he wished to assure himself of his complete understanding of organic life. He heralded most of his opinions with a preamble somewhat like this:

"I do not feel myself fully qualified in this particular case either to dissent from, or in any way to qualify, the extremely interesting theory you have advanced, notwithstanding a considerable period of my life devoted to—what I think I may adjudge—an exhaustive study of collateral theories. I am handicapped, perhaps, by my allegiance to the never-to-be overlooked doctrines of Herr Professor Eitel von Strumpfmeyer, whose constructive system of ethics and high spiritual outlook has always been an inspiration to me. Nevertheless . . ."

He and Mr. Burwell occasionally looked at each other as though each was observing an almost unbelievable relic in a museum of curiosities.

II

When Laura had had three glasses of champagne she began to ask Mary about Madeline. She adored Madeline, but she seemed to have peculiar moods about the child. There were times when she disliked us talking about her, and other times when we couldn't talk enough. Auntie Laura was always a great favourite when she honoured us with a visit, and no one found such wonderful and uncommon toys. From the subject of Madeline she flew at a violent tangent to the subject of the great success she had had two nights previously in Birmingham.

"The place was packed. They simply loved the Boellmann."

Silver and glass sparkled on the dark oak table. Carnations and gentians snuggled in little beds of moss beneath the modulated lights.

Edgar raised his glass and looked across it at Laura with an expression which seemed to signify that some crisis was passed.

"Laura had a great success," he said, addressing us all. "An enormous success."

"Good! good!" exclaimed Mr. Burwell, with his mouth full of quail. "That's what I like to hear. Do you know what my old uncle used to say, Beyfus—and he was a successful man, if ever there was one: rose from nothing, fought his way up."

"What did he say, Mr. Burwell?" asked Laura.

"He said to me, 'Success has its price, Henry.' Now what do you think of that? He said it not once, but a hundred times.

"'Success has its price!' That's what the old boy said. Well, he worked hard, I must say. Always trouble with the work-people—lazy, shifty lot of devils. Ha, ha, ha! you're a lucky one, Mrs. Beyfus. You don't have anything of that. No one to worry you—all on your own—leaping upwards to fame and fortune, eh?"

The student cleared his throat and drank some water. Then in his steady voice he said:

"Will you tell me precisely what you mean by success, Mr.—er?"

Mr. Burwell looked annoyed. Damn these foreigners! He waved his hand contemptuously.

"Success? Why, success is getting on, making money, getting talked about, of course. What else do you suppose?"

Edgar nodded and smiled indulgently at the boy.

"How would you define success, Herr Freitel?"

The young musician blinked and looked timidly at Laura as though for support. Then he lowered his eyes and pinched a piece of bread into a pellet.

"Success? ... It is to know one's heart when one is alone on the mountain-tops."

There was an uncomfortable pause, shattered by a rude guffaw from Mr. Burwell. It was Mary who saved the situation.

"I think Herr Freitel's is much the nicer definition," she said, smiling.

"Are we to have coffee in the other room, my dear?" Edgar almost yawned, and rose to fetch the cigars.

After dinner we seemed to fall away into groups. The drawing-room appeared too large for our small company. On an ebony stand by the piano was a large gilt basket filled with pink roses arranged in festoons. In had been presented to Laura two days before by some influential person in Birmingham. We gathered round it.

"Isn't it a shame!" Laura remarked. "They only gave it me two days ago, and the roses are already beginning to die."

Freitel murmured something. I caught the word "success."

"Well, of course, they're wired," exclaimed Mr. Burwell. "They never last when they're wired."

Mrs. Burwell exploded: "Oh, Henry always knows about anything to do with—he, he, he, he."

Her husband barked, his way to the most comfortable chair, and Edgar stood with his back to the fireplace and talked to him. Laura and Freitel whispered over a pile of music. Mary and I tried to prevent Mrs. Burwell from having a fit of hysterics because of some incident she was trying to tell us about a bishop losing his overcoat at a flower-show. The atmosphere of the room seemed charged with an almost unbearable sense of nervous tension. I don't know how long this went on before Mr. Burwell bawled across the room: "Won't you play us a piece, Mrs. Beyfus?" Laura did not look at him. She replied curtly: "No, I'm not playing any pieces ' to-night. But Herr Freitel is good enough to say that he will play to us."

III

We all gave that murmur of approval which is expected of a company at such an announcement. Herr Freitel sat down at the piano.

I am no great judge of music, but I do not think I have ever heard the piano sound so beautiful. All the academic, dogmatic exterior of the man seemed to vanish. He became a poet. This academic side was probably busy with the technique, but it was too carefully concealed for me to detect. He played the Schubert Impromptu and two small pieces of Schumann's. His playing moved me tremendously. Laura sat in the window-seat alone, with her head averted. She was frowning, and her face looked old. My eye wandered from her to the gilt basket of flowers ..."already dying."

"Laura either loves this boy or she is jealous of him," I suddenly thought.

Laura, whose name was a household word in several countries, jealous of an unknown student! And yet I could not believe that it could be the other thing. Laura must be thirty-five; the boy was uncouth, short-sighted—to me physically repellent. But still he went on, and I didn't want him to stop. He was alone on the mountain-tops, knowing his heart Whilst Laura's flowers were dying, and her "manager" was standing on the hearth-rug, talking to a rich accomplice.

Yes, I could understand that. Success has its price, Henry, A topsy-turvy and difficult world. Mr. Burwell's uncle and Laura had both set out to chase the braggart down the hill, and having started to run—they could not stop! At that moment I even felt sorry for poor old Uncle Burwell, A long struggling, nagging life, sweating people and bullying and being bullied, bartering, bargaining, scheming, looking ahead, and afraid to look away in case someone snatched the bauble from his hand. On he rushes, tripping and skipping over the boulders. The will-o'-the-wisp is here, there, and everywhere. Then suddenly a crater opens under his feet. It is too late. In that concentrated moment as he hurtles through space he realises that all that he has struggled for is a chimera. The products of his toil merely serve to supply a braggart nephew with the wherewithal to laze and slay.

"Laura could not play like this. She has lost it."

I knew that was true. Where was Laura rushing to? She was far, far more brilliant than Herr Freitel, but she was not alone upon the mountain-tops. She was rushing down the hill, chasing the braggart. Her heart was freezing. She was afraid. What was she giving to the uplifting of our common life?

When the flowers were dead, and the gilt basket buried in an attic, the press-notices forgotten, what then? . . . One must know one's own heart. There is something bigger than what we call Success.

I have an idea that there was some scheme for inducing Mr. Burwell to put money into Edgar's business. When Freitel had finished playing Edgar came over and said to Laura:

"I wish you would play, dear. Mr. Burwell is very anxious."

Laura bit her lip, and snapped out: "No, I'm not going to play to-night"

One had only to know Laura, and to hear her say that, to recognise that the decision was absolutely final. Edgar knew it too. He made no comment, but I observed a slow, malevolent look creep at the back of his eyes. He shrugged his shoulders and returned to the fireplace. The maids brought in trays, and decanters and glass pitchers of lemonade. Blue smoke drifted about the room.

"We had a screaming time in Cape Town. Do you know what Henry did one night in the Victoria?— he, he, he, he."

Mary was politely attentive. Laura suddenly came over and pinched my arm. Dark rings encircled her eyes. She said nothing, but I knew she wanted to speak to me outside. I followed her into the hall, and across the passage into a little boudoir. She shut the door.

IV

She stood swaying in the middle of the room, her face buried in her hands.

"What's the matter, old girl?"

She could not speak for some moments. Then she said suddenly:

"Oh, Tom, take me away from here . . . take me home with you."

Some awful climax had come. I felt no call to question her. I simply knew that she was desperately unhappy.

"Of course you can come, Laura, but—"

"It's nothing to do with Freitel. Don't think that. And yet it is, in a way. When he began to play . . . Oh, Tom, I've lost it all. You make me madly jealous, you and Mary. I'm slipping down, slipping . . . slipping."

"Edgar?"

"I'm his bond-woman. Can't you see? Oh, of course I love him. But we are going on together slipping down. I sometimes think I hate him, and then he comes and puts his arms around me, and I am helpless. . . . That disgusting episode about the fiddle—that was the beginning. One thing leads to another, and you can't stop. You go down and down, Tom. Whatever I do I know I can't get back. Oh, let me steal back with you. ... I would like to take Madeline away with me to some cottage right away in the country, where no one knows me . . . where there's just an old piano, and wild flowers, and simple people. I want to start again."

"You're unstrung, old girl. Of course we could arrange it, but hardly to-night, suddenly like this."

"Yes, yes, I want to go to-night. If he suspects me, he won't let me go. I have no power when he . . . Oh, Tom, let us creep away at once."

"But Mary?"

"Write a note and pin it on her cloak."

"Laura, my dear, it's not workable. Edgar will know. He'll simply follow and fetch you back."

"No. I shall tell him I have gone up to the mountain-tops for a time—any old lie. I shall come back to him, of course. I know that's inevitable. He is my fate, the partner I have chosen for this dance of fame. But to-night I am suffocated. I want to be free. Please, old boy."

I thought the matter over. A thousand difficulties presented themselves. Why must Laura always do these abrupt and disturbing things? I required an hour to think the matter over, and here she was tugging at my arm. If she could only be reasonable and wait till to-morrow I It would be quite a natural thing for her to come and stay with us, or to take Madeline to a cottage in the country for a few days. But tonight—like this, with an inadequate explanation, in a gorgeous frock of old gold and jade, as though she was fleeing from a sudden threat. Edgar would naturally suspect Freitel. Visions of duels, and broken heads, and scandal, and police-court scenes flashed through my mind. At the same time, Laura was unhappy . . . desperate. She might do something even more—unbalanced. I picked up a sheet of paper and scribbled: "I am taking Laura home to stay the night with us. Will send the cab back for you in half an hour. Tell Edgar she will be back to-morrow."

I pinned this on Mary's cloak and we went out into the hall. Laura put on a fur coat and feverishly twisted a shawl round her head. Just as we reached the hall, the drawing-room door clicked open. Freitel came out of the room, followed by Edgar. Freitel was saying:

"I trust that my departure does not seem precipitate, ill-mannered. I find that late hours are detrimental to my work. Will you convey my regrets—"

Edgar did not see me at first. He was leading Freitel to the cloak-cupboard. He appeared quite satisfied with the sudden departure of this guest. Then he looked along the hall and observed Laura standing there in her coat and shawl . . . waiting. For the fraction of a second he started. Then he said in his purry voice:

"Hullo, dear! Where are you going?"

I thought Laura was going to faint. She held on to the handle of the door.

"Oh," she exclaimed jerkily, "Tom and I . . . Tom and I . . . were just going out . . . for a stroll. The room is so warm. We—"

And yet she did not move. Freitel was helped into his coat. He made a pretty apology to Laura and kissed her hand. He brought his heels together and bowed to us all and took his departure. We all stood there in an embarrassed silence at the open door, listening to the clumsy beat of Freitel's heavy boots as he marched downstairs. They squeaked a little. A party of people came out of the flat opposite, laughing and talking. An old gentleman in evening dress rang the bell for the lift, exclaiming as he did so: "Really, now, really! . . . that's too bad!" Edgar closed the door. With a caressing, insinuating movement he put his arms round from behind and gently released her shawl.

"I don't think I should go out to-night, dear," he said. "There is an east wind. It is very late. And—the Burwells might not understand. They are not yet accustomed to the—ways of artists. . . . There, there; now let us go back to the drawing-room."

The following night I paid one of my periodical visits to "The Duchess of Pless." I found father and Uncle Stephen in the little room at the back of the bar. They both seemed in very good spirits. Uncle Stephen was smoking a churchwarden, a form of pipe which no one could possibly enjoy, but which gives a good picturesque, sporting appearance to a man. They are now only smoked by 'Varsity undergraduates, who are always willing to suffer for a romantic pose. Uncle Stephen was in one of his hard-headed, genially oppressive moods. He called out:

"Hullo, Tom! How are you getting on?" I gave him some of the details of my new venture with Jevons, and he replied:

"Well, it's about time you began to bring off something, old boy. You'll never be a success like your sister, unless you start doing something big soon."

I answered that I was afraid I wasn't so clever as Laura. Indeed, I had no special ability for anything. Laura was a genius.

"Yes, but look here, my lad," he replied, "you don't have to be a genius to get on. Work, industry, ambition—that's the ticket. I know a man who's a perfect fool, and he's earning six thousand a year."

"Will you have a drink, Tom?" said my father.

"Oh, thanks, dad. . . . Could I have a brandy-and-soda?"

"Never drink spirits, my lad," exclaimed Uncle Stephen. "Spirits are the curse. Beer will do you no harm, wine will do you no harm, but spirits eat up the vitals. Never touch them."

"What are you drinking, uncle?"

"Whisky-and-water, my boy."

We all laughed. It seemed gay and simple in the little parlour. Father asked after Laura, and I told him that we had been dining there the previous evening.

"Oh, la, la!" he broke in. "Yes, I know. I dined there one evening. I wasn't invited to meet anyone, mind you. But we dined, you know. All sorts of little faked-up dishes, and French wines. Not for me. Give me a cut from the joint and two vegetables and a tankard of ale, any day in the week. But still— there it is. That's Laura. It's her affair, not mine."

"Anything more been heard of the Cuban assassin, Tom?"

"No; I think he must have left the country."

We sat talking for some time, and Uncle Stephen had several glasses of the stuff which eats up the vitals. We tods our departure at the same time, and as the night was fine, we decided to walk as far as Portland Road station together.

We talked about various matters, when suddenly Uncle Stephen said:

"I don't mind telling you, Tom, that your father's very relieved that you hardly drink at all. He was very worried about you at one time."

"Worried about me! But I never showed any disposition—"

"It's not that. Didn't he ever keep on at you that he didn't want you in the licensing trade?"

"Yes, he did. But why—"

"You've got to have great strength of character to keep your head in the licensing trade—like he has himself. He thought you might be—you looked rather like it—one of the weak, poetical, easily-led people, you see."

"Well, perhaps I am still."

"Yes, but you didn't show the predisposition. When he found you hadn't got it, he didn't mind offering you a glass now and then. Moderation's all right."

"I still don't quite see."

Uncle Stephen stopped by a lamp-post and gripped the lapel of my coat.

"You don't see, because you don't know, old boy."

"What don't I know?"

"You don't know about—your mother."

"What about my mother?"

"She was something like you and something like Laura. She used to be all over the shop, you know; you didn't know which way she was going to jump. Full of ginger, like a three-year-old; very fiery, touchy—a good woman, though, boy. She was a good woman, until she started—well, you know, your father dreaded that you might inherit her taste."

"What did she start?"

"Drink, of course."

"Do you mean to say that my mother drank, that she drank herself to—"

"It certainly hastened her end, old boy."

CHAPTER XIII

THAT WHICH IS ALWAYS CHANGING IN ME

There comes an exact instance in human stress—whether of pain or pleasure—when things must either snap or recreate themselves. There came such an instant to me -one day when I was polishing a brass bedpan in the basement of the antique-and-curio shop which Jevons and I had started after the failure of our scene-painting venture. I trust you to suspect my capacity for suffering. At the same time I do not see why you should suffer with me. You, too . . . you doubtless have felt the unbearable wrack when there seems no escape, when even death offers no solution, when you are cabined between the narrow walls of your material existence, the flames of sentimental association eternally licking your heart and blood. The empty days, the empty nights, the bleak years stretching out before you; nothing but dreariness, hopelessness, and that ever-present gnawing vacancy. I do not want to tell you of my sufferings, because if you have not experienced them, believe me, you are born to them. They are our heritage, and I have nothing to offer you except my kindred understanding. I think it was only Madeline who kept me sane. Madeline, and a few surprising people who forced me to weep by their unexpected quickness of sympathy. ... I remember Jingle coming, and the tears streamed down his battered face.

How could I tell Madeline that Mummy had left us and that we should never see her again? One day, in a state of despair, I drew for her a picture of us three all meeting again in some elaborate paradise. And I hated myself for doing it, for I did not believe it at all. I do not believe this aspect of human love to be a permanent factor in evolution. Everything changes. That which we call Shakespeare, or Lincoln, or Gladstone must have gone on and by now be something entirely different. And it is well it should be so. I rejoice to think that Shakespeare as a man is quite extinct. It makes the universe seem less stuffy. I don't want to be bunged up with my grandmother and my grandchildren. Let them, too, rejoice in this realisation of the eternal flux. The brass bedpan glowed like silver under the influence of my rubbing.

"Some snuffy old fool probably warmed his bed with this a century ago. Thank God he is dead! Even the art of warming a bed with a brass pan has died out. No one will ever do it again. We hang it on our walls as a sentimental relic."

This is my great enemy—sentimentality, going back. In the early months of the struggle I realised that I should have to be ruthless with this enemy, or he would kill me. When Jevons mooted the idea of the antique shop I helped him by stocking it with every scrap of antique furniture which Mary and I had collected. I asked him to sell it for whatever he could get for it while I was away, and I started out for Italy. When I had spent a week in Verona I realised that it was the worst thing I could have done. Italy was simply Mary, and nothing but Mary. . . . We had planned so often to go there "later on." ... I returned suddenly. Jevons had not sold the furniture. I snapped down some shutter in my mind and helped him. I even haggled with people over the price. I polished brass as it had never been polished before. . . . looking back on it I am aware that my behaviour may seem to you cowardly, even disloyal. It possibly was. I can only state just what I did. Please remember that I was in a desperate comer, fighting this thing, and I wanted to come out whole, for Madeline's sake.

Father suggested that I should go back and live at "The Duchess of Pless." Laura wanted us both to go and live with her. Both of these offers I rejected. They would have entailed a state of going back, and the essential thing was to go on, keep on doing things, changing.

Jevons was a delightful person, with whom I got on admirably. He was a thin, aesthetic, impatient, lantern-jawed young man, very gentle in his manners, but quick and sympathetic, with a profound knowledge of the antique, and a useful knowledge of values. However, he hated selling anything which he liked very much. He would hop around the little shop like a bird. (He had a club-foot.) Suddenly he would pull himself up, and gazing for a long time at a piece of majolica, with his head on one side, he would exclaim:

"Oh, Tom . . . that's too beautiful. I know some swine will buy it."

I had very little knowledge of the antique, and it is surprising that in spite of the rather temperamental way we conducted the business, it paid fairly well. I kept on the little house in St. John's Wood, only rearranging the rooms. Our bedroom was now Madeline's. The drawing-room was the dining-room, and vice versa. New furniture was placed where furniture had never been before. I secured the services of an admirable woman named Mrs. Whittle, who acted as caretaker and looked after Madeline. Madeline was now twelve, a difficult age. She tortured me with her likeness to Mary, but she was too young to be a companion for any length of time. I loved to have her, and to talk to her, and to bring her presents, to feel her arms around my neck; then suddenly she would make me impatient. I had been spoilt, perhaps. With Madeline I had to give all the time, and I had become accustomed to receive so much. I never went down to Woodstack. I simply could not do it. The evenings were the worst time, when Madeline had gone to bed. Sometimes I went back to the shop, or studied some book on pewter or glass. Whatever I did had to be hard, technical. I could not read fiction, or listen to music, or go to a play. The newspapers brought a lump in my throat I dare only think about practical affairs. Jevons said he thought I was a very good business man. I believe I must have been, at that time. I developed a fund of driving power. I studied carpentry and upholstery, and did many of our own repairs and restorations. On the night I have mentioned I was alone in the basement Jevons had gone for the day. A November fog had filtered its way down the narrow staircase and hung in little drifts, revealed by the flare of the incandescent gas. All around the room were stray pieces of furniture, brass and crockery, some broken, some awaiting adjustment or polish. A mouse scuttled across the floor. I felt a quiet glow of satisfaction as I regarded my over-polished bedpan.

"Jevons will be pleased, to-morrow," I thought; and then, "What an ass I am! The fog will undo all my labours." And still I went on polishing. All sorts of thoughts jumbled through my mind. One was:

"Suffering is good for the soul."

I had heard that often—quite a trite saying, but somehow very true. Was my soul—whatever it was—hardening, being made a finer thing by what I was enduring? Was I becoming a bigger man, a stronger personality? If it were so ... a sudden vision of infinite possibilities presented themselves. I felt a kind of pride. One digs down and finds powers. Suffering is a stimulus, a creator. Up to fifteen months ago I did not know what suffering was. My life had been a pleasant drift. If I could harden a little like this, why could I not do more? I did not mean to be . . . successful in Laura's sense but to be somehow successful in myself. To contribute something to life, to leave something of myself behind. Men die, ideas go on. Everything changes. Laura, with her réclame, and her bouquets, and her expensive dinners, had not grasped the true significance of change. Aided by Edgar, she was failing . . . failing all the time, in the glare of lighted halls and the plaudits of a mob. Suddenly in that little room I seemed to realise it all. Everything curves, and therefore changes. That which we take to be static is only a breathing space in a moving episode. That which we take to be established is only the dust in a new cycle of vibrations. Life is only a temporary arrangement; incomplete, indefinite. As I shape the change in me, do I become in touch with God? God is not power, or love, or beauty, but that which is always changing in me. Even in the short span of my life I am a hundred people, driven by hereditary taints and impulses, linked by sentient episodes, loosely wrapped in an amorphous and unreliable material called memory. Yesterday I was a small boy putting flies in a spider's web in my father's garden. To-morrow I may be Leonardo da Vinci planning the fortifications of Florence. I change because God changes. When I confine myself to material things I am obstructing the natural sweep of the curve. The eternal question kept raging round my heart:

"Where is Mary at this instant!"

But I mustn't think of it in this way. It doesn't happen like that I must dig about inside. My life is like the reflection of a star bobbing up and down on the dark waters of a trackless sea. These other particles are reflections as I am. We meet and mingle and twinkle and ogle each other in our passage, and one after another we pass away. But somewhere away up there in the heavens is that real star which is ourselves, a thing incomprehensible and permanent and yet which is always changing. One must learn to be proud, so proud that one will not demand the thousand and one little appearances of stability. It is the stumbling-block of our faith—that we are always striving to establish permanent combinations. We want to found a race, a family, a religion or union, and to say, "This is it. This shall stand for all time. When the earth cracks up it shall survive in some superior and more indestructible condition." We are cowards because we will not face the fact of change. There is no evidence of such a stagnation in the rulings of the Universe. Am I to believe in the formula of a religion, when one after another I have seen them come and go? Am I to believe in the dominance of a people, when one after another I may read their story in the brief chronicles of a book? Am I indeed to believe in the complete "establishment of my own entity as a permanent record, when I observe the ambit of its little circle fringed with identical manifestations . . . bobbing up and down? That's just all it is. All my life is bobbing up and down. . . ."

III

The room grew chilly, but I felt no desire to move. I believed that I was passing some important landmark. Powerful resolutions were forming in me. It was imperative that I should focus this new aspect. The intense realisation of the simple fact that everything changes seemed to come to me in the light of a revelation. It put everything in its place. One must not expect too much of life, just what it gives and what one gives to it, and nothing else at all. One must be too proud to demand more. On the day of his death, they say that Confucius went into his garden and said:

"The great mountain must crumble,
The strong beam must break,
And the wise man withers away like a plant."

He threw no sops of "permanence" to his disciples. All other religions seemed to be founded on an implication that we were leading up to some perfect individual. What this perfect individual was to do when he arrived was not stated, but the hint was that everything would become static. The people we happened to be loving at that fateful moment would become our permanent possession. "The dead shall rise from their graves"—surely the most disgusting idea ever put forward! If the dead rise from their graves, the unborn are cast into oblivion. Life reels backwards. The idea is worthy of a people who desire to tabulate and card-index every experience. They must see it in terms of a story with a prologue and an epilogue. It must afterwards be sat upon by the leading critic, and stowed away among the archives of the museum of mammals. But life is not like that. It is fluid. Christ and Buddha are no more permanent than Mr. Timble discoursing on funerals in the saloon-bar of "The Duchess of Pless."

Therefore . . . how shall I live my life? In the first place; I have to be so proud that I can face the circumstance that Mary is gone from me for ever. Our love is blinding and consuming, but some change has occurred which we cannot control. She will always be vivid to me, but every year, owing to the fortuitous circumstance of her death and my life, she will become slightly less vivid. Thirteen years ago I did not know her. Thirteen years hence I shall not have forgotten her, but I have got to face the fact that her hold on me will be less vivid. Perhaps all human love is a fortuitous circumstance. It was only by chance I met her. I might have met another woman and loved her equally well. But no, no—I could not believe that. But memory does fade. If memory survived eternally, then indeed there might be justification for a belief in hell. For this would predicate another static condition. Memory, with its fugitive adjustments, is the merciful veil to the grim enactments of the first law. It hides the anguish in the human heart which is always craving for perpetuity.

There must, then, be something else . . . soma justification in our being, something greater than the love of man and woman, of father and child, of brother and sister. What was it that produced in me a sudden moment of serenity as I was polishing the brass bedpan? I was working, truly, but work itself is not enough. Why was I working? Only to serve my own ends. I had thought, "Jevons will be pleased." I was helping Jevons. Perhaps there was something in that I was serving. Was the secret of it all—service? I do not know, but I was oddly conscious that at that particular instant I experienced the only almost happy thrill I had known for fifteen months. I had passed an invisible barrier. Existence seemed possible.

I took off my overall and fetched my hat and coat.

It was past ten o'clock, and I was about to turn off the light, when I heard someone rap on the door of the shop above.

"I expect it's the police," I thought, "to see if everything is all right"

I left the light on, and went upstairs, where a dim gas-jet was burning. I opened the door. A woman in furs stumbled into my arms.

"Lemme come in, old boy," she said. It was Laura—drank!

IV

I slipped the door to quietly, and put my arm round her.

"I wanna sit down," she gurgled.

"All right, old girl," I said. "Come downstairs. It's a little warmer."

She hung heavily on my arm, and I had to save her from falling down the narrow staircase. I tucked her into a comfortable Chesterfield.

"F'you got anything to drink?" she asked.

I stroked her hands, and took off her hat, which was balanced at a ridiculous angle.

"Laura," I whispered, "what's the trouble? You've been drinking. I've nothing here but water. I could make you some tea."

"Oh, hell to tea! Gimme some water."

"What is it?" I said, fetching a glass and a pitcher.

"I've left that swine," she said thickly.

I cannot say that I was inordinately surprised. Troubles in the Beyfus family had been working to a head. Laura had threatened to do this several times since the night of the Burwell dinner, and it was inevitable that she would eventually do it abruptly like this. But it was deplorable that she should get drunk.

"D'you know what's happened now, Tom? Blast him I how I hate that man!"

"Tell me."

She began to say something; then she cried and I could not stop her. When she had had a thoroughly good cry, and drunk some more water, she seemed calmer. She held a handkerchief over her eyes, and said:

"D'you know what he's done? . . . Pm going to have a baby."

The news startled me. They had been married six years. She began to talk rapidly and incoherently.

"We always arranged we wouldn't No good to an artist like me—muck up my career, too. He says it was accident. ... I don't believe him. He—"

"But, Laura."

"Wass good of talking? You know everything, don't you?—married man—I can say anything to you, can't I?"

"Yes. But, Laura . . . how awful. But now, as it's happened, why not?"

"I'm too old, old boy. Too old. . . . Besides, there's this American' tour in the spring. It's not only that—everything about him. He's cruel. He's a beast He does beastly things to me. No one could ever imagine. And I can't help myself. You don't know what I've been through. I don't want a child of his, though God knows"

She cried again, and I soothed her forehead and stared at her helplessly.

"You must come home with me, Laura, and we will think out the best thing to do."

She clung to me.

"Tom, old boy, I know I'm a rotter. I'm drunk. I'm beastly drunk. You don't know it, but I've been drinking for years, ever since I married that . . . No, old boy, I daren't go home with you to-night. I'm not good enough. With that kid of yours in the house and everything. Lemme stay. Tommy. You've got some rugs and things, I bet Any old thing; juzza sleep it off. . . . I'm so tired, Tom. So damn sleepy."

She snuggled into the Chesterfield. I fetched some curtains and any heavy material I could find. I piled them on her and tucked her in.

"Poor old girl!" I thought. "Poor old Laura!"

She was already in a heavy sleep, breathing noisily. What could I do? I dare not stay the night with her. Mrs. Whittle would be alarmed. I had been in to dinner and told her I should be back about ten. Madeline might wake up and ask for me. The light would be burning in the hall. I put the tea-things and some biscuits on a chair near Laura, and left a note for her. I said I would be back at half-past eight in the morning. I turned out the gas. My last impression as I did so was her black hair scattered in profusion over a piece of Italian damask, and just in the background the bedpan upon which I had lavished so much energy, gleaming like a watchful moon.

Poor Laura! I locked up the shop, and made my way out into the fog.

Our shop was in Paddington Street, and it was barely fifteen minutes' walk to Plane Tree Road in the ordinary way, but somewhere in the Edgware Road I lost my way. The streets were nearly deserted. Eventually I groped along a wall and arrived at Lord's Cricket-ground. It was half-past eleven before I found my house. The light was flickering dimly in the hall. I opened the door and saw the fog rush past me. How cheerless and deserted the little house had become! I heard someone moving in the drawing-room. My nerves, unstrung by the events of the evening, presaged burglars. I shook with cold physical fear. But—Madeline was sleeping in the room above. I gripped my stick. A man came out into the hall. It was Edgar.

His throat was muffled up in a white scarf which emphasised the pallor of his cheeks. His eyes looked wild and slightly bloodshot. He bore down upon me.

"Where is Laura?" he demanded. "She has left me. She would come to you, I know. Where is she?"

A sudden detestation of this man came over me. I had not observed before how close together his eyes were. His face was dirty with the fog. Without die smug contentment of material comforts, and the grooming of the cultivated citizen to mark it, it appeared a weak and horrible mask. Here was I, broken in grief, half a mile away Laura, drunk to insensibility through his swinish behaviour, and all he was thinking of was—himself. I felt it He had come to demand his rights, his bond-woman. I flashed out:

"What the devil business is it of yours?"

Across his face there crept a look of cunning and amazement. I had shown him that I knew where Laura was. At the same time he was surprised at the ferocity of this negligible brother, who had always been so tame and friendly. He shifted his ground a little.

"I'm sorry to trouble you, Tom. I'm very worried. We had a little difference this evening. She swung out of the flat and said she was never coming back. Naturally I thought she would be here. If not, where would she be—on such a night?"

"I know nothing about her," I replied stoutly. He looked at me, and I know he wanted to say that I was lying. If he had, I should have struck him, and I think he knew that. He sighed and muttered:

"It's very distressing."

"For you, or for her?"

"For both of us, Tom."

"I can't help you. If Laura chooses to leave you, it's her affair. There must be some reason."

Suddenly he shouted:

"If that man Freitel is in this—"

"Hush!" I said. "This is my house. You may wake up my child."

And I opened the door for him. As he hovered on the step, I added:

"If Laura chooses to come and stay with me, you must please understand that this house for you is—out of bounds."

He gave me a quick look, and snapped:

"What has she been telling you?"

"Nothing which reflects any credit upon either of you," I answered enigmatically.

He glared at me, and the fog swallowed him up.

"I don't mind him suspecting Freitel," I thought. "But this other business . . ."

CHAPTER XIV

THE SEARCH FOR PROPORTION

At half-past eight the next morning I found Laura drinking tea. She appeared comparatively fresh and cheerful. She rallied me about our somewhat limited washing arrangements, and said that the towel was a disgrace to both of us.

"I'm awfully sorry I was such a beast last night, Tom," she said.

She appeared to be very anxious to please me, and she began examining all our stuffs and furniture. But I could tell there was something at the back of her mind she wanted to have settled. She suddenly remarked quite casually:

"I can't remember what I told you last night, Tom. Did I explain—"

"You said you had had a quarrel with Edgar, and you weren't going back."

"Yes, yes, that's it. We are always quarrelling, you know. He appears so calm, but he's got a beast of a temper. And—well, there's no getting away from it, he—to put it crudely—exploits me. I told you that, didn't I?"

"Yes."

"I didn't Did I say anything else?"

I began to put on my overall.

"Oh, you didn't say much. You were awfully squiffy, old girl . . . rather incoherent."

She seemed relieved. I somehow could not bring myself to remind her of what she had said.

"Can I come and stay with you as a p.g.? Fortunately I've got some money in the bank. I always kept my own account going. It's the only clever thing I've done."

"Of course you can come. You mustn't talk rot about p.g.-ing."

"I don't know what will happen about my engagements. He's my agent, you see. He'll muck everything up if I desert him."

"You'll have to chance that. You are still determined not to go back?"

"Worse than ever."

"Well, we must buckle to, and think of the best thing to do."

Laura was masterful. At ten o'clock she called at another agents' called Pealls, and got them to promise to do what they could for her. Then she telephoned to Lydia, the parlour-maid at the flat. Lydia said that Mr. Beyfus had instructed her not to send away, or allow to be taken, any of her mistress's frocks or property. This was easily settled. Laura took over Lydia, too. Lydia adored her. At three o'clock in the afternoon, when Edgar was away at the office, a small van arrived, and took away all Laura's property, including frocks and jewellery, and even some of the furniture which Laura said was hers; as well as the faithful Lydia. The whole contents were deposited in my house in St John's Wood. Madeline was thrilled with delight at this advent.

"Oh, Auntie Laura, how scrumptious! You must stay for ever, and ever, and ever."

The house underwent a further transformation. Laura's furniture adorned the most conspicuous places. Madeline insisted on giving up "the" bedroom to her.

The drawing-room became her music-room. Lydia shared a room with Mrs. Whittle. We were all rather congested. I expected another visit from Edgar, but he did not come. He wrote a formal letter to Laura, apparently under legal advice, and requested her to return to him. She replied, also under advice, and said she could not see her way to accede to his request For a few weeks the little house almost assumed an air of gaiety. Madeline and Laura were both gifted with that quick instinct of recovery which characterises youth and genius. Madeline was in higher spirits than she had been for a very long time. Laura and I both assumed an attitude of blustering joviality when we met. We talked crisply above the surface of things. We each had tragedies incommunicable to the other. We were sorry for each other, but less intimate than in the old days. Laura was right about her "agent."

Pealls informed her that the engagements secured for her by Mr. Beyfus had not been confirmed. They could get no satisfactory statement from him. Loeb she could not go to. She had lost the kind of name that Loeb handled. Between the two stools of the older societies—the more serious musical ventures, represented by Loeb, and the lighter, more popular undertakings of Beyfus—her career seemed in danger of collapsing. To my surprise she did not seem unduly distressed. She was content with her freedom. She went for walks with Madeline, and took her to matinees, played little pieces to her, and discovered that she had musical talent

II

This reasonably-contented existence endured for nearly three months, and then one evening when I arrived home I found Madeline in tears.

"What is the matter, darling?" I said, pressing her to me.

"Auntie Laura won't teach me any more. I think she is angry with me. Oo-oh!"

Laura was out. She did not return till late, looking pale and exhausted. When she had rested a little, I said:

"Madeline says you won't teach her any more."

She looked at me, and then turned away. She did not speak for some time. At last she exclaimed in a bitter voice:

"Oh, Tom, don't let the child get fond of music. It's hell."

I knew it would be no good arguing with her. I poked the fire, and thought the matter over. Then I said:

"Is anything wrong, old girl? You seem down."

I could not get her to reply. She was inwardly choking. I pressed her hands in mine, and said:

"It's a rotten old world, Laura, but we've got to make the best of it. I'm trying to."

Suddenly Laura kissed me.

"I know. I know. You're an awful brick, Tom. I think it's fine the way you've faced this thing. I never thought you had the strength—but it's somehow different with me. I suppose I haven't the stuff to fall back on. I'm miserably weak, Tom. And now, I'm—"

"What are you going to do, Laura?"

"I'm going away for a time—some months, perhaps. You're not to worry about me. I shall—be all right."

"You're going away to play?"

"No."

I could not ask her where. . . . The fire crackled in the hearth, A fine rain was beating against the windows.

"You won't do anything—foolish, will you, Laura?"

She replied with an almost inaudible "No." A sudden wave of fear swept over me. I felt myself in the presence of some disturbing menace. I wanted to act, but my limbs were cold. I paced the room, and lighted a cigarette, hoping to relieve the nervous tension. Then, steadying myself by the mantelshelf, I said:

"Laura, that night when you turned up at the shop in Paddington Street . . . drunk . . . you told me something. I knew afterwards you would be ashamed. ... It's no good pretending I don't know. . . . Promise me you won't be a fool . . ."

Laura jumped up, and her eyes flashed angrily.

"Oh, you . . . it's all right for you, you men. . . . What business is it of yours? . . ."

"But, Laura, I only want to help—"

"Oh, don't! Don't talk to me."

She flashed across the room and disappeared.

III

A few days later Laura left us, and she would not say where she was going. It was springtime, the most trying time of the year. I felt it more than Madeline, who was always being absorbed by some new and consuming interest. She made friends very easily and was popular with the other girls in the school. I just went on doing things, trying to keep the shutter of my mind snapped-to against the vivid light of emotion. One day Jevons came to me in a great state of excitement.

"You are a perfectly priceless old josser!" he said.

I could not make out what it was all about for some time. He kept on darting backwards and forwards from the shop to a room at the back, where we kept our superfluous stuff.

"What made you buy all that old junk at the Baughan sale?" he asked at last

I had been down to a sale in Sussex a few days previously. They were selling up the effects of an old recluse who had recently died and who had, apparently, left no relatives.

"Do you mean the pictures or the pots?"

"The pots are all right, of course, but—the pictures! There are seventeen of them—the most mixed crowd I've ever seen."

"I know. But they were sold as a lot. I rather liked those two old prints of Lewes, and I thought some of the others might be worth something. I know nothing about pictures, as you know. I paid twenty-seven pounds ten for the lot."

"Good Lord! 'Out of the mouths of babes and sucklings'" Jevons went back into the other room. A customer entered. A dear old lady, who admired everything enormously, talked for twenty minutes, borrowed a piece of string, said she would consult her husband, and then departed. When she had gone, Jevons once more hopped back into the shop.

"Tom Purbeck," he said, "I believe you're the greatest genius of the age. You are the coming Duveen,"

"Of course I am," I replied. "What about it?"

"Come with me."

We both went back to the inner room. Jevons had spread the pictures all over the place. One fairly large oil-painting was balanced on a chair. Jevons swept his arm round in a circle and said:

"This lot are worth fourpence. But just examine this oil on the chair."

It was a dexterously-painted landscape, with cottages and figures, and a mass of cold green foliage.

"I don't much like the damn thing," I said.

"Perhaps you don't, you silly old gump; but that's not the point. Look at this signature in the corner."

I examined it carefully, and deciphered the letters "Ruysdael."

"Well, who is he?" I said. "I've never heard of him."

Jevons shouted with laughter.

"You are undoubtedly destined to end your days in Bond Street and Park Lane I If this is a genuine Ruysdael, and I have every reason to believe it is—well, our shares will go up."

Ruysdael? Ruysdael? Oh, yes, of course. I remembered Ruysdael in the National Gallery. I never liked him very much. The name had slipped my memory.

"I expect it's a bally old fake," I said, feeling rather ashamed of my stupidity.

"Fools rush in where angels fear to tread. You leave the dealing of this to me."

I will not ask you to follow the immediate machinations of Mr. Jevons. Odd, mysterious people called and examined the picture. It was not even framed, but Jevons soon remedied that. Negotiations went on for six weeks. Someone was introduced to someone else. Handsome commissions were offered all round. At length a wizened old gentleman with snow-white hair drove up in a large car. He looked ill and worried and rather shabby. He asked petulantly to see the Ruysdael. He never gave a glance at us or at anything else in the place. He produced a horn-rimmed microscope. He went all over the picture, muttering:

"Ah! um—um—yes—um—um."

Then he drove away.

"That was old Bleatley, the millionaire and soap king," said Jevons, when he had gone. "He has the finest collection of Ruysdaels in the country. In the course of time we shall hear whether he has bought it. He always buys through Röder."

Three days later we heard that the picture was sold. I do not to this day know how much old Mr. Bleatley paid for it, but our share amounted to three thousand two hundred pounds! It seemed more wonderful than the victory of "Baionnette."

IV

It would be idle for me to claim any credit for the surprising run of luck which favoured the house of Jevons & Purbeck from that day. Neither do I think that Jevons himself would wish to boast of his part. To me there was something ironic in this twist of fortune. After all the years when we had been so indifferently off . . . My mind was being constantly bombarded by these disturbing reflections. ... "If this had happened before!—I could have done so-and-so, and so-and-so."

I just hardened myself, and went on. I accepted the good fortune without regret and without elation. Jevons was always quicker at the uptake than I. It was he who insisted on extending our premises. And it was he who eventually introduced a kind of fairy-godmother into our little premises. She was an elderly, kind-faced person called Lady Stourport. Her husband was Sir Andrew Stourport, a big man in the Glasgow shipping world. To Lady Stourport money seemed to be of no consequence at all. I think she liked us. Apart from liking us, we seemed to amuse her. She had apparently never seen anything quite so queer as ns in the part of the world she came from.

If she liked anything, she just bought it without asking the price. It was a cruel thing to do. It left Jevons and me arguing by the hour, after she had gone, as to how much we could decently demand. I suppose I inherited something of my father's instinct for the "fair price." Jevons was in favour of charging fancy sums. So we usually ended by a compromise of a fair price plus about fifty per cent.

One day she came in, and after making one or two purchases, she said:

"Now, Mr. Jevons, I have just bought an old house at Richmond that wants entirely renovating and redecorating. Do you do that kind of work?"

"Why, certainly we do, madam," promptly replied Jevons. I gasped. Jevons must be going off his nut! She gave him the address and a card to the agents.

"Whatever are you up to?" I said when she had gone. "We know nothing about decorating and renovating."

"My dear old mugwumps, it's as easy as falling off a tree. We only have to go to several builders and get estimates. We can sub-let the whole bally thing. A lot of these swanky firms do that. They don't do a stroke themselves."

I was astonished to find that Jevons was quite right. Lady Stourport's house at Richmond was a stately Georgian building in the precincts of the Park. It had not been occupied for ten years. We reconstructed several rooms, put in staircases, installed a new system of lighting and heating, papered and painted and panelled. We even launched out into landscape gardening, and introduced fauns and females in marble. When it was finished we began to fill it with antique furniture and old masters. If we had been quite unscrupulous we could have made a fortune out of Lady Stourport. On the other hand, she might not have come to us. She was by no means a fool. She thought we were two queer young men. She probably knew she was paying more than necessary, but it did not matter very much to her, and she had no great opinion of her own taste. We took all the worry and responsibility off her shoulders. I must say that, having once taken the plunge, I took a delight in trying to make Belhampton House as attractive as possible. I visited other old houses of the same period and made innumerable notes and sketches. I went to South Kensington Museum and looked up every book on the subject. I spent days in the builder's office, planning with him the best arrangements, and examining samples and patterns. My experience in the scene-painting profession was not entirely wasted. When the work began I haunted the place. I made the foreman explain to me every little operation. I worried the poor man's life out. I discovered imperfections, and ordered them to be done again. I did not know very much about it, but I did the very best I could. Jevons left me to grapple with all these technicalities, whilst he instinctively looked after the business side. I was happier than I had been for a long time, not because we were making money, but because I suddenly found a chance of serving a purpose.

Sometimes the thought occurred to me: "Is there any real satisfaction in doing this—just helping a rich and possibly selfish old woman?"

A few moments' reflection told me that there was. It was not as though she wanted something showy and vulgar. She wanted the best. I was helping to shape something—make something more beautiful. I had never been attracted by the unsolvable problems of social reform. Doubtless many people would say that in my mood at that time I should have been better advised to have worked among the poor, to have definitely pledged myself as a champion of moral rights.

That the only real satisfaction is a complete negation of self, I should have lived entirely for others.

I can only say that I am not made that way. The world appears to me more in need of fining down than of bolstering up. I would always rather subscribe to a spiritual idea than to a material advancement. At that time I was convinced that it was far more important for the cornice in Lady Stourport's drawing-room to be the exact proportion than that some unfortunate creature should be prevented from drinking too much beer or not eating enough bread. If the cornice was exactly right it would be observed by thousands of people in the course of time. The majority of them wouldn't stop to think about it, but it would gradually impress itself on their mind. They would get to feel that that was the right and true proportion, and they would notice when other cornices were not. In time a wrong proportion would offend them. I was contributing towards the evolution of a finer thrust of humanity—towards a better appreciation of beauty, towards an idea. On the other hand, if I gave bread to a starving man, he would be hungry again to-morrow, or, expecting my presence, he would make no attempt to get bread for himself. I was not helping his ideas at all. Indeed, I was rather contaminating them. If I arrested the hand of the drunkard as he raised his glass to his lips, and said, "Hold, my good fellow! Don't you know that that is the way to damnation?" he would probably answer:

"Right, old sport! Have one with me." And, being of a friendly disposition I should probably fall in with his request, and we would make a merry evening of it. I don't say that I am right about these things. I only repeat that I am made that way. I honour the people who think just the opposite.

I heard nothing from Laura all the summer, and her name did not appear in any musical announcements. At the beginning of September, however, I had a letter from her—a most unusual attention. It ran:

"Dear old Tom,

"I have been most frightfully ill. I am now all right again. I am leaving for the Pyrenees with Lucie van Stael to-morrow. I expect to be away two months, to recuperate. Heaps of love to you both. I am sending Madeline a large parcel by this post. I shall come and see you directly I get back.

"Your loving old fool of a sister,

"Laura."

She had been a fool, then! There was no address, but the envelope was stamped "Buxton." I had never heard of Lucie van Stael.

It fell out rather fortunately that Madeline had made great friends with two little girls in the neighbourhood. Their mother was a charming Canadian woman named Mrs. Maguire, and she invited Madeline to go and stay with them at their cottage at Lulworth Cove for the summer holidays. I was delighted for her to go. I went down there myself for several week-ends, which I conducted in a business-like way. I always took some work with me, and when not working I was bathing with the children, or learning to manipulate a sailing-boat, or discussing the question of education with Mrs. Maguire.

One morning I discovered two streaks of grey hair on either side of my temple.

"You're beginning to fade, old man," I thought to myself; and the reflection produced in me no sense of regret.

CHAPTER XV

NOT A NICE THING TO HAVE HAPPENED

I looked out of the window into the little garden. Yellow and violet crocuses were forcing their way through the earth. For March the day was warm and sunny. Madeline was very busy. For a time I could not determine what she was doing. She had a spade and a trowel and a ball of string. Then I realised that she was planning a bed of standard roses. Her movements were vigorous and concentrated. There was something about the poise of her young body which gave me a sudden feeling of surprise. Madeline was growing up. She was no longer "just a kid." In a few years she would be a woman, with all a woman's potentialities and troubles. A disturbed sense of misgiving crept over me. Was I giving her all of myself that I could? Must not her life be rather cramped and drab? I wanted to go out into the garden and throw my arms round her and kiss her. But I had schooled myself to give way to these impulses as little as possible. I was somewhat restive concerning the emotions in those days. Was I becoming too hard and set? . . . a solemn, dull, middle-aged father? The birds were already active in the branches. The old cycle of this age of re-birth had come round again. I opened the window and called out: "Midgkins!" She looked up at me with one of her quick smiles of greeting. Her eyes were very alive; tiny lights seemed to sparkle in their blue-grey depths. Her face was square rather than oval, the eyes wide apart Light brown hair tumbled in little curves and sweeps around her cheeks, that glowed with exercise. Her features appeared small in detail but broad in effect. She was lightly built but with the poise of an athlete rather than a student. Her mother must have looked exactly like that in the days before I knew her.

"What do you say to a day in the country?" I said.

"Oh, ripping! I won't be a minute. I'll have to wash. My hands are filthy."

"You must buck up. There's only one train that's any good, and that goes in forty minutes."

"Right you are, daddy!"

I believe she was very surprised at my sudden invitation, but she gave no evidence of it. Going down in the train she told me the details of two rival systems of education, one—the proper one, of course—being instituted by her beloved Miss Delarme at her own school, the other by a "simply frantic old lunatic" at a rival school at Hampstead. It was all rather complicated, and I'm afraid I did not follow it very closely. I was looking at Madeline, her animated face beneath the scarlet tam-o'-shanter, her plaid skirt, brown gaiters and walking-stick, and I was thinking to myself:

"It won't do. It won't do at all—to shut everything out."

Madeline was not at all of a sentimental disposition. She seemed to adjudge my outlook exactly, and to adapt herself to it. We were a very sensible couple. I found, moreover, that at this school of Miss Delarme's, where she was being co-educated, an entirely novel attitude towards life was presented. That is to say, it was novel as far as I was concerned, but not novel to Madeline. She accepted it as a matter of course. It was all very, very different from the grammar-school in Camden Town which Laura and I had attended. These children—Madeline and her friends—seemed somehow freer and more independent in thought and action. Hero-worship apparently had died out. Nothing cast a spell over them. At times this attitude shocked me. You felt as though you could not impress them. When Laura and I were at school someone had only to mention Pitt, or Gordon, or Milton to put a class into a kind of trance. But now they wanted to know exactly all about these people, and what they did, and why, and whether it couldn't have been done better. They questioned, and criticised, and modified, and qualified. In effect, they were more concerned with ideas than with individuals. Pitt was not a god, he was just a competent politician, with many weaknesses, and who made many blunders. What was Gordon doing in Egypt, anyway? "Yes, I like the opening part of 'Paradise Lost,' but a lot of it is very dull."

II

What arc you to do with children like that? When I first came up against it, I confess it made me angry. But after a time I realised that the effect it had on Madeline was on the whole wonderfully beneficial. If she had been a hero-worshipper like myself, she would never have been able to withstand this great blow which had come upon us with such fortitude. The blow struck her as heavily as it did me, but after the first stunning effect she immediately began to think rather than to feel. And when the truth of this dawned upon me, I knew that I was witnessing a definite human advance. In my time we were encouraged to treat such a catastrophe as a lifelong companion. We were encouraged to sustain it with every mark of recognition and perpetual endurance. Madeline was as unselfish a child as any I have known, as quick in her sympathies, as loving, but after the first few months she made no display at all of the grief which consumed her. She thought furiously. I do not know what conclusions she came to. After my rather futile attempt to portray for her benefit a vision of St. John's Wood being perpetuated in heaven, we did not discuss religion. We were a little shy of each other. It took me a long time to realise that I was learning more from her than she was from me. Wordsworth has put this very clearly, but there are remarkably few of us who accept it. Everything that is of any value we learn from children. They present us with the produce of our own experience.

On that Sunday I had a wonderful day with Madeline, and we said nothing at all. That is to 9ay, we said nothing that mattered. She chatted the whole time, and I invented some fantastic stories for the fun of watching her eyes light up. We tramped over the hill beyond Wendover, and sat on a fallen log, and ate our sandwiches. The great panorama of the Vale of Aylesbury lay before it, and we discussed its topography, and argued as to the pace of a tiny train puffing miles away below us. We were remarkably "sensible." We even discussed the site for a house I was to build the following year, its plan, and necessary accommodation, and garden.

"I don't think I'd like to live in the country all the year," said Madeline. "I like people."

Very well; then we would have a week-end cottage, and a motor-car, and still keep on the house in St. John's Wood; or perhaps have a flat nearer in town. I, too, like people.

"Are you going to make a lot of money, daddy?"

"Heaps and heaps."

"Oh, how fine! Well, I'd like to—"

"What would you like to do, Midge?"

"I'd like to have a good time, of course But there's lots of things—"

"What sort of things?"

"Oh, I don't know. I'd like to spend it all, not just on that, but on—well, you know, science, and helping people to find out things. Wouldn't you?"

"Of course. That would be fine. Would you like to help poor people?"

"Yes . . . but I think if you can help people to find out things, perhaps there needn't be any poor."

"No, perhaps not. We must think about that a lot"

"Elspeth and Dolly Maguire are going back to Canada next year. They wanted me to go and stay with them. Do you think I could, daddy?"

"Go to Canada and leave . . . Why, yes; why shouldn't you?"

"I would love to travel heaps. I'd like to see America, and India, and China, and Japan. I'd like to go to those islands in the South Pacific—you know, Samoa, the Cook Islands, Solomon Islands."

"What makes you think of them?"

"We've been having them at school. And there's Robert Louis Stevenson who writes scrumptiously about them."

"Do you have him too?"

"Of course. Have you read 'Treasure Island'?"

Good Lord! How ignorant I am. I glance at Madeline's face, all glowing with the walk. She is fourteen. Talking geography, Robert Louis Stevenson, helping people to find out things. What were Laura and I taught at fourteen? What ages ago! I could not remember. I squeezed her arm.

"You want to be a pirate, I can see."

"Only for a time. Not a permanent pirate. Just long enough to see what it's like, and then come back where all the people are that you—that understand you, and then tell them all about it"

"Write it up, you mean?"

"Yes, or paint it."

"That would be a good idea."

"It doesn't matter what you do so long as you give it away."

I was about to say, "What do you mean, my child?" and then I saw. I blushed in a kind of confusion. I seemed to see in that instant why I had never been an artist, why Laura had never been quite an artist, why Radic had been one, and why Madeline might be. It is to be moved by something so profound that your only idea is to give it out of yourself.

"I take off my hat to Miss Delarme," I thought. "My education is just beginning."

III

We arrived home in time for a very late tea in which boiled eggs played a conspicuous part Madeline was ravenous. After tea the Maguires paid us a visit, and we played a game called "Uncle's in it!" a game played with towels and cushions, of which I have now forgotten the rules. It seemed to have been specially designed to make me look a silly old fool, but the children enjoyed it immensely, and Mrs. Maguire said she had no idea I could be such a comedian. About seven o'clock Mrs. Whittle came in and announced that a lady bad called to see me, and said she would rather not give a name. I went out into the hall. In the dim light I observed a middle-aged, actressy-looking woman, rather floridly over-dressed. She smiled and held out her hand:

"Mr. Tom Purbeck?"

I shook hands automatically and murmured:

"I'm afraid I—er—haven't the—"

"My name is Lucie van Stael."

"Oh I . . . Oh, yes, a friend of Laura's. Will you come into the study?"

She laughed familiarly, and looked round the room.

"What a ducky little house! I've heard all about you, and Madeline, of course. Laura is always talking about you. Sweet! Perfectly sweet! Where did you get that dear little escritoire?"

"As a matter of fact, it belongs to Laura. Won't you sit down?"

"Oh, thank you so much. I must really apologise for calling like this. The dear child was so anxious. It was her last injunction: 'Now mini you go and see Tom at once.'"

"I haven't seen Laura for over a year."

"Isn't it dreadful how time flies! My poor husband used to say—he was an American, you know; he died at the age of thirty-seven, after making a fortune in twelve years—he used to say—now, let me see: what was it?—Ah, yes! You can make money but you can't make time. Ha, ha, ha!"

I felt that I disliked this woman intensely. I broke in with:

"Have you any message for me from Laura?"

"She has been so harassed, so tried, poor child, it is quite difficult for me to take up the threads. I am not sure how far the position had developed when she last wrote to you. She was emphatic on the point that an interview is so much better than laboured correspondence. Don't you agree with me? One may so easily misunderstand in a letter, but in talking you can clear up every point There is, of course, the difficulty of your father."

"I'm afraid I don't quite follow. What is the difficulty about my father?"

"From a distance it is so difficult to judge. One is apt to make harsh distinctions ... if one doesn't foresee all the eventualities. You see, the marquis comes of one of the best families. But he is so much more than that. He is a hon enfant, serious, an intellectual indeed. There is no case of—"

"Excuse me, what marquis do you refer to?"

"Why, the Marquis de Thor Bohunville, of course. It is all quite commendable. It is only the preliminaries that are a little difficult of arrangement. You see, it is necessary to take the decisive step in order to secure freedom. The dear child is so convinced that you will entirely appreciate her position. But I think that she worries a little about the opinion of the father. If it should appear in the newspapers first! . . . You know what they are—scurrilous! And then, a title. There is almost sure to be."

"But what do you mean? Is Laura going to marry this marquis?"

"When she has secured her freedom. That is why she thought that an interview would be more satisfying to you than—anything else. One can so easily misjudge. The elegant suite of apartments which—they occupy at St. Jean de Luz, and you, as an artist, I assure you."

I jumped up.

"Do you mean to say," I exclaimed, "that Laura is already . . . that she is living with this?"

"A most admirable and distinguished man, destined for the Académie. Nothing, I assure you, the least intriguant. You will appreciate the fact that these are mere formalities. The law demands such."

I glanced at this woman as though I held her responsible, as so, indeed, to a certain extent, she was.

"How do you know that Beyfus will divorce her?" I demanded.

"It almost goes without saying. He will b6 given every encouragement and assistance. To be happy it is necessary sometimes to take risks, to act contrary to one's principles. But the poor child is distressed that you should think—uncharitably of her, not completely understanding all the circumstances, not appreciating how admirable and well-intentioned is the other parti, quite removed from what one might expect. She is anxious that you should do your best ... to make the information as acceptable to your father as . . . Indeed, the child loves you both very dearly and she would not cause you unnecessary distress. She wept."

Damn Laura! Why must she always do these things?

IV

On the very day when life appeared to be holding out to me some semblance of gladness, when I detected within myself the slow dawning of reviving hopes, when I began to see through the eyes of Madeline, and realise that here was something "worth while"—this frowsy, foreign blockhead comes butting in with this corroding counterblast from Laura, announcing what amounts to be an acknowledgment that she has been seduced by a French marquis, who is keeping her in an "elegant apartment" at St. Jean de Luz! And, forsooth, I am to go and break it to my father! I am to go to "The Duchess of Pless" and convince him that it is all quite all right That the marquis is "well-intentioned" and "distinguished," That what they have done is a mere formality. He means to marry the girl. Madame la Marquise de Thor Bohunville! Of course. Admirable!

Probably a drunken old roué, who will throw her in the gutter at the first opportunity.

"How old is this man?" I snapped.

"Monsieur le marquis . . . Quite young; indeed, a little younger than Laura."

Very well, then; probably a young roué and café-lounger; an adventurer. Just as bad.

"Ah! I wish I could impress you: I see you are sceptical. Mister Tom. I assure you he is in every way bon enfant. He is quiet, reserved, studious, good-tempered, charming. And he adores her. . . . My God, how he adores her!"

I don't know what made me, but I got up and laughed bitterly. She looked at me without malice. Indeed, she smiled coyly and also rose.

"Dear Mister Tom, you must not take this too much to heart. I promise you there will be no cause for regrets. I can almost call you brother Tom. Do let me see dear Madeline before I go."

I felt a keen antipathy to the idea of this woman meeting Madeline. Madeline belonged to me. I would not have her even run the risk of being examined by this creature of ill-omen, who seemed to carry in her person the essence of cabarets and casinos and the antechambers of decadent aristocrats. I answered offhandedly:

"Oh, Madeline has gone to bed. She's not very well. She's very tired."

It might have been a satisfactory explanation if the door had not at that moment opened with a bang, and a face glowing with animation had not been thrust into the room.

"Daddy! Oh! . . . I'm sorry."

She was about to withdraw, when my surprising visitor threw out her arms and exclaimed:

"Madeline! Madeline! Oh, isn"t she sweet!

Dear child, let me look at you. I am a very old friend of your Auntie Laura's."

Madeline found herself effusively embraced. Her face was a study. At the mention of Auntie Laura it lighted up with interest It was bewildered by the embrace, but straining to be gracious. It wanted to be polite, but plainly showed it didn't approve of the visitor. At the same time it was determined to hear about Auntie Laura.

"Where is she? Is she coming?"

"Not yet, my dear. Mercy, what a pretty girl you are I What lovely hair!"

"Where is Aunt Laura?"

"She is in France, my darling."

"Is she playing?"

"Not just now, dear."

"Why not?"

This was a drastic method of cross-examination. I dreaded what might be said. So I interrupted with:

"She's been having a long holiday—travelling about, and staying with friends, dear."

Madeline looked dubious, but she held out her hand and said primly:

"Give her my love if you see her again—"

I could not help laughing. It was so formal and old-fashioned, and it also implied that the visitor was dismissed, or in any case that her presence was no longer desirable. Lucie van Stael looked a little annoyed, and I could not help being impressed by the fact that, whereas I had been pointedly rude to her and had been caught out telling her a lie, she seemed to bear me no ill-will, but Madeline's indifference nettled her. She took her departure with less show of effusion. The door had hardly snapped-to on her before Madeline exclaimed:

"What on earth can Auntie Laura find in a person like that?" And then very breathlessly: "I say . . . can we ask the Maguires to stop to supper?"

V

I put off my visit to "The Duchess of Pless" for five days. It was only the haunting dread that something might appear in the newspapers which eventually drove me on to fulfil my unpleasant task. How would father take it? Of one thing I was convinced—it would upset him greatly. It is a curious fact that although he saw so little of Laura, and not a great deal of me, I know that we were ever present in his thoughts. Our welfare was one of his living preoccupations. He had grown accustomed to our neglect of him. It was quite natural that we should go off and get married. The great gulf of years between him and us indeed created a certain barrier of uncompanionableness. His interests were not our interests. At the same time he was very alert to our well-being and conduct, and I knew that he had a ponderous—not to say Victorian—respect for what is called honour. I dreaded his sense of honour. It was like a sledge-hammer. He had never realised that there had been a serious breach between Laura and her husband. He knew that she had gone away, but he did not know the conditions. He believed it was to do with her work. He viewed artists as queer, irregular people, likely to do queer, irregular things. They were essentially creatures to be laughed at and pitied, but at the same time—there is only one standard for all Christian people when it comes down to fundamentals.

I found him upstairs with stepmother in the parlour. As I entered the room there flashed through my mind a kind of myopic vision of our concentrated lives there. There was something about this house which never changed. It seemed to be the only place in the universe not susceptible to the friction of time. I believed that whatever I did, whatever experiences were in store for me, I should always come back and find father in the horsehair chair, reading the Morning Advertiser, stepmother sitting primly on the couch, knitting, the wax fruit and "The Death of Wolfe," the paraffin lamp with the green shade—he greatly objected to electricity—the crowded furniture, and the faded memory of many teas, Laura coming home from the Royal Academy, the brown-paper parcels, the Kings of North and South Carolina. It required an effort of will to see beyond this vision to the larger issues of my visit. Father cried out:

"Hullo, Tom! Glad to see you."

Stepmother was getting a little feeble. She did not seem to recognise me at first, but when she did she held up her cheek to be kissed, and said:

"We're just going to have a cup of tea. Will you have one, Tom?"

I said I should be delighted, and I sat there talking to them both about my business, and the weather, and the coming general election. I felt embarrassed and uncomfortable. I could not tell father about Laura with stepmother in the room. I could not be sure how he would take it. And he might not wish her to know. At the end of an hour I felt I must make a desperate move, so I said suddenly:

"I wonder whether you would come down to the little room at the back of the bar for a few minutes, dad? I want to consult you about a business contract"

"Yes, yea, of course. Won't be long, Annie."

We went downstairs, and I felt my heart beating. We heard the drone of the bars and the popping of corks. Father turned up the light.

"Well, my lad?"

I fidgeted from one leg to another.

"It's like this, dad. It isn't about my business I wanted to speak to you at all. It's something else. It's to do with—Laura."

"Oh?"

There was a tap on the door, and Mrs. Beddoes' bepowdered face appeared.

"Excuse me, Mr. Purbeck. Johnson is asking for sherry. We've nothing except that lot that came from the Bennison sale. Shall we open some?"

"No, no. I won't have that served. It's inferior rubbish."

"They won't take it back, sir."

"Then we'll pour the lot away."

"All right, Mr. Purbeck."

She vanished. It did not seem an auspicious start.

"Well, Tom, what's this about Laura?"

"I don't know whether you know, dad, her marriage with Edgar Beyfus was not a success. She has left him."

"What do you mean—she has left him?"

"She has gone away. She refuses to live with him any longer."

Father's eyes rolled menacingly.

"What has he Has he been unfaithful?"

"I don't know. In any case, they have quarrelled."

"But they are still man and wife. She can't go off like that."

"She has."

"A woman can't leave her husband without proper justification."

"But she has left him, dad."

"I must write to her. She can't do that. She must go back."

"You know what Laura is, dad. She won't go back. Besides—there's something else. She wants to marry another man—a Frenchman."

Father was speechless. He took out his pipe, and put it back in his pocket He gave me a searching look as though he held me responsible, in the same way that I had held Lucie van Stael responsible. The position of the bringer of evil tidings is never an enviable one. In the old days they used to kill them.

"How can she marry another man when she's already married?"

"Divorce."

"But, damn it, boy! you say she has no grounds for divorce."

Poor old chap! Why must I torture him like this? But it had got to be done.

"I'm afraid the fact is Beyfus may divorce her."

"Do you mean to say."

For a moment I thought he was going to strike me. He looked ugly; very much like he did on the day when he turned out the unfortunate Zuk. His eyes protruded, his cheeks appeared shiny, his hair bristled. He thrust his head forward, and opened and clenched his fists. Then he seemed suddenly to fall to pieces. He turned away and said in a choking voice:

"It's not a nice thing to have happened, Tom."

The mildness of this verdict moved me more than any explosion of anger. It was pitiable . . . finished. He had read the truth in my eyes, and he knew that the position was irrecoverable. He fixed his eyes upon a coloured print of a stag-hunt, and suddenly he made a comment which surprised me:

"I was a fool to have sent her to that Royal Academy."

In those brief seconds he must have focussed her whole career. The unfortunate institution in Tenterden Street had been primarily responsible. It had filled her head with false ambitions. She had come in touch with all these restless, undesirable people. I could not help following father's eye, and also studying the stag-hunt. A lady in a bowler hat and a stiff black frock was gracefully taking a hedge, surrounded by a pack of dogs. A huntsman in front had been thrown and was picking himself out of a ditch. What a much more enviable life! Doubtless in good time the lady would marry the fallen huntsman. They would lead normal, healthy lives. They would hunt, and eat, and bring up a large family of sporting. God-fearing children, who would do the same. They would suffer no misgivings, have none of these complicated twists and turns of the soul.

Poor Laura! . . . Poor old dad! . . .

CHAPTER XVI

A FIRST-WICKET MAN

During the following two years the firm of Jevons & Purbeck made surprising progress. Our success in the first place was undoubtedly due to the two instances of sheer luck which I have recorded, but as time went on we established a more solid reputation. Jevons said I was a demon for work, and I think it was true. This passion for accomplishment was the legacy of my suffering. I was driven to it blindly, and having once started I felt no desire to relax. It was never a frenzy for making money; it was just the impetus to do something that was worth doing worthily. I made an exhaustive study of the decorative trade. However busy we were, I always found time for museums, and books, and old buildings. I got to love the work, and in a very short time we moved our premises to Soho, and had our own workshops.

Madeline realised her ambition of a week-end cottage, which we found near High Wycombe, and we moved to a rather larger and more comfortable house in St. John's Wood. We extended our circle of acquaintanceship, and frequently I took her to theatres and concerts. Even if I was still a victim to the emotional stress of these experiences, I realised that that was no excuse for starving the child. We made many new friends, but the most delightful surprise in the way of friendship was that with Monsieur le Marquis de Thor Bohunville.

Laura's divorce was accomplished with considerable publicity, but without much fuss. It might have been more difficult had it not been that at that time Edgar had made the acquaintance of a South American widow, who was extremely wealthy and who had dark, languishing eyes. Laura was married to the marquis in Bordeaux a week after the divorce had been pronounced. A honeymoon under the circumstances, I presume, must have seemed superfluous, for they came to London immediately. You can imagine with what trepidation I awaited to see this "well-intentioned" and "distinguished" bon enfant. They stayed at the Metropole, and I went to dine with them on the evening of their arrival. I must say at once that Lucie van Stael had not lied. He was indeed a delightful young man. He must have been five or six years younger than Laura. He was as different from the usual British conception of a Frenchman as he could well be. He was fair, with deep blue, reflective eyes and an extremely reserved manner. He spoke in a rich, low voice, and without gesture. When I saw them together it occurred to me that in effect Laura might be a Frenchwoman married to an Englishman, instead of the reverse. Laura had not worn well. She looked much older. Her face was lined and, I thought, over-powdered. She had developed some cunning way of doing up her dark hair which made her look very foreign. People stared at her, and it was not surprising, with her striking, almost bizarre effect of black velvet and white skin, with carmine lips, and the little diamonds glittering at her throat: a touch of green somewhere—I think a green velvet flower at her breast. She looked happy enough, but as though she had been through an awful experiences. She was very moved when she saw me, and kept pressing my hand and murmuring:

"Dear old man . . . dear old man,"

We had hardly seated ourselves at table before she said:

"Henri, let's have some champagne to-night—just to welcome Tom."

I noted that Henri made no comment. He ordered the champagne but he did not drink any himself I had two glasses, and I believe Laura drank the rest.

She quickly warmed to me, and we became intimate. She was the Laura of old.

"I have not made a mistake this time," she said suddenly, smiling at Henri, who smiled back solemnly in response.

She talked quite simply about her love-affairs, and talked of Henri as though he were not there, or as though he were a little boy whose presence hardly counted. She told me all about his lovable character and his work. He was, indeed, a scientist, and he had written books on metallurgy, and sublimates, and conglomerates and such things.

"What I like about Henri," she suddenly remarked, "is that I can tell him everything. He understands so . . . Oh, it's wonderful! I didn't know I could be so happy, Tom. He knows everything, every little thing about me."

Henri turned his reflective, adoring eyes upon her and said:

"Foolish woman! Your brother will think I am a paragon, a—what do you call it?—a prig, eh? I am, on the contrary, a very wicked man, married to an abandoned woman, who drinks champagne."

Laura sipped her wine and exclaimed:

"Isn't he perfectly sweet I You must love each other, you two."

We grinned at each other in that foolish way that men will when put in an embarrassing position. As a matter of fact, I think Henri already liked me, and I certainly felt drawn towards him. Laura chatted on:

"I have told Henri all about father, and he quite—understands. How is dad?"

I answered that he was well, but I did not tell Laura how father had taken the whole affair. I am sure that Henri would not have been able to understand. He considered that he had acted honourably, but father's ideas of honour were different. I dreaded what might transpire when they met. We arranged that they should come to us the following night, as Laura was crazy to see Madeline again, and that on the following night we should all visit "The Duchess of Pless." Laura was still a little dubious about Henri. She kept on repeating:

"It's a queer place, Henri. You mustn't be shocked."

And he replied promptly:

"I shall be most entertained. I have a great respect for your father, from what you have told me of him."

II

The meeting at our house was almost hilarious. Madeline and Henri hit it off at once. My daughter at last had met someone whose mission it was to find out about things. He talked to her quite solemnly, as though she were a grown-up person. He told her all kinds of interesting things about the stars, and the formation of the earth, and the tides, and the law of gravitation. He did not attempt to patronise her. Her eyes gleamed with interest. I believe Laura was almost jealous—not of Madeline but of Henri. She wanted to have the child to herself, but Henri almost monopolised her.

As I listened to Henri and observed his kind, candid, fatherly manner, I thought to myself: "How fine it is for Laura I There is no doubt she has found the right man this time. It is like a miracle. Dear old Laura! I'm so glad."

We eagerly discussed our future plans. Laura and Henri were to have a house in Curzon Street. It had already been negotiated for. They were to spend part of their time in London, and the rest in Paris and down the South. Moreover, the old ambitions were again stirring. Henri offered no objections to her continuing her professional career if it made her happier. He had given her a Strad.

"I shall only go for the good things now," she said. "No more of these flap-doodle ballad shows for me."

She was in the highest spirits. We discussed taking a furnished house in Cornwall for August and September, which we were to share.

"And I should like," continued Laura, "to get the dear old dad and stepmother down for a bit."

We laughed and talked and plotted. We were a merry, congenial party. At half-past nine Madeline dashed out into the hall to answer to the postman's knock. She returned with a letter which she held out to me.

"A letter from grandpa," she said.

"Good!" I answered. "I wrote to him last night. This will be about our going to-morrow."

I opened the letter, and stared at it. I read it through five times. I could not put it down. I tried to crumple it up in my hands, but Laura snatched it from me.

"What's the matter, Tom?"

I could not prevent her reading it. I sat there like one paralysed. Madeline looked over Laura's shoulder. This is the letter they read:

"Dear Tom,

"I have a son but no daughter. I have no wish to meet the Marshoness of wherever it is.

"Your affectionate

"Father."

Henri looked enquiringly at his wife, who went quite white. We none of us spoke until Madeline blurted out;

"Whatever does he mean? Why does he say he has no daughter when Auntie Laura is sitting here all the time?"

Then Laura burst into tears.

"It's just my luck! It's always my luck!" she gasped.

It was useless to pretend to Henri that nothing was amiss, so I took the letter and handed it to him. He read it through at a glance, then he patted Laura's shoulder.

"My dear," he said quietly, "he does not understand. He cannot know that we are married."

"Oh, yes, he does. You don't understand. You can't understand—father."

Henri looked extremely perplexed. He knew that he had acted sincerely and honourably. His friends had told him he had acted with extraordinary magnanimity. According to his code his position was unassailable. He had fulfilled his obligations to the letter. He was even on his way to be entirely familiar and friendly to his wife's father, who, he had been told, was a common old pot-house keeper. He intended to show that he did not in any way wish to presume upon this social discrepancy. He would treat him as an equal. How could any honourable and well-intentioned man do otherwise? And then this amazing letter! It was simply incomprehensible.

"Same misunderstanding," he muttered, looking from one to the other.

III

But I knew, and Laura, dabbing her eyes with her handkerchief, knew that there was no misunderstanding. The issues were perfectly clear, and quite irreconcilable. Henri was right and father was right, but neither the twain could possibly adapt his point of view to the other. Henri had his code. He may even have been harbouring a slight sense of liberality in coming to forgive the girl's father for being a publican. He had gone a little beyond the actual prescriptions of the code. But away over there, amidst those dingy tankards and glass screens, the antimacassars and stuffy furniture, was another code. A strange, relentless, Victorian code, something which could not be turned aside or bought. A code which believed in fair dealing, in decent action, in refusing to adulterate wine or to serve inferior sherry. A code which would never under any circumstances forgive adultery.

Henri frankly did not understand. He turned the letter over.

"What does he mean by the 'marshoness of wherever it is'?"

I believe for the moment he was more concerned about this slight to the family name than to the moral imputation. He wondered whether any possible scandal could have arisen connected with the name to produce so gross a breach of courtesy.

Laura snatched the letter from his hand.

"It's no good," she said. "Father is like that. We shall have to—cut him out, dear."

Henri nodded sagely. Of course, now he understood. This old potman was a drunkard. He was probably drunk when he wrote that letter. His beautiful Laura was distressed. She did not wish her husband to meet the old reprobate. There might be an unfortunate contretemps. She had always been a little apprehensive about the meeting. Well, well, it was of no great importance. Regrettable, extremely regrettable that the father should be a drunkard. He must be avoided. His adorable wife must be kept from the contamination . . . Henri suddenly gave her one of his quick, penetrating glances, and moved a little uneasily in his chair. Regrettable, very regrettable. . . . Rather odd . . . did his beloved one sometimes seem disposed to . . . demand rather a lot of wine? Henri continued to stroke the bridge of his nose.

To Madeline also the whole affair was incomprehensible. It was unfortunate that she should have been present. The letter did not distress her so much as Laura's sudden outburst of tears. For a moment I thought she was going to cry herself, then she stamped up and down the room, and exclaimed vehemently:

"I shall go and see grandpa to-morrow, and give him a jolly good talking to."

Henri smiled, and put his arm round her.

"You are a little tigress, I can see."

"Well, it's so stupid; so utterly stupid! He might as well say he hasn't got a pair of trousers when he's wearing them all the time."

We all laughed at that, and the atmosphere seemed to clear a little. I was anxious to change the subject, for I knew that it would be useless to discuss it. Only Laura and I alone could discuss it. I fetched some designs which I had been making for a panelled room. We looked at them, and sat talking till half -past ten, when Laura and Henri took their departure. Laura and I could only exchange glances, but I invited her to come down and inspect our new business premises the following day,

IV

I lay awake that night for a long time, thinking over the unfortunate situation. It must have been about two o'clock in the morning when an idea suddenly leapt to the forefront of my sombre reflections. "Uncle Stephen!" There was something about Uncle Stephen that was very get-at-able. He was less Puritanical than father and more informative. I always felt that I could say anything to him. He was not by any means a clever man, but he had a curious breadth of outlook, and a rather shrewd way of making deductions. I found him in the office of his stationery business just before lunchtime. He called out:

"Hullo, Tom, come to lend me some money? Wait ten seconds, and we'll go and have a bite of something together."

We went to a little Italian cafe near by, where, as Uncle Stephen said, "the food was vile but the best you can get in Notting Hill." He was elated at the success of Jevons & Purbeck, and I could get him to talk of nothing else. It was not till we were regaling ourselves with two very good cigars, and drinking a lukewarm liquid which the management described as coffee, that I got an opportunity of laying bare the full story of our family upheaval. Uncle Stephen listened and nodded and twirled his dark moustache. It did not seem to produce in him any manifestation of surprise, or indignation, or sympathy. He merely kept saying: "Yes? Well?" When I had finished he said:

"Well, what do you want me to do, boy?"

"I only wondered whether it would be possible for you, as his brother, to go to him, and try and make things all right? Explain exactly how it came about, and make him see that Laura and Henri did the wisest and best thing."

Uncle Stephen leant across the table and tapped me on the shoulder with his long first finger.

"Tom, did you ever see Arthur Shrewsbury batting for Notts on a plumb wicket, with a schoolboy pitching him up long hops?"

"I can't say I ever did."

"He never took any risks, whoever was bowling. I should stand about as much chance of getting your father out as the schoolboy would have of getting out Shrewsbury. Oh, no, lad. I've known your father for over sixty years. He's set. He's got his eye in. Nothing could move him."

He flicked the end of his cigar into the coffee-saucer and went on:

"I don't say anything one way or the other about the rights and wrongs of the case. I've seen too much I've never been a Shrewsbury nor even a Jessop. I'm just an ordinary back-garden player. I've not even been a Joseph. I've made love and not regretted it. I've made money and lost it, and made it again. I believe in sport as the best school. One learns to give and take, to take the best with the worst, and never to kick or grouse. But your old man is of different metal. He's a Shrewsbury. A first-wicket man, a man who'll never alter his style. It doesn't matter who's bowling against him. He knows he's got iron nerves and a wrist of steel, and he knows that the honour of the side depends on him. You couldn't get past his defence with a cannon-ball."

"But surely, uncle, he can be made to see that there may be two sides to a case? I've never known him do anything unkind in my life."

Uncle Stephen drew back and locked at me meditatively, as though brooding upon the advisability of a confidence. I pressed my point.

"Have you?"

Uncle Stephen coughed, and looked round the little restaurant. The few stray customers were immersed in newspapers. Speaking in a lower voice, he replied:

"I believe I gave you a tip once, that your mother—drank a bit, eh?"

"Yes."

"He took her from the sunshine of Spain and Chile, and brought her into this filthy climate. She was twenty-four, a beautiful girl—more beautiful than Laura. He took her to the pub in Camden Town. She loved him, but she hated the country. Above all he hated the climate. The fogs, and the wet, and the dulness, and the cold got on her nerves. She put up with it for years, till you and Laura were no longer babies. She was always imploring that you should all go back to Spain or South America. She didn't care which—anywhere where there was sunshine. But your father would not. He was not rude about it He simply laughed and shook his head. No; his business was here, and she was his wife. Do you see? He could not see that there were two sides to the case. Then gradually she began to drink. It was very accessible. Probably it warmed her, or helped to conjure up visions of the land she was craving for. He did not notice it at first, but after a time no one could help noticing it. She nipped secretly all day. Once he found her dead-drunk in—the parlour I think it was. He was furious. He did not see how it had come about. He simply ordered her not to drink again. She was his wife. It wasn't the way to behave. He didn't conduct his house on those lines. The reputation of his well-conducted house would be ruined. But you know what it is, boy, when people once get the craving. She got it outside. She got it by all manner of means. She drank more than ever. They quarrelled incessantly. Once she was picked up in the street at the comer of your road. The weaker her character got, the stronger and sterner he became. He could simply see nothing except that she was his wife he was anxious to love and support, and she was behaving dishonourably. One day he found her in one of the rooms in the arms of a fellow-countryman. Tour father thrashed the man, and turned your mother put into the streets. You ask me whether he ever did an unkind action? ... I tell you he's a very strange man, boy."

"But what became of mother?"

"She died in Paris. I don't know the circumstances. I know it nearly broke his heart. He adored her, really. He's a strange man. I tell you he has a heart of gold, but everyone has got to play the game according to his rules."

V

I was already late for my appointment with Laura, but I did not feel eager to go. I had certainly nothing very helpful to lay before her. I lighted a cigarette and tried to appear as tranquil as I could. I said:

"Thank you very much, uncle."

He laughed. "You might just as well say, 'Curse you, uncle.' It's not a very pretty story, is it, Tom?"

"I would rather know the truth, anyway. It's good of you to have told me."

Uncle Stephen continued his ruminations.

"He's the strangest card I ever met. I found out when we were boys that he was too strong for me. He has his rules and principles and nothing else simply counts. He won't concede an inch. They are not always reasonable, but he thinks they're the most important thing in the world. Money! . . . Have you any idea how much money he has?"

"Not the slightest. He told me once we were hard up. It was just after I left school. He said a partner had let him in, or something."

"That was true to an extent. But it was only a small amount He's certainly one of the richest men in Camden Town. He could buy them all up. He's a hard-dealing man. He's kind to the people he loves, but he must keep the control in his own hands. All the money he's made he's made by hard work and fair dealing, and he believes that everyone else ought to do the same. He could easily have afforded to send you to college, or abroad to study, or have put you into one of the big professions. We argued about it. But no. The boy must make his own way, as he had. I knew the kind of lad you were, and that was why I pitched up that yarn about 'Baionnette' winning the race."

"What!" I exclaimed. "Do you mean that it wasn't true?"

"It was true that 'Baionnette' won, and that I won a couple of fivers."

"Uncle! You ought not to have done that!"

"It was touch-and-go. I waited till you were over age. I thought there might be an infernal row about it. We were, I know, all on the edge of a volcano. It was Laura who put the lid on it. When he saw that she meant to take the money whether he liked it or not, he compromised with himself, I should think for the first time in his life. But he has never quite forgiven me."

"I wonder ... if he gave in to Laura on that occasion when he saw that she did not mean to give way—perhaps he would on this."

"There's no comparison at all. After all, the money was not dishonestly come by. There was no disgrace about it. It was a fair win and a fair gift. It was only that he was superstitious about it, don't you see? He kept on saying, 'No good comes of it.' But this affair! . . . Mind you, I'm not criticising. But however you like to explain it away, you can't get away from the fact that Laura gave herself to this man when she was already a married woman. It was adultery. He turned his wife out of the house for much less reason. I'm sorry, old boy, but I simply wouldn't have the pluck to go and tackle him about it I know him too well."

"Well, uncle, I'm very grateful to you. I must be going."

I found Laura in one of our show-rooms. She was in a very bad temper.

"You said you'd be here at half -past two, Tom."

"Sorry, old girl; I've been kept by a business engagement. Let me show you round."

But Laura's interest in our new premises was extremely apathetic. She said she felt tired and had a headache. She wanted to sit on one of the comfortable Chesterfields. We sat in silence for some moments. Then I said:

"I'm afraid it's going to be difficult—this business with dad."

Laura scowled at me. Then she said fiercely:

"Do you think I care—whether the old fool wants to see me or not?"

I looked at her and answered quietly:

"Yes, I think you do."

And then, of course, she cried.

Jevons thrust his head outside the door of the inner office. He did not notice Laura. He called out to me:

"We've got that Wychley Court job, Tom"

CHAPTER XVII

ADEQUATE ENCOURAGEMENT

The occupants of Wychley Court were most delightful and sympathetic people. Jevons and I had been introduced to them by Lady Stourport. They consisted of Mr. and Mrs. Waynesfoote and their daughter Stella. Mr. Waynesfoote was a courtly old gentleman with charming manners. He had been in the diplomatic service, had owned newspapers, and written books on sub-tropical fauna. He was deaf in one ear and he had a habit of holding his hand cup-shaped at the back of his other ear, and leaning forward and saying:

"Really! Now that's most interesting!" Quite ordinary remarks appeared to impress him as being profound revelations. In spite of his deafness, he was the best listener I have ever met. He wanted to know everything, and he never forgot anything you told him. At our very first interview he was not content only to discuss the alterations he proposed to have at Wychley Court, but he wanted to know all about myself, my life, my work, my moral and spiritual outlook. He was a far more intellectual man than I, but he had that genius of suggesting that it was just the other way about. He would ask me my opinion as though it was a matter of the utmost importance to him. He must have been a good diplomat, for he always made me give myself away. I simply rattled on to him like a babbling child. After our second interview he invited me down to spend the week-end. Mrs. Waynesfoote was one of those compact, grey-eyed New England women, who had lived in this country since the day of her wedding—twenty-eight years ago—but still retained the strong characteristics of her race. Stella was something of a contrast to her parents . . . unexpected. Fair, jolly, and on the surface rather a tomboy. Always dressing up, and wearing striking effects. Even her face and hair were not, I suspected, free from artificial attention. But you felt that all this was not vanity, but just the joy and fun of doing it. She loved an effect, and dancing, and the friction of social life. She inherited the parents' keen interest in everything and everyone. The very first time I went there I felt that they were old friends. Before I had known them a month Mrs. Waynesfoote asked me to bring Madeline down. We went, and the visit was an unqualified success. Madeline said afterwards that she had never been asked so many questions in her life. And she did not require any encouragement. She prattled on quite unselfconsciously. They were all very amused with her. Mr. Waynesfoote listened to her opinions with the same rapt attention he had paid to mine. She had never been to such a beautiful and luxurious house, and she did not hesitate to say so, or to go around and examine everything in detail. She and Stella became fast friends. The friendship came at an opportune time, for Madeline was feeling the loss of Elspeth and Dolly Maguire, who had gone back to Canada. Stella must have been ten or eleven years older than Madeline, so that they could not have been quite as intimate as the Maguire children, but she was extremely kind. When they were in town Stella visited us in St. John's Wood, and sometimes she took Madeline for a run in the car to Roehampton, or Hurlingham, or Henley.

Laura and Henri had gone back to France. The breach with father was never healed. It was I who eventually had to go and plead, and then for the first time in my life I beheld an aspect of him which during all these years I had never suspected. Uncle Stephen was right. He was absolutely immovable—almost brutal to me. He accused me of conniving at vice, of condoning my sister's unchastity. He said that on the occasion of that interview when I had hinted at what had happened, he was simply ashamed of me. He would have been prouder if I'd gone to France and "thrashed that blackguardly marquis to a jelly." He said he didn't know what was going to happen to this country. All the young people seemed to have no honour, no morals, no religion. I made a final plea that perhaps we had charity. He fumed at me.

"I have charity too—for the poor and weak, but I should be ashamed to use it as a cloak to licentiousness. If we are to have charity for every vice—by God! what will happen to this country? I couldn't flee why he wanted to keep on talking about "the country." I wanted to say I didn't give a damn about the country; I was concerned with Laura. And then I flaw that this would be weak. It was true, father believed implicitly in the country. He was a staunch patriot. He believed in England, the

Church, the King, honour, and the licensing trade. I could do nothing with him. Our two points of view were irreconcilable. And I felt that mine was the weaker case. It was nebulous, difficult to explain, and it had no figure-heads. I could have talked till Doomsday without convincing him one iota. And afterwards I could not help being impressed by the spectacle of a man sacrificing someone he loved dearly for a principle. I was not myself capable of such an exalted attitude. To me love always comes first.

II

As was to be expected, the idea of sharing a furnished house in Cornwall with Laura and Henri for the summer holidays did not materialise. They were staying at their chateau on the Loire, near Amboise, and they invited us to go over and stay with them; but I did not feel at that time that I could leave the business for so long, as Jevons had been ill and had had to go away for a complete rest. Neither did I feel eager to let Madeline go alone. Somehow I had got a little out of touch with Laura, and I did not know Henri sufficiently well. I could form no idea of the kind of life they lived, or of the kind of people they entertained. Madeline was very precious to me. I wanted her to have a good change, but I wanted her to be easily accessible. I explained all this one day to Mr. Waynesfoote, and the following day I had a letter from Mrs. Waynesfoote inviting Madeline to stay with them at their country house on the Sussex downs for August, and inviting me to go for as long and as often as I could. I hoped they did not think I had fished for this invitation, but it was very acceptable. The Waynesfootes were becoming more and more intimate. They were so easy to get on with. In spite of some aristocratic streak in the family, there was no fuss or side. Probably Mrs. Waynesfoote had brought a bold streak of democratic unconventionality into a life which might easily have become stereotyped. In the country they were at their best. They wore shabby old clothes, although Stella always managed to make herself arresting, with vari-coloured jumpers, bright plaids, and daring scarves. She was a fine horsewoman, and Madeline, to her delight, was taught to ride. I went down for sundry week-ends, and in September managed to stay for a whole week. Madeline eventually stayed on till the school re-opened in the third week in September.

There was a continuous house-party. The people we met there were as removed from the Woodstack people as Woodstack was from "The Duchess of Pless." It was a different world from any I had been used to. There were members of Parliament, knights of industry and science, people eminent in the arts. But they were not invited for their reputations but because the Waynesfootes liked them. They were not tuft-hunters, neither was there any attempt to accentuate social distinctions. I sometimes wondered what some of these people would have thought if they had known that my father was a Camden Town publican. I blush to say that I had not even informed the Waynesfootes themselves of this fact. I have no excuse to offer. It was just the inner streak of snobbery which we nearly all possess in some form or another. I had never given Madeline any advice about the matter, but I am quite sure that she avoided the subject also. I wore my dinner jacket, and sat on the terrace, sipping coffee, and talking to some woman who had never ridden in a public conveyance, or done up one of her own frocks in her life, and we talked quite familiarly about Villon, or George Moore, or the diseases of dogs, or the ideal way to run a state; and I thought to myself:

"It's a queer world!"

I confess that I easily fell a victim to the narcotic of these social nuances. I suppose, as Radic said, I "went down the sink." But what is man if not a social being? And if so, why not do it as well as possible? It is in the social hour that man surveys his story. It is the moment of his triumph. Outside the beasts are still fighting in the wood, the stubborn roots of trees are struggling in the ground, the rocks are wasting against the pressure of the wind . . . . everything that he has sprung from. Within, cunning lights reveal the rich display of his imagination, materials of fine texture and design, things old and nobly wrought . . . . all that he has wrung from the cold heart of Nature, the story of his day. Above all . . . . those others whom he needs with a passionate insistence—their eyes seeking his. Lively thinking, the little corridors to high adventure, leading hither and thither. The eternal experiment, with his mind crystal-clear reading the portents. A rower cannot see the beauty of the river or realise the distance he has coma It is only when he rests upon his oars or glides between the reeds, and sees the martins swing above the willow-herb ... it is all clear then; the distance, the colour, the majesty of changing life, the significance of his place in it.

Heigho! I suppose I was changing, too.

I was becoming a comparatively successful man, hardening, developing a material crust. The impetus to being "a successful man in myself" was slackening, or being modified by insufficient support I was content to follow behind Madeline, learning from her, watching the white ribbon of the road ahead.

III

One day in the autumn I was sent for to go and see my father. I found him only partly conscious. He was lying on his back in bed, and his face was quite yellow. Stepmother and a nurse were hovering about the room. He pressed my hand and said:

"Tom . . . they've got me." And then he mumbled something of which I only caught the word "kidneys."

I turned away to the nurse. "Do you mean to say?" I gasped.

She nodded her head, and whispered, "It's very serious."

I was terribly alarmed. I waited for the visit of the doctor, and he gave me no hope at all. I wandered about the house disconsolately, I could not believe it. The only permanent comer in the universe suddenly brought face to face with dissolution. My father would die, and this house, sacred to the thousand memories of our united lives, would crumble and pass away. Here was the spot where Laura and I did Hubert and Arthur, and she had caught my eye, and laughed. . . . Here, probably, mother used to sit, and watch the rain splashing down in the dull streets, dreaming of Spain. The dark passage and the print of Queen Victoria, the comer where I used to climb up on the steps and look into the private bar. Why must all these things be so vivid? I went into the bar, and spoke to Mrs. Beddoes. How sordid and dreary it all seemed. Probably, coming fresh from Wychley Court helped to emphasise the gaping ugliness. How could I have ever found pleasure in this atmosphere? A few dingy men were huddled together in the public bar, the private was deserted, but a fat old man was seated in a comer of the saloon, apparently asleep. Mrs. Beddoes was whispering to a barmaid. "Poor old fellow!" I heard her say, but the eyes of both of them were bright, not with grief, but with that kind of excitement which a death or a funeral always excites among certain people.

I had never thought of my father dying. He was not the kind to die. He loved life. It was all such a simple process to him. Why couldn't he be allowed to live—laughing, and joking, polishing his brown boots, and doing things properly? They would talk of him in years to come—"Old Purbeck's Paradise"—a queer old crank—but they would never know the secrets of his heart. They would never know that he gave up the two people he loved most dearly for a principle. Strong and incorruptible, imaginative and narrow-minded, kind but unduly cautious, passionate but self-centred—if it hadn't been all so simple to him!

I hung about "The Duchess of Pless" for ten days, going in two or three times a day from our place of business. On several occasions I met Uncle Stephen, and he was a great help and comfort the first time I met him there, he said:

"Well, boy, it's no good pretending. They've got through his defence at last He may keep up his wicket for an over or two, but he won't score any more runs."

I think this brought home the inevitable to me more than any other statement. The whole thing became a dream. Curious people appeared and vanished. Stepmother, who would not leave the room, and would not weep. Doctors, and specialists, and business friends, a succession of nurses. Upstairs the ever-present tragedy, downstairs the eternal drone of the bars and the popping of corks. There seemed to be a kind of conspiracy that, whatever happened, this must not stop. The gods demanded this accompaniment to the rendering of their elegiac. The dream was dominated by the personality of Uncle Stephen darting hither and thither, keeping people on the move, and being sensible. His dark moustache appeared more obviously dyed than ever, as his face appeared bony and lined and hollow, and the short hair on his temple had become quite white. He seemed to be living up to the formula:

"Back your fancy. If you lose, don't grouse or kick. Sport is the best school."

On the tenth evening I was alone with my father. I did not know whether he was conscious or not. Suddenly he looked at ma

"Tom!"

"Yes, dad?"

He did not speak for some minutes. He seemed to be pulling himself together for a great effort Then he said:

"Tom . . . what really happens when you die?"

I was taken at a complete disadvantage. I never felt more fully the inadequacy of my own convictions. I stammered and muttered:

"Oh, I—I expect it's all right, dad."

"Yee; but what really happens?"

I was amazed. He was afraid of death. This strong man of iron principles and religious faith was suddenly become a child afraid of the dark.

"You go on ... I expect."

"Yes . . . but the people we love? . . ."

I leant over him. It was an opportunity I had been seeking.

"Dad! do you hear me? . . . Laura is back in town. Laura is here—only ten minutes away. Do you hear me, dad?"

I do not know whether he heard me or not. I fancy not. His eyes were closed, and his face was set in that mask-like pose of absolute concentration which only the dying possess. I repeated my statement, but he gave no sign. He appeared to be absorbed in this new problem which has disturbed the imagination from time immemorial. The minutes ticked away. Once he sighed. It must have been a quarter of an hour before he showed a disposition to speak again. Then he muttered something I could not hear. I put my ear close to his mouth.

"Yes, dad?"

"They ought not . . . tell Mrs. B. . . . ought not decant . . . that stuff from . . . wass name . . . people in Leadenhall . . . not before June . . . end of May . . ."

Those were the last words my father spoke. He died at five o'clock the next morning.

IV

Stella married me three months later. It was her suggestion. At least, I have always contended. What would you do if you had a letter like the following? It came soon after she had been spending a week with us:

"My Lord and Master,

"In the first place, perhaps, I ought to thank you for your hospitality. Well, then, it was very nice indeed. There, is that restrained enough for you? Father has given me a perfect duck of a shawl, an old Paisley. I believe even you will have to do more than grunt when you see it. You are always accusing me of thinking too much about the body. But what would you? You have to think about it to get the utmost out of it. The soul is a self-supporting article, a kind of hardy perennial. But, oh, my lord, the body withers and withers. Argh! The great secret is to be always looking ahead, so that you are not taken by surprise. I have already thought about what I'm going to wear when I'm a very old lady with snow-white hair in little festoons of curls. I shall wear a black frock with tiny lace ruffes, that old brooch of Whitby jet and moonstones that used to belong to Aunt Alice and—this shawl. Do you think you will know rue then? Forlorn youth, your mournful face haunts mi. With adequate encouragement I could iron out every wrinkle and frown. Madeline is an angel. You must think of her—I know you do! but even a teeny-weeny bit more.

"Your friend,

"Stella."

When I read the letter through I turned it over and smiled. I was about to take up a pen and reply in a similar strain. Then I thought to myself:

"No; this is too important. I cannot be flippant in such a case."

I put it in my pocket, and all night long and the next day I thought about it intermittently. About four o'clock in the afternoon I got into a fever of restlessness, I prayed for the wings of Mercury, but failing them I commandeered an old car which our firm used for odd jobs and a young chauffeur who also did stencilling, and I winged .my way out of London in the direction of Wychley Court. I found Stella in a greenhouse, potting bulbs. She was wearing an overall, and she dropped a trowel at sight of me.

"Good gracious! What have you come for?"

"I've come in answer to your proposal of marriage."

"My—what?'

"I've given the matter every consideration, and taking into account all the circumstances of the case, I cannot exactly see my way to refuse."

"You are the most insolent villain I have ever met. Go, before I scream for my father to come and horsewhip you."

"In other words, I've come to give you adequate encouragement."

"You wretch I You take advantage of my kindness. Because I offered to remove the wrinkles, you . . . Oh, Tom, no! No violence . . . no, not again. You are hurting me!"

Panting against the wall, her face all flushed, she gasped:

"I don't suppose you have even asked your daughter's consent?"

"She is bound to give it me. We will go together on our knees."

"I have nothing to beg for. Now, do be sensible."

A long interval devoted to action.

"How old are you, Sir Launcelot?"

"I've reached the romantic age of forty-two."

"Then I ought to be half that, plus seven. H'm. It's very curious. It's very awkward. I'm exactly twenty-seven. I'm a year too young."

"We will have a six-months' honeymoon. That will make you half a year older, and me half a year younger."

"I never thought you could be so ridiculous. Oh, dear! I wish I was dressed for the part! Fancy being proposed to in this old overall!"

"Stella, I know I'm a middle-aged old fool. I've no right to do this. You know all about me. I'm lonely, dear. Forlorn, as you say. I suppose it's madness of me, but I want you so much. You know, don't you? I can't keep on being flippant. Tell me. Tell me what I want to know."

She did not answer, but she held out her arms.

When I arrived home that night, I went in very sheepishly to see Madeline. I blurted out my confession, without preliminary. For a moment I thought tears hovered in her eyes. Then she kissed me, and said quietly:

"You are a funny old thing, daddy."

Someone else had called me that.

V

Mellow days in Bellagio. Moonlight nights among the cypresses. Idling on the lake, listening to the Campanello. Is it possible that twice in one's life one may attain complete happiness in that way? I don't know. More mature, perhaps. Different. Everything changes. We talked often and quite simply about Mary. Stella never showed any resentment or jealousy. The great thing is to love—while you can, life is an inexhaustible storehouse of riches. We go on and on discovering them. Sometimes they appear fixed and essential, then one after another they pass away. I accepted Stella as she came to me, as a goddess satisfying every physical and spiritual desire. Our emotions obeyed a unifying demand. Our minds, in all the little mysteries of taste and inclination, dovetailed with a fine adjustment I never asked her if she had loved before, but one night she told me she had had "a terrible affair" when she was twenty-two. A married man, older than herself. Fond of his wife but a union without real passion. "It was perfectly awful, dear. We used to meet ... we loved each other desperately, and we both liked the wife. It seemed so mean. It went on and on. We simply could not let each other go. I believe I—I would have gone away with him. He wanted me to. It was only the thought of father and mother, I think, which kept me from doing it. . . . Oh, my dear, I'm so Happy now to think I didn't—

"Is it all now dead to you?"

"No, not dead. But something which has passed by on the other side. It was a foregathering, perhaps, of all these forces which I feel now. You are the realisation. I know now that I have waited for you."

I pressed her to me. A strange mood crept over me. I wanted to say:

"I don't know. I'm a queer old card. Love comes easily to me. You darling angel, you hold me in the hollow of your palm. But my position is unusual While you hold me like this I am a complete and splendid entity. The world can give me nothing more. But if you were to die—I am hardened to the thought, you see—if I were endowed with some abnormal powers of life—just this life—I believe I could love a thousand women, and each one reverently, passionately, finely—as I love you. Memory fades. Bodily desires are a quicksand, where no trace is left"

I did not say this, but in the darkness she seemed to divine something of my thoughts. She suddenly whispered:

"Do you think, when people love each other like we do, that they are united for ever and ever?"

"No. All this life, and perhaps not beyond, but not for ever. Nothing lasts for ever. Everything changes."

Her cheeks were wet. "It's beastly cruel," she said.

"No. It only seems cruel to us at this moment. It wouldn't be like you think—an awful parting—but . . . somehow different. I hate these people who call themselves spiritualists, who mess about with tables and messages and try to pierce the veil. They are simply fidgets. They have no pride. A man's business concerns his own soul and nothing else at all. . . . Stella, you must not cry."

"Was I crying? ... I don't know why, dear. Kiss me again. Hold me close to you."

CHAPTER XVIII

THE RABBIT

We did not stay away for six months as I had suggested. There was too much to do, and Madeline could not be left. There is, indeed, something extremely primitive in the idea of a honeymoon. A period set apart for the more obvious delights of married life, and for nothing else at all. So obvious that, although it has the sanction of the Church and the State, and the blessings (accompanied by slightly amused benedictions) of friends and relatives, the two victims, blushing from the very precise obligations put upon them in the Church service, feel it necessary to go away and hide. If they have the misfortune to encounter friends on this adventure there passes between them an exchange of knowing glances which makes the position almost intolerable

We stayed three weeks at Bellagio, and a week at Como. Then we. took a flying visit to Genoa, and returned home through Paris. At Paris we stayed for five days with Laura and Henri, in their fine house on the Champs Elysees. The visit was very enlightening to me in several respects. I found that Laura and Henri were leading quite detached lives, although still very devoted to each other. Henri spent most of the day in his laboratory, or at one of the colleges where he was lecturing; Laura was living the life of a Parisian society woman. She had practically given up the violin. Shortly after their visit to us, she had again given a series of recitals, but they had not been a success. Her playing had deteriorated, and her reputation had not been enhanced by the notorious vicissitudes of her career. The only thing that had come of it had been an offer by a music-hall manager to play in a sketch specially written for her. He offered her a princely salary. There were to be coloured lights, and gorgeous frocks, and the incident of burning a violin. There was also to be a murder in it. Laura was to play under the name of "The beautiful Marquise de Thor Bohunville." Henri was, naturally, very opposed to the idea, and eventually it fell through. Laura returned to Paris, and easily drifted into Sie conventional routine of a social life. During the five days we spent there it was easy to gauge the position. Laura never appeared till lunch-time, and then she was pale and irritable. At that time she was forty-five, but she might have been considerably more. In the afternoon she would sometimes drive, but more frequently retire for further rest. At afternoon tea she would appear in a dazzling rest-gown and regale us with some of her social exploits. But it was not till the evening that she appeared to revive completely. In her evening frock, and the artificial light, aided by the professional skill of an experienced maid, she was again a beautiful woman in the very prime of life. She overpowered Stella with affection and flattery. Every night we were bidden to a series of functions. Sometimes we dined at home, sometimes elsewhere, but there always followed a theatre, a reception, or a ball, and not infrequently the whole lot Henri dined with us, but he did not accompany us on these expeditions. He went to bed soon after ten. Stella rose to these attractions with alacrity. Great fun I She wasn't going to let these Parisians outshine her. She would show them that she, too, knew how to carry a frock. She said that she thought that Madame la Marquise was one of the most fascinating people she had ever met. It was impossible to keep track of Laura's friends. We met hundreds in those few days—deputies, scientists, merchants, and actors. Many we absolutely disliked. Others were quite charming. We rushed hither and thither.

Henri would be about when I came down to my English breakfast at nine o'clock. He had already been for a ride. He was about to go into the laboratory. He would look at me with his deep, reflective eyes, and say:

"Good morning. Mister Tom. You enjoying your visit, yes?"

I would reply that we were having a great time. And he would nod sagely, and add:

"For a little while, yes. But one cannot live at both ends of the candle. I fear you will think me a boor. I neglect my guests disgracefully. Fortunately, my wife is a good hostess, eh? I have an important paper I am preparing for the institute. But please come into the laboratory and see me, whenever you feel so disposed."

I thanked him profusely. I only once, however, penetrated into this sanctum. On this occasion Henri was very charming to me, but I realised that I was obviously holding up his work. He had two assistants, and they were all working together, checking some figures. He immediately suspended operations, and gave the impression that he was prepared to entertain me as long as I could stop. I could not, however, take advantage of this, and after a few brief generalities I left him. Stella and I spent most of the day alone, and naturally we thoroughly enjoyed the experience. We visited the picture galleries and museums, the bookstalls on the banks of the river and the pig-fair in Montmartre. In the evening we placed ourselves in Laura's hands.

II

As we were returning home after our fourth evening's dissipation Stella whispered to me:

"I'm glad we're going home to-morrow, dear. I've had just enough."

It was not, however, till we were in the boat train on the way to Dieppe that she said suddenly:

"Tom, I wonder whether you will forgive me?"

"I'll make a bold try."

"You know, I think your sister's a very fascinating person, but . . . there's something about her I don't quite like. I don't feel that I really know her."

"She's a funny old fish. I wish you'd known her twenty years ago."

"I'm sure she must have been ripping. Why is it?"

"Why is what?"

"The change. She's altered, hasn't she?"

"Yes, I'm afraid she has. I don't know. It's all very difficult and involved."

"He seems such a ripping person. So simple and sane."

"I know. I hoped it might make all the difference. It's difficult to know the root of causes. She married a rotter at first, but when she was married to him she seemed to have more hope . . . more ideals. Now that she's married to a really decent chap she seems to have gone to pieces."

"Perhaps it all started earlier than either."

Queer! At that moment I suddenly remembered my father's exclamation: "I wish I had never sent her to that Royal Academy." Absurd! As though a musical career should seriously injure one! Some musicians have been quite nice people. There must have come some moment . . . possibly a perverted ambition. No, it must have started earlier than the Royal Academy. Stella's indictment worried me. I knew it was true, but I had never acknowledged it to myself. Laura had always been difficult, but never . . . quite like this.

"I have an idea," I said abruptly. "She was very upset about our old man ... I told you, I think, he disowned her on account of this affair with Henri. They lived together before they were married. He never forgave her. Laura never speaks of it."

"But, my dear, it seems so . . . unreasonable on both sides."

"It is. When you get two people like father and Laura pulling different ways, it's like the irresistible force meeting the immovable mass."

"And you?"

"I was the kind of go-between. I nearly got squashed between them. On the whole, I think father was the more to blame. A girl with a temperament like Laura's can't be driven. She has to be humoured and managed. She's partly angel and partly Bengal tigress. She rushes to extremes. Father never had the imagination. He never began to understand her. His first mistake was—"

"Yes?"

"When he married our mother. I can see it all now. He fell in love with her—a pretty, dark, Spanish thing. He never had the imagination to see that she was different from him. She was his wife. He bore her off like a dog with a bone. She had to conform to the code of Camden Town or die. Oh, God, isn't it awful! Every trouble in the world is caused by this—this lack of imagination. People go to war because they can't believe that the other fellow has a case. They can't put themselves in his place."

"It must have been rotten for you, Tom."

"It has been rotten. They are both so fine in their way—they both have sterling, fine qualities. And perhaps the greatest tragedy is—they loved each other. And yet when father died, he deliberately ignored Laura in his will. He left quite a lot of money, over twenty thousand pounds. It was all left in trust for stepmother, and afterwards it goes to me and Madeline. Of course, if Laura had not been well off, I should have insisted on it going to her. . . . Lord!"

"What are you thinking of, Tom?"

"I was thinking of that dingy little pub upsetting the palace on the Champs Elysees ... of the far-reaching ravages of—unimaginativeness. Of Henri, sitting there among his bottles . . . thinking, thinking, thinking . . ."

"Don't you think Henri might do more? Why doesn't he try to save her?"

"Can't you see he has tried? Can't you tell by his eyes? The man has suffered agonies. He is like a man preoccupied with a problem, the solution of which he knows will come ... too late."

III

We established ourselves in the country, Stella, Madeline, and I. We found a small Georgian house two miles from Wychley Court. In addition to this we had a tiny flat at Chelsea. Madeline had now left school. She suddenly expressed a desire to take a science course at Cambridge, whither two girl friends of hers were going. I was a little doubtful at first whether this desire was genuine, or whether she felt that her place in my household had been usurped by another. However, she seemed so keen, and she always got on so amicably with Stella, that I decided to let her go. We all settled down to our various activities. Jevons was pleased to see me back, but he said he could never forgive me for my effrontery in marrying one of "our customers." I retorted that I had merely done it for his benefit—to raise the status of the firm. I advised him to do likewise, only to choose one who was very rich. Her appearance and intelligence need not be of any great consequence. Then, to my consternation, I found that my poor old Jevons was in great trouble. He was almost serious when he rallied me about marrying Stella.

"All right for you, old chap. It came over me, a sudden mood, just after you got engaged. I'm not that sort of person, but I got thinking about things—lonely, bored with the whole bally business. What's the good of making money when you've no one . . . I've never had women fall in love with me. Not much. But she kept looking at me, as I passed through the cretonne department. It suddenly dawned on me one morning. Soho Square looked quite gay. I saw her going in—"

"Who on earth are you talking about?"

"Miss Horlock."

"That little girl who serves the chintzes and things?"

"Yes. The thing suddenly got me. Mad. I believed I was in love with her. I kept her behind one night when everyone had gone. I kissed her."

"The devil you did I"

"Then, of course, it was all U.P. She seemed very sophisticated for her age. The whole thing was her idea."

"What was the idea?"

"We went away together for a week-end, to Felixstowe."

"To—where?"

"To Felixstowe. What the devil does it matter where it was? The whole thing was detestable. I was hating myself like fun."

Alas, poor Jevons! No friendly odd socks to save his soul!

"And now do you see what it all means?"

"We must get rid of her gracefully and generously."

"No; it can't be done. She wants to marry me. She means to marry me. Otherwise it will ruin the firm. Can't you see?"

"My dear old chap! That's nonsense. Are you at all in love with her?"

"No. It was just a passing madness. But it was two months ago. She's holding out veiled threats already. There's trouble in the offing. I've never done such a thing in my life before."

"I won't have you marry a girl you don't love, and ruin your whole life, and hers. The firm must take its chance."

"It's decent of you, old chap. But I'm afraid I'll have to."

I could see exactly how it had come about. I was annoyed with Jevons, but I was certainly not the one to throw stones. Felixstowe had all but been my undoing. But the girl? I sent for her the next morning. She was a pretty, warm-coloured little thing, quite unlike Anna. I was quite sure that she had never saved up her lips for anyone. She looked at me obliquely and suspiciously. I remarked casually:

"Oh, Miss Horlock, we are rearranging the soft goods department. I'm afraid that after next week we shall not be able to continue to—avail ourselves of your services."

She stared at me defiantly. Her lips quivered. I turned away as though the matter was at an end. Suddenly she blurted out:

"He's put you up to this."

"What do you mean?"

"He thinks he's going to get rid of me in this way. The coward!"

"Whom do you mean?"

"You know quite well, sir—Mr. Jevons."

Then she began to cry. 'I'm going to have a baby, too. . . . His!"

My attitude of the stem director of a successful firm all went to pieces. I said:

"Oh, no, no, don't cry! I must speak to Mr. Jevons about this. All right. Miss Horlock. Now run along home and don't worry."

To Jevons I said:

"When I look at you, old chap, I am torn between two conflicting emotions. In the first place, what is going to happen to the country if you go on like this? Blast you! Have you no sense of honour, no sense of morality? On the other hand, who am I, to judge? I, to whom love and good fortune have always come like a natural birthright? On one side we have nature and patriotism, on the other, humanity and pity. I have always contended that patriotism is wrong because it has nothing to commend it except naturalness. It is an exclusive, uncharitable, narrow-minded, short-sighted, bigoted thing."

"All this hot-air talk is all right," interjected Jevons. "But the point is—what are we going to do?"

"Give me a night to think it over."

The fact was, I realised that there was only one thing to do—to tell Stella all about it I told her all about it in the dark. It was more comfortable. When I had finished, she said:

"How long ago was it?"

"About two months."

"H'm. How disgusting! In any case, I should think it was rather soon to be certain. Let's hope she's made a mistake."

Oh, this modem generation! What would father have said?

IV

Among other work we had on at that time was the doing up of the house in Curzon Street belonging to the Marquis de Thor Bohunville. Laura had given me most precise instructions. She and the marquis were coming to London for the season in May. I kept Jevons very busy. Fortified by my wife's admonitions, I said to him:

"We can't sack Miss Horlock. But we'll wait and see what develops. If what she says is true, we shall have to see her through her troubles. But the idea of your marrying her is ridiculous. It isn't only you you've got to think about. She would be bored to tears with you in no time."

"Yes, but what about the kid? If it grows up . . . always the stigma."

"Look here, Jevons, I don't see why two people should live utterly miserable lives just to satisfy a public craving for convention. Perhaps by the time the kid grows up the status of illegitimacy will have been raised. Why, Leonardo da Vinci."

"Oh, I've heard all about Leonardo da Vinci. He didn't live at Surbiton."

"Well, what about that estimate from Weils & Scholtz? Shall I ring them up, or will you?"

Jevons required a lot of bustling. Over business matters he sometimes appeared to me to be almost unscrupulous, but over this affair his conscience was jagging him mercilessly. We all have our kinks of virtue.

At that time I had a letter from Madeline:

"Dear old Daddy,

"It is simply ripping here. Adela Shaw, Polly, and I have just come in from a long run on a car belonging to Dr. Parsons. I am taking up physics and moral philosophy. Joppleson, our physics master, is a perfect dear. We call him 'Pea-nuts.' Only because he is a vegetarian, I think, and boils and drinks hot water during a lecture. His inside is all wrong, but he has a lovely mind. Makes everything seem big. Do you know what I mean? I have joined the hockey club. I am pretty good at it, I think. Anyway, it keeps my inside all right. By inverse ratio I expect I have a nasty mind, and make everything seem teeny-weeny. It is a jolly life, so much going on. Some of the girls are awful cats, but most of them are ripping. My love to you both.

"Yr. affect
"MADELINE."

Bless her! Moral philosophy! Hockey! People's insides! I am miles behind her. I can only just see her over the ridge. If we could only get Madeline's advice about this affair, she would be able to tell us all about it. I have an idea that she could write a quite closely-reasoned and dispassionate essay on "The Future Status of Illegitimacy." But I can't ask her, because she is the other side of the ridge. It is in her hands, however, and the hands of her babies, that the fate of Milly Horlock's baby lies.

I had the good fortune, a few days later, of relieving Jevons of, in any case, some of his anxiety. We employed an old porter named Peel, who used to wear a green baize apron and wheel carpets about on a trolley. One day, as I was going through the show-room, I heard him say to another porter:

"'Arry, where's the Rabbit to-day?"

"Dunno. Gorn 'ome sick, I think."

I did not take any notice of this remark, but later in the day I was told that Miss Horlock had telegraphed to say she was too unwell to come to business. Then I suddenly remembered old Peel's question. I began to ponder. After a time I sent for him.

"Peel," I said, "whom do you mean by 'the Rabbit'?"

He grinned.

"Miss Horlock, sir."

"Why do you call her 'the Rabbit'?"

"Oh, I dunno. Everyone does, sir."

"Why?"

He sniggered, and wiped his hands on his apron.

"It's just a nickname, like."

"But every nickname has an origin. Pea-nuts! No, I mean Rabbit—why Rabbit? She doesn't look like a rabbit. I'm only asking out of curiosity."

Old Peel glanced furtively at the door.

"Well, I suppose, quite between ourselves like, sir—you know, they say she's a bit—of course I know nothing. It's only hearsay. But I'm told that any feller—if you know what I mean. She's like that, see?"

"I see. I thought there must be an origin of some sort. Thanks, Ped. Don't let this go any further— that I asked you, I mean."

"That's all right, sir."

I went straight to Jevons.

"Jevons," I said, "I have reason to believe that if that girl has a child the credit is due, not to you, but to some other blackguard."

"What do you mean?"

"That she is in effect what is known as a fairy. She got into trouble. Then she compromised you because she thought that you were better off than any of these other seducers."

"How have you heard all this?"

"I can't tell you, but I believe it is true. If it's true I shouldn't think it would be very difficult to prove. One has only got to probe about and ask a few questions. If she has conspired against us, we have a right to conspire against her. We can even employ private detectives."

"My God! if it's true—I'll chuck her in the street!"

"No, no, Jevons; don't be a fool. You're none the less a criminal because you happen to escape. We are all responsible. The next generation won't think any better of us because we chuck her in the street. Whoever the father is, we must patch her up, and give the kid a chance. No one has ever designed a man. We are all accidents. Let justice be done, though the firm of Jevons & Purbeck fall!"

CHAPTER XIX

THE INSTRUMENT AWAKENED

"You are the Marquis de Thor Bohunville?"

"Yes, monsieur."

"You are a Knight of the Legion of Honour, the holder of many diplomas in various scientific and learned societies, both in France and elsewhere?"

"Yes, monsieur."

The little grey-faced man looked over his spectacles and shuffled with some papers. One felt that he was neither very interested nor very bored; he was just getting on with it.

"You have heard the evidence of the witness Angele Ballonet with regard to the finding of the body?"

"Yes, monsieur."

"And of the Doctors Gascoigne and Waterspon, who have both affirmed that death was due to narcotic poisoning resulting from an overdose of heroin?"

"Yes, monsieur."

"Will you kindly tell us precisely what transpired, as far as you know, on the evening of the twenty-first and on the morning of the twenty-second?"

Henri looked down at his hands, and spoke in a low voice.

"The twenty-first was my wife's birthday. We had a small dinner-party at Curzon Street. Her brother, Mr. Thomas Purbeck, and his wife were there, Mr. Raymond, Sir Theodore Cartmill—about a dozen of us. Quite a merry party. Afterwards my wife and most of the guests went on to the ball at Lady Chamwood's at Bede House. Sir Theodore and I stayed behind. We talked for some time. Sir Theodore left soon after eleven. I went to bed soon after. I arose at seven o'clock on the morning of the twenty-second. I was very occupied all the morning. I had an interview with Mr. Fiennes of the Royal Society. I returned to lunch at one o'clock. My wife had not yet appeared. Angele informed me that she had been in to see her an hour before, and that the Marquise was sleeping soundly. I did not think it advisable to disturb her. We had lunch and I went into my study. At a quarter to four Angele came knocking on my door and screaming, "Monsieur! Monsieur! Vite! Vite!—la Marquise!'

"I hurried up to my wife's room. She was lying perfectly still. Her face was a strange colour. Oh, monsieur, need I—"

"All right, all right; thank you. . . . Now, I understand that you and your wife were in the habit of occupying separate rooms?"

"Yes, monsieur."

"On the evening of the twenty-first you say she was in good spirits?"

"Yes, monsieur."

"Have you knowledge of any trouble or depression that was weighing upon her?"

"No, monsieur."

"Was she normally a woman of cheerful disposition?"

"She was—variable."

"Would you describe your married life as a perfectly happy one?"

"I—I think—I can hardly answer that question, monsieur."

"Monsieur le Marquis, I presume that, being a man immersed in scientific studies, your time was principally occupied in that way?"

"Yes, monsieur."

"Was your wife interested in science?"

"No—not very. Not at all."

"May I ask in what direction her interests lay?"

"She was musical. She had her friends. She entertained."

"At one time she was a professional musician. Isn't that so?"

"Yes, monsieur."

"I suggest from these circumstances that you led rather—shall I say detached lives? You went your way, and she went hers?"

"That is—true."

"Was there any definite estrangement?"

"No, no; none at all. We loved each other."

"You loved each other, and yet you lived detached lives?"

"Yes; it is difficult."

"Now, Monsieur le Marquis, I must ask you—were you aware that your wife was in the habit of taking drugs?"

There was a long pause. The court-house was quite still. Suddenly Henri buried his face in his hands and sobbed:

"Yes . . . yes, I knew. God forgive me!"

II

The grey-faced man scratched indifferently on a piece of parchment and quietly observed the witness until he was more composed.

"How long had this been going on?"

"Oh, for six—seven years, as far as I know."

"What did you do when you first discovered the fact?"

"I did my utmost to dissuade her."

"When you first married her did you suspect then that she had acquired the habit?"

"No, monsieur. I do not think she had. She . . . drank champagne, sometimes more than wisely."

"You were at first, I presume, entirely devoted and attached?"

"Yes."

"When did this spirit of detachment first show itself?"

"It came gradually."

"You do not ascribe it to any special cause?"

"No."

"From whom did your wife obtain these drugs?"

"Latterly—I do not know. At one time there was a man, Rene Salzmann. He supplied her. His body was found in the Seine."

"Who else?"

"I do not know."

"Have you made no effort to find out?"

"Yes. I made great efforts. But what could I do? My wife knew hundreds of people. She was always about. I should have had to keep by her side the whole time, and even then—you did not know her. She would have had her way."

"The Marquise, I understand, came of humble origin; she was a professional musician, and she was also the divorced wife of a London concert agent. She was, I take it, a woman of lower mentality than yourself. You state that even at the end you loved her dearly. Now you, Monsieur le Marquis, are a man of great intellectual attainments, and, I am sure, strength of character. She loved you. The moulding of her character was to an extent in your hands. You had the power to control, to direct, to influence; you—"

It was then that the voice of Henri, playing on a vibrant chord, rang through the court.

"I could teach her everything there is to tell of life, monsieur, except—how to live!"

Those were the last words he uttered in the court He collapsed, and had to be helped away.

III

It may sound incomprehensible, in cold print, when I state that on the night of my sister's funeral I went to a concert. But so it was. Stella and her mother and I dined alone at our flat at Chelsea. It had been raining, and the night was humid. I had no desire for food, and their sympathy for once failed to arouse any response. They had not known Laura as I had known her. Perhaps no one—not even Henri—knew her as I had known her. Suddenly I pushed my plate away and rose.

"Will you forgive me if I go outside?" I said.

They both said, "Of course," and Stella came out into the passage with me.

"The fact is," I whispered, "I must go and hear music."

"Music!"

"Yes, dear. I'm all right. You mustn't worry about me. But I must either hear music or go mad."

"Would you like me to come with you?"

"You'll understand me, won't you?—but I would rather go alone."

Stella held me a long time, and then let me go. I hailed a cab. I was in a fever that there might not be any music on, or that it might not be good. I drove to the Queen's Hall. To my delight I found Sir Henry Wood's orchestra playing. I sat in a dim corner of the gallery, with my hat over my eyes and my collar turned up.

"The charm of London is that no one knows or cares anything about you," I thought. The hall was packed. The same curious, solemn, detached concourse drawn from their innumerable "business and desires," seeking something. We none of us knew each other, none of us cared very much; but we all wanted something . . . terribly. The orchestra began playing, and I looked down. I saw the top of Sir Henry Wood's head, and his arms waving, the sombre, business-like-looking gentlemen drawing their bows, and blowing through long pipes, and beating on drums; the girl at the harp, the red electric light shades . . . the people. I do not know what they played. It did not seem to matter. I was so eager to find what all these other people were seeking.

Something was very solemn and big: a broad theme with a simple line, and then, fluttering round about it, dancing like a will-o'-the-wisp, the intriguing graces of a second theme. It was not what is known as descriptive music. It was just music Just what you and I are . . . what we want. Music analyses nothing and explains everything. It fills up all the crevices, as ether fills up the holes in a bar of steel. I seemed to go right out of myself, and then to come back and find new springs ready to be tapped. Everything receded and came into proportion.

And there, in that prosaic hall, looking down on to the top of Sir Henry Wood's head, I seemed to find Laura. I seemed to know and understand Laura for the first time. Laura and her life.

Is it beauty? Is it honour? Is it happiness? What is it we seek? The bubbles go racing through the wine and vanish. We raise it to our lips. . . .

Through the window we see the yellow leaves of the plane-tree drifting in the autumn breeze. Soon the trees will be stripped and bare. Another will hold this self-same cup, will ask the self-same question: What is it we seek? One after another, things pass away. . . . But there is something there, and we cannot find it

The small, unhappy boy, impatient of his youth—he wants to be a man, or perhaps an engine-driver. He is an engine-driver. Is he satisfied? No, no; the stations and the signals flash by. The day finishes and starts again. He peers ahead, still seeking the elusive answer. Moments come when, blinded by beauty and ecstasy, we think we have found it. But alas! they pass. This is not what we are looking for. These are but pin-pricks in the vast carcase of our being. So we go on, searching, backwards and forwards, up and down. We listen for sounds and portents. We peer into the eyes of our fellows. Do they know? Have they found it? No, no; they are peering into ours for the self-same reason. They cannot find it They, too, are searching and waiting. The priest talks of God, and we nod knowingly. The philosopher repeats something he has read in a book written by a Greek three thousand years ago, and we say: "Yes. Well?" The scientist dissects a beetle, and makes something go faster or slower, and we murmur, "Wonderful, wonderful!" The artist throws the shadows of his various calf-loves on the screen, and we applaud him, because for a moment he diverts us, and gives a vague hope that he may stumble across it. Whatever it is, it must be the most wonderful thing in the world, because it is so intensely believed in. . . .

"We can teach them everything there is to tell of life, except—how to live."

Laura never knew how to live. She never had a chance. Life overwhelmed her. It was unmanageable.

It was all too much and not enough. She believed in this thing profoundly, and if she had found it she would have been a goddess. Possibly father found it, in his way, but he would never have been more than just himself. If you are satisfied with that, you may find it to-morrow. Laura was linked to the movement of the rushing wind and the stars, to the exegesis of these stirring chords, to the visions of Parnassus. This life was but a tiny bit of it all to her. She wanted to crowd it into something even smaller, taste it and throw it away. Music frightened her. It made her see herself as she was—her power and her smallness; the little bit screaming for Olympian interpretation. She never began to understand . . . she sought vicarious substitutes, anything which came most readily to hand. The visions must be sustained.

The seeds of this disruption were probably in her at her birth, the deliberate outcome of our father's obstinacy. But the point of cleavage came when she was living with Edgar Beyfus. When she began to—prostitute her art. From that time on the gods mocked her. She knew she had destroyed the spirit for the letter. She sought the little paraphrases. The big thing passed her by.

IV

A woman came on to the platform to play a piano concerto. I don't know who she was or what the concerto was. She played well, but she had the conscious platform manner. A lot of little things were bothering her. Nerves, ambition, her frock, her friends, the Press, dread of not catching the conductor's beat. Poor wretch! No good while this lasts. We are moving again. Out and about among the rushing torrents of rhythm which make us what we are. Music interprets us. It is nothing to a cow or even to a Chinaman (not this music). It is us. The beat of our heart, the ebb and flow of our story ... all the half-awakened dreams, the best in us, the worst in us. Laura.

The woman is playing well. She has forgotten about her frock and her friends and the Press and her fears. She is with us—leading us forward. She is exultant. Her soul is flooded. We don't exist. I have seen Laura like that. Conscious of her mastery, and yet flooded. The great thing pouring through her. Giving it away and yet with something of herself added. In those days before she began to wear red carnations in her hair. Before the accident to the Guarnerius. Laura, you are intensely with me. All the little episodes of your life stand out clear and vivid. Do you remember how you fought me about the spiders? Do you remember how you came into my room to brush your hair? and your discovery that Evie was a white rabbit? Coming home from the Academy, your cheeks flushed with the damp fog. Zuk. The awakening of formless ambitions. I remember thinking how you were like a musical instrument yourself, something to be played on.

Poor old girl. It has been like that. The world has played upon you, broken the strings, and thrown you away. Is it your fault that you were a musical instrument and not a plough or a sewing-machine? A plough is used, a sewing-machine is worked, but a musical instrument is awakened. It has something of itself to impart. A Strad has a sentient life, alert to the fingers of a master. And yet a Strad is made as the bodies of you and me are made, by a process over which we have no control, and not an ounce of responsibility. These "balanced" people! How easy it all is I Suffering is a science, and living is a trick. You can either do it, or you can't. No one can teach you. You've got to practise it hard by yourself, and be always struggling to "find out things." Even then you may fail.

Old girl, you failed brilliantly. Perhaps that is better than succeeding meanly. You took so much away with you. Even now you are living in all this—the gorgeous colour of this slow movement, leading on and on. . . . They could not rob you of that. All they can do is to tabulate and card-index you. Oh, yes, we know what the little grey-faced man meant. "A professional musician, a divorcee of humble stock, took to drink, and—h'm, yes, very distressing. My dear sir, you, an educated man, why did you indulge in this mésalliance? Lost your head probably, eh? But why did you not keep her in order? Forbid her these things? Point out to her the evil of her ways? You mean to say you were fool enough to make her your wife, and yet you could not teach her how to live! Preposterous! Is there not machinery for every eventuality of this sort? What is going to become of all the automata of State? Where is the power of property? Above all, my dear sir, what do you suppose is going to happen to—the country?"

V

How pitiless is the wind driving through the dark wastes where only water and marsh sustain the torpid protozoa! Pitiless the million, million years. The slow, the almost imperceptible thrust of rocks and reptiles. The barren centuries where nothing lives but cruelty. Darkness, and water, and rushing wind, the slow development of fighting-powers. Claws, and talons, and raging hunger. The birth of poison, and protective colouring. The struggle, never-ceasing, just to live. A thousand centuries the wind has listened to it, and nothing else. Blows in the darkness, screams of pain, lingering death, exultant torture. Just to live. Then from femur-like creatures arises a type that arms itself with stones, and then with iron and bronze, the better to kill, and mutilate, and destroy. The better just to live. Pitiless. In the heart of nature nothing lives but relentless cruelty.

Oh, you funny little people! As I look down on you on this night, standing in a compact mass in the body of the hall, with your solemn faces, your pipes, and your drab clothes, I suddenly realise how wonderful you are. Your life has been so brief in the measure of this story. You are a mushroom growth. I wonder what the wind thinks of you? For in all the chronicles of nature you, and you alone, have known the element of pity. You do not know how wonderful you are. You are so occupied with all your little affairs, going, and coming, and loving, and grieving. You think you're rather clever, don't you? You can do nearly any old thing you like with the little earth, which you have taken over as your property. You can link it up with chains and ships, and read its story in the rocks. You can twist the rivers, and bore your way through the earth or the waters. You can make it produce just what you want. You can make it do nearly everything, except perhaps revolve in the opposite direction. But that is not the remarkable thing about you. Please realise this. You are a mushroom growth, a nouveau arrive, and you have discovered pity. And pity is the only thing worth discovering. It did not exist till you came.

If you would only always keep this in perspective—you, John Perkins, down there, in the mackintosh and the straw hat—there would be no need for you to get angry with your wife because the bacon wasn't cooked exactly as you liked it in the morning. Just think how wonderful you are, and that it is you who are also in this big thing—the dawn of love. No, I don't mean what you mean, Agatha and Francis, nudging each other there in the sofa stalls. That was done in the neolithic age. I mean love in the big sense. It has all come so suddenly. You, Lord Clancy Pelville, leaning back in your cushioned seat, listen to the music of this scherzo, and realise how wonderful you are. It is out of all proportion to be jealous of that other fellow at the Foreign Office. That is the way wars arise.

You are all in this, and the measure of your life shall be the measure of the way you use this gift. That is what Henri meant when he said he could not teach you how to live, old girl. He gave you all his love and all his pity, and he had nothing else to give. In truth, you did not treat him very well. I do not think you loved him very well, or all might have been different. But you were not to know. Your angle of perspective had become distorted by an earlier injustice. The people we love are the people we want to tell things to. I do not think you told Henri very much. You were already consumed with those little paraphrases of the big thing. When I hear this music I love everyone—all humanity, the good and the vile. It explains everything. Everything is filled up. My heart is beating wildly. I want to make up for all these countless aeons of emptiness and suffering. I want to suffer myself, so that I know. I want to hug you closely to me, to whisper in your ear, to hear every little thing you want to tell me. Let me live it and make it mine. I cannot teach you how to live. ... No one can do that. I can only live myself because you want me. . . . . Mary . . . Madeline . . . . Stella . . . Laura. . .

CHAPTER XX

THE SCIENCE OF SUFFERING

Ave atque vale, Roger and Stephen. Let me examine you and wish you God-speed. You are so absurdly alike, I am not quite sure now . . . Ah, yes, Stephen, I know you by your slightly tilted nose, and the greater breadth of upper lip. All right, old boy, don't wake up. 'Sh! There, there; that's right. Nurse is out, you know—she must have one evening a week—and Mummy has gone down the road for five minutes. Do you know what she said to me? "Just keep an eye on these little brats for half-a-shake!" Wasn't it rude, Roger? We do that, you know, we grown-ups. We take all kinds of advantage of your lack of understanding. I heard Mummy say "Damn!" this evening because you upset your bottle, Stephen. We call you awful names. You are little brats, too—savages. If ever anyone was neolithic! ... I want to give you some advice, though. Of course it will bore you, but it may all come back to you in after-life. I shall write it down so that some day you may read it. Don't believe all the stories you hear about me, you chaps. I know I'm a queer fish, a fusty old crank. And in after years all these stories get exaggerated. One becomes a myth, a type to whom certain stories are automatically ascribed. Why I'm so concerned to give it you is because it is not likely I shall live to see you into manhood. I'm not that sort.

This rheumatism gives me gyp! I get so crusty and bad-tempered. You will hear all kind of records of my bad behaviour.

You must allow, in any case, that it is pretty creditable to be your father at my age. The father, of twins at fifty! Come, now, isn't it absurd? To be sure, the credit is more due to your mother, who is—now, let me see; what is it?—half fifty, plus seven, less one. There's a sum for you when you begin to count. She wasn't really keen on having you, you know. And when you arrived, you seemed—well, rather unnecessarily redundant. But now, of course, she is as rabid as the she-wolf with Romulus and Remus. She finds astounding virtues in you. You have established my reputation as a definitely comic figure. You cannot mention the word "twins" without people doubling up with laughter. It's like a red nose on a comedian, or a reference to a mother-in-law breaking her neck. Jevons was perfectly cruel about you. It was particularly mean on his part He must have completely forgotten that only a few years before your coming I got him out of a scrape. The same sort of scrape as you are, only not half so respectable. Twins are ultra-respectable—almost exceeding your obligations.

Do you know what really keeps things going, boys? It's—grandmothers. Grandfathers, too. I have always found that women are keener on being grandmothers than they are on being mothers. The fathers are almost as bad. I think they feel that when they are grandmothers and grandfathers the picture is complete and framed. They can sit down and read the newspaper. All their responsibilities have ceased. They are linked up at each end. When they die there will be crowds of people they can impose upon both coming and going.

How round and absurd you are, Stephen! I must smell your skull in the same disgusting way I used to smell your sister's. You are all inverted. Your knuckles are holes. You have projections where you ought to have holes, and holes where you ought to have projections. You are simply impossible, but the thin down on your skull tickles my nose and makes me want to laugh. No, no, for goodness' sake don't wake up! It is very important that I should write down on this tablet my message to you. We shall never really know each other. You are beginning where I leave off. We are miles apart

II

I have to try to justify myself because everybody laughs at me. And I shall remain in your memory as a kind of old harlequin who failed at everything until he began to sell linoleum. Your sister laughs at me; your mother laughs at me. Do you know what they call me down at business?—Father William. I heard that old ruffian Peel refer to me one day as that. I'm certain he didn't know who Father William was. I suppose the name suggests my atmosphere. They say I'm untidy in my apparel, careless over details, absentminded, often irritable. But I notice that they always come to me when they want favours, the dogs! I know they think they can always wangle things out of me more easily than out of Jevons. Jevons has become quite the proper managing director. He hops down in a top-hat and tail-coat, with spats. He has married a most respectable person—the widow of a magistrate. They live at South Kensington, and leave their visiting cards, with the right number of comers turned down, in people's halls. You know the sort of thing? You can't get a laugh out of Jevons, except sometimes when we are alone, and he forgets he is a managing director.

Well, what I particularly want to talk to you boys about is—success and failure. By all the canons of the game I have been a success; that is to say—I have made money. In other respects I have been a failure. I have done nothing distinguished. I failed at everything until I started with Jevons, and even now we haven't set the Thames on fire. We have developed into a solid, respectable firm, known to a few wealthy customers. The success we have had has been largely due to sheer luck—Ruysdael, Lady Stourport, my marriage. All my life I have, indeed, been very lucky. Ninety-nine people out of a hundred would say I am a lucky, successful man. I know I have failed; but you can keep that dark. I never quite found the thing I was looking for. It is not true that "the evil which men do lives after them; the good is oft interred with their bones." The use of the word "oft" is just one of the tricks of these writing fellows to give him a loophole. I have known some very pretty vices that have been completely buried with a man, and some virtues that have only been discovered after his death. If our poet is referring to reputation, I can assure you that, unless you succeed in getting several square inches in "Who's Who," both the evil and good are buried with you. No one is the slightest bit interested. If he is referring to the effect of character, the evil and the good live after a man in corresponding force. There are hospitals for rickety children, and there are—well, you. Do not forget that. Success is not what you do, but what you leave behind. I do not mean by this that success is being a grandfather, or leaving a large family of healthy babies, or painting a masterpiece. I mean to say, it is what you contribute of yourself to the community. You may not marry at all, you may not have children, but you cannot escape the influence of your character. Every day of your life you are either helping or harrying. Every man and woman you meet, when you look into their eyes something definite takes place. You either help to make or help to destroy. The building is in progress. You may be the architect or you may be a stonemason, but according to the spirit in which you carry out your part of the work, so shall you count success. And we are building, believe me. The man who is staining the wainscot in the spare bedroom, or nailing boards across the joists in the loft, cannot see it He is so occupied with his little bit. He is apt to fret and say it's a rotten building. Never mind; it will be all the better to have the floorboards flush and true,

I believe we are building; in spite of the morning's paper which records the slaughter of countless thousands of young boys on the outskirts of Verdun. The history of mankind is very short. He must at times be conscious of his primordial ancestry. If a staircase gives way, it doesn't follow that the whole building is bad. It simply implies that there have been some indifferent and lazy joiners at work on one part of it. It will be up to you, boys, to see that next time the staircase is built more solidly. And this can only be done by each of you singing in your heart as you work. Not because you are getting an award, but because you know you are helping the whole building.

"Lord!" I can hear you say. "What a prosy old bore our father must have been!" Well, you have escaped all that. You might at least be patient It is a father's prerogative to bore his sons. I have not the faintest hope that you will heed anything I say. Indeed, I hope you won't. You will be right beyond me. I am only trying to impress upon you that it has taken me all these years to discover the formula for success. And if I could only live more intensely up to my formula I believe I could find the thing we are all searching for. It resolves itself into the realisation of the spirit of community. One after another we pass away, with all our little hopes and disappointments, loves and griefs. But the community survives. When all these parochial differences upon the continent have been adjusted, then will come a great chance for you boys. You have got to learn how to live. It has never yet been done.

III

No one has ever yet found out how to live. Jesus Christ nearly did, and then He let the whole thing down with His awards and penalties and dubious miracles. Turning water into wine or loaves into fishes doesn't help the case at all. Buddha thought more about dying than living; Mahomet was too much like the hero of a story by Robert Hichens. The most satisfactory one of the lot was Confucius, who did indeed enunciate a reasonably good way of living, without worrying about the future life. But the whole conception is befogged by ceremonial, which is a kind of "King Charles's head" to him.

You, I know, will dispense with all prophets, and seers, and saviours. I feel it coming. The decay of hero-worship is the first sign. And it is a good sign. It implies searching within rather than without; of acting rather than of being acted upon. Sermons in stones is a fine discovery. Everything lives; everything is a part of the story. I have failed because I have sought satisfaction rather than surprises. A shock is more valuable than a palliative. When you begin to find yourself "settling down," then is the time to get really angry with yourself and to hurl a brick through your neighbour's window. Seven days in gaol would do you no end of good. You have always got to keep on the move, and to remember that life itself is only a temporary arrangement Do you know that there is a Science of Suffering? It astounds me that it has never been written up. Being the inevitable corollary to happiness, it seems odd that the professors have treated it with such scant respect Suffering is the solution of endless problems, but we always regard it as a thing to be avoided or ignored. The Christian certainly uses it as the emblem of his faith, but he treats it as a sentiment rather than a science. The worst amateur of the lot is a person called a Christian Scientist, who professes to believe that it doesn't exist at all. The Christian Scientist is a kind of spiritual strap-hanger. He hasn't got a seat but he believes that because he's hanging on to a strap he's really sitting down. The whole idea bowdlerises the essential value of Christianity. One might as well assert that it's always summertime, or that it only rains in the night, so you needn't take out an umbrella in the daytime.

What fun it all is, Stephen. People, I mean, and talking through my hat, and raging up and down the earth. I wonder whether you will enjoy it all as much as I have? I could go on for ever, living thousands of completely different existences, and loving it all the time. It's no good unless you love it You've got to love even the people you dislike. This war! . . . My dear boys, perhaps in your time you'll be able to focus it. Or your children may be able to find out what it was all about. For my part, I can only selfishly rejoice that you are too young for the sacrifice. A father who boasts that he is "proud to give his sons for his country" is boasting of being proud of giving away something which doesn't belong to him. I have given you life. It is yours. It is up to you to do just what you think with it. I am your disciple, not your master. I have no right to order you about. The world belongs to you, not to ma I am all encrusted in memories, and associations, and prejudices, which, I thank God, you need not share.

IV

There is only one of my memories I want to hand over to you. It concerns your sister Madeline. She is a kind of halfway-house between us. I want to tell you, because she is never likely to tell you herself. There are times when the sensibleness of this new generation drives me to distraction. Madeline is like that at times. I sometimes think she has no feeling; then I know I'm wrong and that I'm an old fool.

One day she came to me and said:

"Daddy, do you think one could be happily married to a man who has been married before?"

"That's rather a leading question, my child'," I answered. "You had better ask Stella."

"I have. Of course she thinks it's all right. But I can't make up my mind. You see, he has three children, and his first marriage was a complete success. He loved his wife—horribly."

"My dear, who on earth is this?"

"Geoffry Storr."

"Do you love him?"

"I'm afraid I do."

What impressed me was the extraordinary detachment of this confession. In my time we didn't behave like that at all. There would have been heavings, and tears, and choking sobs. And yet Madeline was quite sincere. Here was a girl in her early twenties, suddenly finding herself in love for the first time, and she calmly considers the problem. She is weighing all the eventualities.

"I suppose it depends upon—how much you love him."

"I suppose it does."

She said nothing more, but went away. For months, I know, she was carefully weighing the balance of her love for Geoffry Storr against the weight of obvious disadvantages in having three ready-made children thrust upon her. I had nothing against Geoffry Storr. He used to come to our house. He was a pleasant young fellow, rather too "Oxfordy" for my taste, but a decent, clear-eyed boy.

Then one day she came to me, and said:

"You know, I'm afraid I shall have to marry him, daddy."

I said: "Oh, well, don't be afraid. You must surely know your own mind?"

"I love him all right. Only, of course, one must always feel—that other one. I know he'll be unconsciously comparing me, and thinking what a rotter I am."

I ought to have been able to help Madeline enormously over this problem, but all I could think of saying was:

"You'll have to chance that. I don't suppose he'll compare you at all It'll be all quite different. He'll have chained, too."

"Changed from what?"

"From—what he was when he was married to the other girl."

"Do you mean to say he will have forgotten?"

"No; oh, no. But there's nothing to bind him except memories. Memories are manageable."

Madeline gave me a quick look, as though she was suspecting me of infidelity to her mother. It seemed to add a further difficulty to the problem. Again she went away, and the affair drifted indeterminately. I did not attempt to influence her one way or the other. I do not know how long it might have gone on, or what might have been the upshot, if it hadn't been for the war. Geoffry had had some training in the Territorials, and he very easily got a commission. One afternoon Madeline appeared at my office in Soho. Her eyes were very bright. She was no longer the "sensible" modern girl. She said:

"Daddy, he's going to France on Sunday week."

I uttered an exclamation of sympathy.

"Do you think I ought to marry him before he goes?"

"My dear, I didn't know you—I didn't know that you had made up your mind."

"Of course I shall marry him now."

"Well, well; I don't know, I'm sure. It's rather sudden. Perhaps it would be better to wait till he returns?"

"But, can't you see, my dear father?—he's not going on a fishing expedition. Suppose . . . suppose . . . anything should happen?"

I realised that things might happen. Then the old problem presented itself: Is it better to be married for a few hours and then perhaps be a widow for life, rather than not marry the man you love at all? God help the thousands of women who had to spend sleepless nights seeking the answer to this question in their hearts!

V

Madeline had thirty-six hours of married life. Geoffry went. He was at the front four months and three days before a telegram came to say that he was dangerously wounded. I do not wish to distress you with what followed. I can only say that your little sister behaved in a way that made me very proud. We were given permission to go to the hospital in France where Geoffry was taken, but he died before our arrival. He had lost both legs above the knee, and he died under an operation. And on that night Madeline made me hold her very dose. And she whispered through her sobs:

"I wanted him back, daddy . . . anyhow, anyhow. But for his own sake I'm glad he died. He always said it was the only thing he dreaded—to come back mangled or disfigured. And, daddy, I've got to be sensible. I've got to go on being stupidly sensible. You know why?"

"You mean to say?"

"Yes. Thirty-six hours of married life. He knew. He made me promise. If the child lives—and I've got to want the child to live. It's beastly . . . hard lines, isn't it, daddy?"

And so, Roger and Stephen, next month, by the grace of God, there arrives for you an uncle or an aunt one year younger than you are yourselves! This will, of course, be stale news for you. You will probably say:

"Oh, he's talking about old Tom or old Susan."

And Madeline is very calm. She has that splendid, well-poised, "sensible" expression which you only see on the faces of modem women. Her spirituality is a practical instrument The Greek women were just as well-poised, but how can we tell how spiritual they were? Sculpture is blind. Their literature is the literature of fatalism. They worshipped physical perfection, but a fatalist is the last person to know how to live. Madeline is finding out, I think. She has been through the furnace. She will help you far more than I can. What I have learnt from her is that to get the uttermost out of life you have to give the uttermost to it "To get the uttermost out of life" sounds too much like pilfering the nest. You must not pilfer the nest, you must add your little feather or scrap of straw.

Oh, yes, Stephen, I know. You want to wake up and yell for something I There, there; curl your little fingers round my thumb. Clutch it and squeeze it and pretend it's just what you want. Sa You will never know the man you were named after. He was rather a character, Stephen. You could do worse than be like him. A terrible fast bowler and, as he said, "no Joseph." A bit of a rip in his time, no doubt. But he was a clean man—a sportsman to the bitter end. Furious that they would not take him in the Army. He dyed his hair—what was left of it—and swore he was forty-nine. But they laughed at him. At last he joined the Special Constabulary. He got his feet wet lurking around a deserted reservoir at Walham Green, caught pneumonia, and died in the service of his country. A good chap. And to you he will not be even a memory. And, indeed, why should you bother about him? or even me? You are twisting, and turning, and straining at the leash already. Well, the game's afoot, and I promise you it is a great game. It's well worth playing. You have to come to it fresh and strong, with all your thews and sinews taut, your muscles quivering, your eye alert and watchful, your brain the imperious master of the whole apparatus. Your nostrils quiver, the air tickles your sensibilities; you are eager for the swift movements, the assertion of your powers, the lightning precision of your judgment, the miracles of chance, the joy of conflict. You are alive. . . .

Lord, what an old bore I am.

Yes, yes, it's all right . . . It's all right She's COMING! . . . "Stella, for goodness sake!"

Stacy Aumonier – A Short Biography

Stacy Aumonier was born at Hampstead Road near Regent's Park, London on 31st March 1877.

He came from a family with a strong and sustained tradition in the visual arts; sculptors and painters.

In 1890 the teenage Aumonier attended Cranleigh School in Surrey. Although he would later write critically about English public schools (with articles for the London Evening Standard and New York Times) in how they tried to impose conformity on students, records indicate that he integrated well into Cranleigh. Aumonier was a passionate cricket player, belonged to the Literary and Debating Society, and, in his final year, became a prefect.

On leaving school it seemed the family tradition of the visual arts would be his career path. In particular his early talents were that of a landscape painter. He exhibited paintings at the Royal Academy in 1902 and 1903, and 1908. An exhibition of his work would later be held at the Goupil Gallery in London in 1911.

In 1907 he married the international concert pianist, Gertrude Peppercorn, at West Horsley in Surrey. She herself was the daughter of a landscape painter (Arthur Douglas Peppercorn, occasionally cited as 'the English Corot'.) A son, Timothy, was born in 1921.

A year after his marriage, Aumonier began a brief career in a second branch of the arts at which he enjoyed outstanding success—as a stage performer writing and performing his own sketches.

The Observer newspaper commented that "...the stage lost in him a real and rare genius, he could walk out alone before any audience, from the simplest to the most sophisticated, and make it laugh or cry at will."

In 1915, Aumonier published a short story 'The Friends' which was well received (and voted one of the best short stories of 1915 by the Boston Magazine, Transcript).

Despite his age being 40 in 1917 he was called up for service in World War I. He began as a private in the Army Pay Corps, and then transferred as a draughtsman in the Ministry of National Service.

By now he had four books published—two novels and two books of short stories—and his occupation is recorded with the Army Medical Board as 'author.'

In the mid-1920s, Aumonier received the shattering diagnosis that he had contracted tuberculosis. In the last few years of his life, he would spend long spells in various sanatoria, some better than others. In a letter to his friend, Rebecca West, written shortly before his death, he described the debilitating conditions in a sanatorium in Norfolk during the winter of 1927, where the dampness was so severe that a newspaper left beside the bed would feel "sodden to the touch in the morning."

Shortly before his death, Stacy Aumonier sought treatment in Switzerland, but died of the disease in Clinique La Prairie at Clarens beside Lake Geneva on 21st December 1928. He was 55.

Whilst Aumonier's works are now slowly coming back into circulation at the time of his death his works were extremely popular and his loss was a profound tragedy for literary society.

The chief fiction critic of The Observer, Gerald Gould wrote: "His gifts were almost fantastically various; they embraced all the arts; but it was the charm and generosity of his personality which made him—what he unquestionably was—one of the most popular men of his generation." It went on: "The things he wrote will be remembered when the company of his friends (no man had more friends, or more devoted and admiring) are with him in the grave; but just now, to those who knew him, the thing most vividly present is the charm and wisdom of the man they knew."

Of his general appearance and manner Gerald Cumberland gives us this interesting set of observations: "A distinguished man, this—distinguished both in mind and appearance. Self-conscious. Perhaps. Why not? His hair is worn a trifle long, and it is arranged so that his fine forehead, broad and high, may be fully revealed. Round his neck is a very high collar and a modern stock. When in repose, his face has a look of shy eagerness; his quick eyes glance here and there gathering a thousand impressions to be stored up in his brain. It is the face of a man extremely sensitive to external stimulus; one feels that his brain works not only rapidly, but with great accuracy. And at heart, he takes himself and his work seriously, though he likes on occasion to pretend that he is only a philanderer."

In literary terms Aumonier was amongst the best short story writers these shores have produced.

The Nobel Prize winning author John Galsworthy called him "A real master of the short story. The first essential in a short-story writer is the power of interesting sentence by sentence. Aumonier had this power in prime degree. You do not have to 'get into' his stories. He is especially notable for investing his figures with the breadth of life within a few sentences." Galsworthy asserted that Aumonier "is never heavy, never boring, never really trivial; interested himself, he keeps us interested. At the back of his tales, there is belief in life and a philosophy of life, and of how many short story writers can that be said? ...He follows no fashion and no school. He is always himself. And can't he write? Ah! Far better than far more pretentious writers. Nothing escapes his eye, but he describes without affectation or redundancy, and you sense in him a feeling for beauty that is never obtruded. He gets values right, and that is to say nearly everything. The easeful fidelity of his style has militated against his reputation in these somewhat posturing times. But his shade may rest in peace, for in this volume, at least he will outlive nearly all the writers of his day." In summing his up Galsworthy suggested that, through his stories, he would "outlive all the writers of his day."

James Hilton (author of Goodbye, Mr Chips and Lost Horizon) said "I think his very best works ought to be included in any anthology of the best short stories ever written." He cited 'The Octave of Jealously' as his favourite short story for the March 1939 edition of Good Housekeeping saying it was a "bitterly brilliant tale."

Rebecca West said of his writing in 1922 that his ability to blend reality with the imaginary was "the envy of all artists."

Stacy Aumonier – A Concise Bibliography

More than 87 short stories in more than 25 magazines, and in 6 volumes published during Aumonier's lifetime.

Among more than 20 other magazines, his work appeared in Argosy Magazine, John O' London's Weekly, The Strand Magazine and The Saturday Evening Post, as well as being anthologized, and adapted for film and television.

Short Story Collections

The Golden Windmill & Other Stories (1921)
The Friends & Other Stories (1917)
Miss Bracegirdle & Other Stories (1923)

Novels

Olga Bardel (1916)
Three Bars Interval (1917)
Just Outside (1917)
The Querrils (1919)
One After Another (1920)
Heartbeat (1922)

Other Works

A volume of 14 Character Studies: Odd Fish (1923)

A volume of 15 Essays: Essays of Today and Yesterday (1926)